# Like Peaches and Pickles

Muriel Ellis Pritchett

*Muriel Pritchett*

*2022*

BLACK ROSE
writing™

The final approval for this literary material is granted by the author.

First printing

This is a work of fiction. Names, characters, businesses, places, events and incidents are either the products of the author's imagination or used in a fictitious manner. Any resemblance to actual persons, living or dead, or actual events is purely coincidental.

ISBN: 978-1-61296-979-4
PUBLISHED BY BLACK ROSE WRITING
www.blackrosewriting.com

Printed in the United States of America
Suggested Retail Price (SRP) $19.95

*Like Peaches and Pickles* is printed in Palatino Linotype

This book is dedicated to all women who have ever been caught up in office politics.

Special thanks to attendees at national SHARE conferences, who shared with me stories of scandals and politics at their own universities and colleges; to Judy Purdy, who tirelessly edited this manuscript; to members of my Tuesday Writers Group and Advisory Board; and to my computer-guru husband, who is always there for me.

# Like Peaches and Pickles

# Chapter One

Georgia Anne Davis stepped out of the walk-in shower and dried off with her new pink, fluffy, over-sized, bath sheet. Monogrammed with her initials "GAD." A birthday gift from her mother, who told her it was the perfect gift for a 55-year-old body that was getting a little bit fluffy around the edges.

Georgia sighed, toweled the steam off the mirror and took a step back to view her aging, fluffy body in all its naked glory. She turned sideways, sucked in her stomach as hard as she could and decided her side view didn't look all that bad. Thirty years ago she would have worried that someone might think she was pregnant, But not a problem now, she assured herself. Not a problem at all.

Turning to face herself in the mirror, Georgia could plainly see a hefty bulge over both hip bones. Gravity. That was the problem. And middle-age spread. She tugged her hands up her rib cage towards her armpits, lifting the bulge upwards and smoothing out the curve of her hip line. With each passing birthday, Georgia became more worried about her looks. Her unyouthful looks, to be exact. Her dream of becoming Vice President of Public Relations at Georgia Central University was finally within her reach and she didn't want to screw it up by looking older than dirt.

Sighing louder, Georgia ran her fingers through her short damp wavy hair that seemed thinner every time she washed it. She couldn't deny the small streaks of white hair just above the temples, either. Georgia chuckled to herself remembering how twenty years ago she paid an obscene amount of money at the salon to put streaks in her hair. Now she had streaks for free. With her nose almost against the mirror, Georgia fretted over the seemingly increasing number of wrinkles above her upper lip. The wrinkles were making her lips look sort of prune-ish. "Caused by smoking," her dermatologist told her, when she asked him about it. He shrugged when she told him she'd never smoked. "Then in your case, it has to be genes." Ah, yes, she thought, how the doctors loved to play the "gene card" to explain the unexplainable.

Still facing the mirror, Georgia stepped back, and pulled and tugged up the hip bulges, again. "All I need is an armpit lift." But was there such a thing? She'd have to Google it later to find out. If surgeons could lift boobs and butts and balls, why not armpits?

Her wishful plastic surgery thoughts were halted by loud banging on the bathroom door. "Georgia," yelled her mother. Georgia barely had time to cover her nakedness before Eula Mae Davis charged into the room.

"Mom, I just got out of the shower."

Her mother, wearing a Star Wars-themed nightgown and Chewbacca slippers, halted in front of her daughter. "So? You got any body parts I haven't ever seen before? And I did knock first, just like you said I should oughta." Eula handed Georgia her smart phone. "Here, it kept squealing and squealing, so I answered it. You're welcome. It's that campus police fellow with the twangy voice."

Georgia grabbed the phone out of her mother's hand. "Charles? What's wrong?" She knew something had happened. Lt. Charles Cassidy, who worked with the campus police at Georgia Central University, never called after midnight for mere social networking.

"Sorry to bother you this late," he said with his Texas accent, "but we have a big crisis on our hands."

That was not what Georgia wanted to hear. Georgia Central University was just breaking in a new president. Some Yankee guy from a university in Michigan, who already thought GCU was a walking disaster. They did not need a crisis to fuel the fire for this line of thinking. "Wait one minute, Charles." She nodded to Eula Mae. "Thanks, Mom, I have this. Why don't you go back to bed?"

"You're welcome," Eula Mae said. "I hope this doesn't mean you'll be out till the cows come home?"

"Good night, Mom."

Eula Mae set her jaw, nodded and exited—slamming the door behind her.

Georgia rolled her eyes. One day her mother was going to drive her stark raving mad! There were days when she thought having her mother move in with her was a huge mistake on her part, but after her dad died last year, it seemed like the best option for both of them. Vero Beach was an eight-hour drive. Having Eula Mae living with her was not only convenient, but also gave her peace of mind. Even on the days her mother told her what to do and fussed about her being an old maid. Even on the days Eula Mae made her feel like a misbehaving teenager, again.

Georgia put her phone on speaker and began wiggling into her comfy Haynes hip-hugging panties. "Charles, sorry about that. You have my full attention. What's the problem tonight?"

"Chief Swanson asked me to give you a call. There's been an incident at the Mu Rho fraternity house. I think you better get yourself down here as soon as you can. You know how tongue-tied I get dealing with reporters."

• • • • •

Georgia saw the flashing red and blue lights of emergency vehicles from three blocks away. The lights from the Mu Rho fraternity house windows illuminated the front lawn in the pre-dawn darkness. Her heart was in her throat as she pulled her old Corolla up behind the campus police SUVs and scrambled out of her car. "Thank God," she said to Lt. Cassidy, as he crossed the fraternity's front lawn to reach her, "the media isn't here."

"You mean, not yet, don't you?" asked Lt. Cassidy, who was carrying two cups of Jittery Joe's coffee. He handed her one—her very favorite coffee.

"Thanks, Charles." Georgia took a sip and sighed. She and Cassidy had worked together for eight years—since he had arrived from the University of Texas to take a position with the GCU campus police. During his first year at GCU, they dated off and on. But once Charles realized Georgia was married to her job, he moved on and married a divorceé with two teenage daughters. Now Georgia considered Charles a close friend and ally.

"You're probably right about the media," she said between sips of hot coffee. "Let's hope it's more *later* than sooner." She pulled a strand of white-streaked brown hair out of her face and tucked it behind her ear. It was 2 o'clock Friday morning. Most likely the police reporter from the local paper hadn't called the station yet to see if anything interesting had happened during the night.

"Okay, Lt. Cassidy, I'm wide awake. My adrenalin is pumping. How bad is it?" Much of what Charles told her over the phone had not fully penetrated her brain. As soon as she heard about an incident at the Mu Rho house and "an unconscious student," she hung up, threw on some clothes and ran out the door. Literally leaping over her mother—guardian of the door—in her escape.

Charles led the way towards the front door of the fraternity house. "It's really bad, Georgia."

"Please tell me it wasn't hazing?" The Student Affairs Office and the Campus Council of Fraternities had worked hard to end hazing, which more often than not resulted in injuries, angry parents and law suits. While reports of hazing were rare now, during fraternity rush, traces of the old tradition still occurred.

Charles stopped and faced her. He rocked back and forth on his toes and heels. "The fraternity members insist it wasn't, but I think they were forcing the pledges to play a stupid drinking game. Otherwise, why would any normal student binge-drink until they passed out?"

Georgia felt a twinge in her abdomen. She had seen this problem many times over the years. Especially with underage drinkers, who were at a higher risk for alcohol overdose. Too much alcohol in the bloodstream and life-support functions started to shut down— leading to brain damage and even death.

"We're talking about something here far-worse than just a little hazing," Charles said.

She sucked down a mouthful of air and gasped. "Go on."

"The student who's in the coma isn't *just* any ordinary student."

"What do you mean? Who is he?" She held her breath, steeling herself for the worst.

Charles leaned over and whispered, "Sherrod Orson Wittick V."

"Senator Wittick's grandson?" Georgia's pulse began to race and her head pounded out a migraine in her temple. For a second, she thought she might even throw up her coffee. This would have to be handled very carefully. One misstep could affect not only her boss, Evan Bradshaw, and President Paul Van Horne, but also the university's reputation and her career at GCU. How she hated politics!

"Yes, ma'am, that's the one. The EMTs rushed him to St. Agnes about 10 minutes ago."

Georgia shuddered. Not only was Sherrod Orson Wittick III a powerful force in the Georgia State Legislature, but he also came from a well-known prominent family—a long line of wealthy businessmen who had lived in Georgia since the 18th century. And he was one of the top donors for the GCU Foundation. His family's money recently paid for a new wing on the law school building.

"Holy crap!" Georgia brought the back of her hand to her mouth. Her stomach lurched. She closed her eyes. Her office needed to get out in front of this story before it became an issue of crisis management and damage control. She didn't see any way to put a positive spin on this. "How I love my job! I really love my job." She thought if she repeated it enough times, she would believe it. It was barely Friday; the weekend was just beginning, and she'd already heard from Campus Police several times last night. She rubbed her throbbing temples as she remembered the first call of the evening.

Right in the middle of "Hawaii 5-0"—just as a shirtless, tanned and sweaty Steve McGarrett was embracing the new love of his life. Just as Georgia and her mother were leaning closer to the TV screen in anticipation of a hot love scene, Lt. Cassidy called to report the arrest of a male and a female student caught strolling leisurely through campus hand in hand—buck naked. She wondered how happy their parents were when the police called. This was followed half an hour later by the arrest of a drunk football player caught urinating in a downtown alley.

And now this. Not one of her better evenings, Georgia reflected. But it was spring semester and strange things did happen. Now that Georgia thought about it, the entire spring semester had been particularly bad. At least student behavior-wise. She guessed the most memorable thing had to be the "peeping Tom" incidents in the women's showers early in the semester. Most of the "perps" had been horny, hormone-high male students seeing what they could see. But one creative student with his cell phone on a stick managed to take several photos of his naked victim and post them online. Even though the photos were quickly removed, the photographer had to face the wrath of the girl's preacher father, who had the student arrested.

In April, during a wild fraternity party, three pledges, high on marijuana, decided to end the evening on a high note by stripping off their clothes and painting themselves with stolen yellow paint—the kind used for making no-passing lines down streets and highways. Then while a co-conspirator pulled the fire alarm in the freshman women's residence hall, the pledges danced and wiggled in front of squealing freshman women pouring out of the building. After firemen tried unsuccessfully to hose off the paint, the pledges ended up in the hospital emergency room, where their skin was scraped raw to remove the toxic paint.

Now tonight's hazing incident had left one student in a coma. And not just any student, but a member of the wealthy and politically powerful Wittick family. The current patriarch of the Witticks, Sherrod Orson Wittick III, was a seasoned, well respected and well connected state senator—known for always being able to get whatever he wanted, through one means or another. Georgia cringed at how this man's influence could cripple the university just by funneling desperately needed funding away from upcoming projects, like the $50-million research center now on the architect's drawing board or the visual and performing arts complex, scheduled for groundbreaking next year. Without a doubt, the new president, the legal affairs office and the university's foundation would be working overtime in the coming weeks to prevent any political disaster.

Georgia left Lt. Cassidy and walked up the sidewalk toward the front door of the fraternity house. The trashed front yard was littered with the remnants of an obviously wild Thursday night party: two sofas on the lawn, overturned folding chairs, extra-large plastic cups, paper plates and napkins, a half-collapsed tent pitched over a mound of empty beer kegs, several large ice chests and what looked like a used condom. She sighed and gingerly stepped over it. Totally disgusting. Were all Millennials raised in a barn?

As she reached the wide porch with its four elegant white Grecian columns, Campus Police Chief Bill Swanson exited the front door.

"Georgia," greeted the chief.

"Bill," acknowledged Georgia, offering him her hand. "Charles says the senator's grandson is in a coma and even if he survives, he may be brain-damaged. Could this day get any worse?"

Swanson glanced down at a notepad. "This will come as no surprise, but the fraternity brothers don't know anything about anything. Everything was fine and dandy until their pledge Wittick fell over unconscious."

"All of them are clueless?" She and Bill both knew that wasn't what happened. The fraternity brothers were trying to cover up a hazing incident gone wrong. Everyone present at last night's party knew the truth. Even the poor pledges who were falling down drunk.

"We're pretty sure hazing was involved, but fraternity members say it was just a party—that everyone was drinking and carrying on and having a good time. Then the next thing they knew, Wittick fell over, his face turned bluish gray and he stopped breathing," explained Swanson. "At least they didn't just dump him outside the emergency room door. They called 911 and attempted CPR."

"Every Mu Rho brother backed up this story?" she asked.

"Plus all the pledges," said Swanson. "At this point about all we can do is charge them with underage drinking."

Georgia shook her head in disgust. "Is there a chance Wittick might not make it?"

"We'll have to wait and see. The EMTs said the kid overdosed on alcohol and it doesn't look good," Swanson said.

Georgia turned and looked at Charles, who had come up behind her. "Yep, that's exactly what they said, all right."

Georgia shrugged and turned back to Bill. "Have you notified the president or Evan?" Paul Van Horne had been president of the university for only nine months, and Evan Bradshaw was her boss, the vice president of public relations. He had been her mentor since he'd hired her as a writer about thirty years ago—a new GCU grad with a master's degree in media relations.

"You know I did!" said Swanson. "Anything bad that happens involving a Wittick or a top athlete, folks at the top want to know instantly."

"Then Evan will have been in touch with the Wittick family," she said. She knew her boss would be distraught as he reached out to the senator. Both men were close friends and allies. The senator, an alumnus of the GCU School of Law, was a very strong supporter of the university.

"The senator's helicopter should be landing at Garner's Field in about fifteen minutes," Swanson replied, glancing at his watch. "Care to join me?"

Georgia sighed. "As if I have a choice." It was expected as part of her job as associate vice president of public relations. The job she loved so dearly—except at times like this. The job that was the most important thing in her life. And, according to her mother, the reason Georgia never married or produced any grandchildren for Eula Mae to love and spoil.

# Chapter Two

Garner's Field, a small private landing strip, was located five miles from downtown Southern Pines and the Georgia Central University campus. The Air Force used it during World War II to train new recruits. Nowadays it saw little business, except on football weekends at the university. Most visitors to town or campus arrived at the Macon airport and rode a shuttle bus to Southern Pines.

When she arrived at the air field, Georgia immediately spotted President Paul Van Horne and her boss, Evan Bradshaw, vice president of GCU Office of Public Relations. After watching Georgia get out of her car, Evan walked toward her. Georgia thought he looked tired. Maybe it was a good thing he was talking about retiring. The strain of breaking in a new president not familiar with the South or its culture and customs had not been easy for him. Or her. Or the entire university, for that matter.

Evan reached towards her as they heard the approaching helicopter and saw its flashing lights. He grabbed her shoulder and leaned close to her ear. "The senator wants to hold a press conference this morning. I'll let you know more as soon as I hear something." He backed away as the noise grew louder, becoming almost deafening. Lights from the helicopter circled the ground. Slowly the large flying machine descended to the tarmac. Before the powerful engines could shut down, a doorway opened on the side and several men hopped out, hurrying toward the waiting officials.

Georgia followed Evan and the president over to the senator and his entourage. The senator nodded curtly to Van Horne, before grabbing Bradshaw's hand and slapping him warmly on the back. She wasn't surprised at the senator's cool greeting for Van Horne. The president had on more than one occasion called out the state legislature's favorable treatment of the University of Georgia when it came to appropriating funds.

"Evan, it's been a long time," said the senator.

"Since the SEC playoffs last fall," replied Evan. "That was a great day."

"Too long my friend. I appreciate you calling me about my grandson, and thank you for being here with me now, Evan."

"I'm sorry about your grandson, Sherrod. It's terrible what happened. I regret we have to meet under these circumstances. Trust me when I say your grandson is in good hands at St. Agnes." Evan, upon seeing Van Horne edging over, stepped back.

The president reached out and shook hands with the senator. "Anything I or the university can do, Senator Wittick, please let me know." Van Horne called over Chief Swanson and introduced him to the senator. After Swanson explained what little they knew, Senator Wittick was whisked away in Van Horne's private car.

Georgia and Swanson watched the caravan depart. She sighed and headed toward her car. "I don't know about you, Chief, but I'm going home for a shower and a cup of coffee before I head to work. I have a feeling it's going to be a very long day."

• • • • •

Georgia Central University, located in Southern Pines in the Georgia plains, was home to nearly 40,000 students from throughout the United States and 150 other countries. It was up to the public relations office to promote GCU to the world, covering everything from minor student achievements for hometown press releases to significant scientific research discoveries for national and international media. Unfortunately, it also meant getting information out to the media on negative events at the university such as fraternity hazing incidents. While it was difficult to put a positive spin on this kind of news, it was important to work toward maximum damage control. When it involved bad news, Georgia's goal was always to report it first, report it fast and report it correctly, in order to preserve the university's credibility and minimize speculation and misinformation.

The Wittick family and the Mu Rho fraternity filled her every thought as Georgia headed to her office on north campus. Today she would have to use everything she'd learned from her boss and mentor, Evan Bradshaw. And the one thing that Evan had hammered into her head—his number one rule—was "Never lie to the media." Also, as a spokesperson for the university, Georgia knew that one wrong word to a reporter meant you were in serious trouble. Reporters were like camels. They always remembered who did them wrong, and one day—when least expected—they would exact their revenge.

Although she would have preferred to sleep for three or four hours, Georgia only had time to change clothes and throw on some makeup—an absolute necessity now that she had a few "old age spots" on her face to cover up. She was not surprised to find her mother sitting in the recliner with a cup of coffee and watching *Good Morning America*. Eula Mae was up by 7 every morning. "Mom, why don't you sleep later?" Georgia asked not long after her mother moved in with her.

Her mother had snorted. "When I have to pee, I get up. When you gotta go, you gotta go. Then I'm too wide awake to get back to sleep."

However, Georgia couldn't help but notice that her mother always dozed off mid-morning. Didn't matter if she were watching TV or reading or crocheting or working crossword puzzles. Eula Mae could close her eyes and totally zonk out.

"Good morning, Mom!" Georgia threw her keys and purse on the table and slammed the front door behind her. "Don't mind me. I'm only here for a few minutes."

Eula Mae looked at her daughter. "You were out all night," she said accusingly. "That job is going to do you in, one day. Mark my words."

"Yes, Mom, I hear you." Like a broken record, she thought. Or to be more accurate—like a looped YouTube video.

"Eat some breakfast before you take off."

"Can't hear you, Mom." Georgia shut her bedroom door.

A few seconds later, Eula Mae opened the door and stuck in her head. "I said to eat breakfast. It's the most important meal of the day."

Georgia pulled off the plaid cotton shirt she'd thrown on last night to get out the door quickly. "Mom, I don't have time to eat." She slipped out of a pair of trousers and put on a white silk blouse and long black skirt. "I have to get to the office and organize a quick press briefing this morning."

Eula Mae opened the door wider. "Something to do with all the shenanigans last night?"

"Yes, exactly. I also have to get information out to the wires, and state and local news outlets." Georgia ran a comb through her hair.

"Don't forget to let Norm know. Such a sweet boy!"

Georgia rolled her eyes. "No, Mom, I will not forget to email the news to poor Norm." She patted cover-up under her eyes and sighed. Norman Brewster was the police reporter for the daily *Southern Pines Press*. Georgia always made sure he received the news before the other reporters. They had gone through journalism school together and dated for many years. But as soon as Norman mentioned the big "M" word, Georgia had balked. Her parents—especially her mom— were devastated. They both loved Norm like a son.

A husband and marriage were always way down Georgia's list of life's priorities. But every now and then, when her job became stressful—like today—she regretted that she didn't marry Norm. If she had, she could be living a life complete with children, a modest home in the suburbs, a sheep dog in a fenced-in yard and a small garden out back. In between carpooling kids after school, she could be busy writing a series of supernatural thrillers and appearing on talk shows. She was married all right, but it was to the job she loved and not to Norman Brewster.

•  •  •  •  •

At 7:45 a.m. Georgia turned right onto University Drive and brought her Corolla to an abrupt halt. Traffic on the two-lane road that cut through the middle of Georgia Central University campus was already at a standstill. Faculty and staff lined up bumper to bumper to get into the gated-parking deck by the administrative office buildings. Late arrivers parked in the outlying lots and hiked or caught a campus bus to work. No one working at the university spoke kindly of the "hunting permits" that allowed 50,000 faculty, staff and students to search for 25,000 parking spaces.

At precisely 8 o'clock, Georgia pulled into the last parking spot in the seven-story deck and smiled smugly as the admissions office director drove up behind her. "Let me have your space, Georgia," pleaded Al Donovan. "I'll be late for staff meeting if I have to park in the perimeter lot."

Georgia slammed the car door and smiled apologetically. "Sorry, Al, but I have a media crisis to handle."

"Don't tell me . . . our new dictator president resigned?" He looked at Georgia expectantly and hopefully. Like many administrators and faculty members on campus, Donovan disliked the new micro-manager president. Georgia didn't exactly find him endearing either, but it was her job to support him. She frowned and shook her head.

Donovan smiled sheepishly. "Okay, my bad. What's going on?"

"Oh, let me see." She closed her eyes, like she had to think about it. "Last night, two students were arrested for indecent behavior."

"That's rough," Al said. "Sounds like the beginning of a typical weekend at GCU."

"I'm not finished, Al. Wait until you hear what happened in the wee hours this morning." Georgia stepped over to Donovan's car, her hand resting on his open window. "Sherrod Orson Wittick V is unconscious in ICU from alcohol poisoning."

Donovan's eyes widened in shock. "The senator's grandson?"

"Yes," she acknowledged.

He covered her hand with his own. "Frat party?"

She looked him in the eyes and did not reply.

"Yikes! Not another hazing incident? What are you going to do?"

"Haul out my media crisis plan and try to convince the reporters that the university is not falling apart." She pulled away her hand. "You, my friend, are late for your meeting." She turned away from his car and walked briskly toward her office in the President's Building.

Donovan stuck his head out of the window. "Call me if I can help."

She threw him a wave and a kiss and kept moving. Yes, Georgia, she told herself, it's going to be another terrible, awful, bad day to add to an escalating scandalous semester.

• • • • •

Georgia hurried through the iron gates and passed the Class of 1955's fountain, which students occasionally laced with detergent to keep the maintenance people on their toes. As she walked up the eleven steps to enter the building that housed the university's public relations office, she thought how glad she was that her office was on the first floor. Her best friend Marina Roberson, assistant vice president of development, had to climb to the third floor every day. Marina said the stairs kept her in good shape. Having younger knees than Georgia was helpful, too.

Sandra Gibson, senior secretary and office manager, stood as Georgia pushed open the front door. "I have a reporter from the *Macon Journal* on the line for you," she said worriedly. "Barbara Clayton?"

Not even a chance for a cup of coffee, thought Georgia, as she continued down the hallway. "Put her through, please," she called over her shoulder.

Sandra followed her a few feet. "Here are the rest of your messages, and Dr. Bradshaw wants you in his office right away."

"Tell him I'll be there as soon as I take care of the media."

Georgia shut her office door and crossed to her medium-sized, inexpensive oak desk. Sitting down in her slightly worn, upholstered chair, she dropped her shoulder bag on the floor and reached for the ringing phone. Her stress level rising, she lifted the receiver.

"Good morning, Barbara. Georgia Davis, here. How can I help

you today?" She stood and reached to straighten her framed Central Georgia diplomas: a bachelor's degree in public relations and a master's in media relations. She was Georgia-born, Georgia-bred and Georgia-educated.

"Good morning, Georgia. I'm glad that I caught you. I need to ask you a few questions about the Mu Rho fraternity pledge who was rushed to St. Agnes ER early this morning."

Georgia leaned back in her chair and took a deep breath, trying to relax. Another aspect of her job in the public relations office was being a spokesperson for the university. She was already crafting a reply, even before the reporter spoke. "Barbara, you probably know as much as I do." Georgia knew this particular reporter was not a slouch. She always did her homework and by this time had already talked to students and the police.

"I spoke to several Mu Rho fraternity brothers who identified the student as a pledge, Sherrod Wittick, grandson of Senator Wittick, but the police would not confirm this."

Yes, thought Georgia, this woman was good. "Now Barbara, you know I can't give out that information until the immediate family has been notified."

"Are you saying he is the senator's grandson?"

Georgia shook her head. "I'm saying that information cannot be released yet."

"I see." Barbara sighed heavily. "Okay, then can you tell me if this was the result of fraternity hazing?"

"No, I can't, Barbara. The police are still investigating." Sandra stepped into Georgia's office and placed a memo on her desk. Georgia glanced down at the note from Evan: *Press conference set for 10 o'clock, President's Cabinet Room. Please notify media.*

"You're killing me here, Georgia. Are you saying all I can say is that some Mu Rho pledge is in a coma from alcohol poisoning? No name or anything else?" The exasperation in Barbara's rising voice was audible.

"Yes, for now, but if you'll come to the 10 o'clock press conference in the President's Cabinet Room, I'm sure you will be able to leave with more than enough information for an excellent news story and still make your noon deadline."

"Oh ... press conference ... good ... thank you," replied a flustered, but mollified reporter.

"See you later, then. Bye." Georgia quickly fingered through her morning mail before heading to Evan's office. She paused at a pink sticky note stuck on her laptop—a message to call her mother. She was probably just checking to see if her wayward daughter had eaten breakfast.

"When were you going to tell me about the press conference and the senator's grandson?" The soft, baritone voice was only a few inches from her ear.

Startled, Georgia jumped to her feet and nearly bumped heads with Norman Brewster. As always, her heart rate quickened at the sight of his shaggy blond hair, now streaked heavily with grey. Currently divorced from his second wife, a number of single middle-aged women in Southern Pines considered him one of the best good-looking eligible men in town.

"Sorry, my lady," he apologized, "I thought you heard me come in."

Georgia frowned at his use of her college nickname and stepped away from him. They had met through an organization that celebrated medieval life and culture by acting out the lifestyle as realistically as possible. When they began dating, Norman continued to call her *my lady*," even outside group activities. "No, Norman, I didn't hear you come in and you know I didn't."

Norman smiled impishly and sat down in her chair. "So, my dearest, my lady, my love, what's the scoop?"

Georgia sighed in frustration. Sometimes she just wanted to strangle him for treating their relationship so casually. Because of their many years of sexual intimacy and friendship, it was difficult for her to draw a line that he wouldn't hop over. "Mr. Brewster, will you please get out of my chair."

"Ah hah!" He leaped to his feet. "Methinks I hear my lady's voice full of serious rebuke. Methinks there is some serious crap going on around here." His smile turned to a frown. "How bad is it, Georgia? My sources say Senator Wittick's grandson was nearly killed in a fraternity hazing incident ... alcohol poisoning."

"Who told you that?" Georgia demanded, but knew Norman would never say.

"My source is not the issue here. I'll just say the person is a reliable source, so I'm sure the information is true. Besides, the expression on your face just verified it for me. Thank you and ta, ta, my lady." He bowed elegantly. "See you at the press conference."

Before she could think of a brilliant, appropriate comeback, he was gone.

Frustrated, Georgia sat down and quickly placed a few calls to alert other members of the media about the morning press conference. After her last call, she headed out of her office, waving Evan's memo at Sandra. "Is *this* what Evan wants to see me about?"

"Partially, but I also think it has something to do with last night's meeting with the president," said Sandra, handing Georgia a cup of coffee and a stack of phone messages.

"Thanks," said Georgia, accepting the cup. "I'd forgotten about that meeting, what with everything else happening." She frowned thoughtfully, took a sip and thumbed through her messages quickly. Dr. Oliver Betts, geneticist and award-winning researcher, had called to say he didn't have time to be on the *Today Show* because he was needed in the lab. The science editors at the *Washington Post, USA TODAY* and *the New York Times* called to say Dr. Betts was not returning their calls. Georgia waved Betts' message at Sandra. "You'd think that if God could give this man the brains to make genetic miracles, Dr. Betts could at least find the time to toot his horn to the media."

Sandra smiled half-heartedly as Georgia passed her desk and headed toward Evan's office, reading her messages as she walked.

Georgia knocked on Evan's door and entered. "Evan, thanks for sending me the note about Van Horne's press conference. I'm assuming this will accommodate the senator, his staff and any members of the Wittick family? Do we need to do anything or is the president's office handling the particulars?"

Evan, his back to Georgia, stood gazing out his window that overlooked the Trustees Garden, which was full of his favorite stately, live oak trees, dripping in Spanish moss. He ran his fingers through his thick white hair. "I'm glad I'm not bald like my brothers."

Georgia smiled and walked over to the window. "I'm glad you aren't bald, too, Evan. Everyone thinks you are much younger than 72." Just like Cary Grant, the actor her mother loved, Georgia thought. Eula Mae always said that even in his seventies and eighties, Cary Grant was still "a sexy, handsome old devil of a man."

Evan slowly turned around to face her. "Summer will be here soon, Georgia. The temperature will soar into the 90s and the humidity will become thick, suffocating and full of gnats."

Georgia bit her lower lip to prevent herself from laughing. Everyone knew summer was not Evan's favorite time of the year. He preferred fall with cooler temperatures and exciting football weekends. How she loved and appreciated her boss! She owed her successful public relations career to him. He was more than her mentor; he was like a second father to her. She would do just about anything for this man, and she felt he would say the same thing of her.

"Relax, Georgia. Paul and Senator Wittick have the press conference under control. Of course, we'll be expected to be in the front row to assist if things get nasty." Evan turned back to look out the window in silence for a few minutes.

Georgia stood beside him and placed her hand on his arm. She could always tell when something was bothering him. "Evan, what's wrong?" She looked up into his kind face, softly etched with what he referred to as character lines. But even with a few character lines, Evan did not look like a septuagenarian.

As a wisp of thick white hair fell down across his forehead, he raked it back with his fingers. Evan looked down at her hand. "You know, Georgia, if life went along as one expected, it'd probably get boring. It's those curve balls that God throws from time to time that give you a challenge, make you strong and keep things interesting."

"Yes, but more like lemons, Evan."

"How's that?"

"The other night I went to the opening reception for a watercolor exhibition at the art museum. The artist, Missouri Rothman, talked about her work and how she became a portrait artist. She said her work was the result of life tossing her lemons. Missouri took her lemons, went to art school at the University of Georgia, studied art in Italy and made the best lemonade possible. And now she is recognized far and wide for her extraordinary portraits."

Even though this brought a brief smile to Evan's lips, Georgia noted how sad he looked, and she felt apprehensive. "Evan, don't get all doomsday on me. Wittick's grandson hasn't died yet, and he could come out of this coma without any brain damage."

Evan looked directly at Georgia. She thought his white hair seemed even whiter in the early morning sun that streamed through the window. He was tan and physically fit, thanks to his regular visits to the campus tennis courts and jogging around the track.

"Sit down, Georgia," he said.

Georgia backed a few inches to the sofa and sat, her eyes never leaving his face and his bluish-gray eyes, which seemed to have lost some brightness. Oh, God, she prayed, please don't tell me he's dying.

"There's no easy way to say this." Evan walked over and sat down beside her. He looked steadily into her dark brown eyes. "The president asked me to retire at the end of this semester."

Her whole body relaxed. "Evan, you've been saying you were ready to retire. Dr. Van Horne is just helping you make up your mind." And then I'll be vice president, she thought—the realization of her hard work paying off at last. Her dream come true. Vice President Georgia Davis. Evan, her mentor, had been grooming her for the position since she'd graduated from GCU almost 30 years ago and started work as a beginning news writer in the public relations office. Slowly she'd worked her way up to senior news writer, news editor, media coordinator and associate vice president. Now at 55, she'd be the only female vice president on campus.

"Are you afraid I'll make a lousy vice president, Evan? You taught

25

me everything I know."

Evan reached out and took her hands in his. He sighed. "I'm afraid you won't be the new vice president."

Georgia's eyes widened. She drew back her hands from Evan's. "What are you talking about? You've always said I'd move up into this position."

Evan looked down at her. "Things have changed. We have a new president. He has named a selection committee."

Georgia relaxed. "Who's chairing the committee?"

"Dr. Eddings."

Georgia smiled. Maria Eddings, head of the English department, was one of her good friends. "Maria doesn't worry me. Who else?"

Evan ran down the list. Georgia knew every single member well. Each person considered her more than competent and half of them were in her debt. "Sounds like a well-chosen selection committee. If I'm the best candidate, I should get the nomination."

"It doesn't matter if you are the best candidate or even if the committee nominates you."

Georgia's head jerked around. "You're scaring me, Evan. What are you saying?"

"Georgia, do I have to spell it out for you? The president has someone else in mind for the job. He wants to bring in someone from the outside. Someone he thinks can promote GCU and help make it the top research university in the Southeast."

"But no one knows this university like I do. This job is my life." And no one knows that better than you do, Evan, Georgia thought, biting her tongue to prevent herself from screaming out loud.

He walked slowly back to the window. "I know how you've given everything to the job," he spoke softly, not looking at her. "You've worked evenings and weekends and never complained. You could have married and had children, but you chose your career. Every assignment I've given you, you've exceeded my expectations. Your work has been exemplary from the first day you walked into this office. You've never disappointed me. Your ideas, energy and loyalty have made this public relations office what it is today."

He turned to face her, pausing briefly to clear his throat. He wiped his eyes and appeared to blink back tears. Georgia had never known him to be sentimental or emotional, no matter the occasion. He mumbled something under his breath. "Georgia, you've worked hard for your alma mater. That's why I'm sick and devastated to tell you that you will not be rewarded."

Georgia was shocked. She didn't know how to respond. Someone else was opening her mouth and shouting. "But Evan, I have to apply for the position. I have to try. Isn't the university an equal opportunity employer?"

But even as she spoke the words, she realized it was a lie. She remembered too late the unequal job opportunities that were associated with Paul Van Horne's first months in office. She recalled the staff members all over campus who had been forced to leave, to be replaced with younger men and women from northern colleges and universities, all friends and former associates of Van Horne.

"It's politics, Georgia, and let's face it, you were never good at it. It's one of the things I admire about you, your political *naiveté*. It's refreshing to know there are people who make decisions and perform daily tasks without political motivation."

Evan gently guided her back to the sofa. He sat beside her and clasped her hands in his own. "Georgia, you are one of the smartest women I know. Please try to understand. It's nothing personal. Paul just wants top administrators who will be loyal to him."

"But haven't I been loyal to you?"

"Yes."

"And I would be just as loyal to Dr. Van Horne."

"I know that, but he doesn't. This is the way it's done. A new boss takes over, old managers move out. New blood moves in. It's life."

"It's a bunch of crap, Evan!" Georgia pulled her hands from Evan's grasp and jumped up from the sofa. Her cheeks were burning and she was finding it difficult to breathe. Instinctively, she wanted to flee Evan's office. She had to get away and sort through everything he'd said. Evan grabbed her wrist as she ran for the door, but she twisted out of his grasp and opened the door.

"Georgia, wait!" Evan reached out to her, again, pleading for her to stop.

She looked back at Evan. "You know me well, Evan, and you know I won't just sit in silence," she said softly, but vehemently, as she stepped out of his office and slammed the door behind her. Heads turned as she bolted down the hall.

Richard Henry, media coordinator in the office—head media screw-up to those who worked under him—was abruptly pushed aside as Georgia ran blindly down the corridor. Richard regained his balance, only to be shoved aside by Evan, who tried to follow her.

"Georgia!" Evan shouted in frustration as she exited the office.

Georgia refused to stop, rushing past Latifa Benedict, the broadcast editor, who was always peering from her office like a hungry vulture observing the death throes of its impending dinner.

"Dang it all," muttered Georgia as she reached her office door. By lunch-time—maybe sooner, if Latifa had her way—the entire campus would hear that something juicy happened between her and Evan. Before she shut her door, she heard Evan ask Sandra to hold his calls and saw Richard edge his way into Latifa's office to gossip and plot. Please, Georgia thought, will someone remind me why I love this job?

# Chapter Three

For once, Georgia did not notice the three flights of stairs she had to climb to reach Marina's office. She was focused on one thought: "They can't do this to me!" By the time she marched trembling into Marina's office, her tears had been replaced with cold numbness and growing anger.

Taking one look at Georgia's face, Marina shut the door and led her to the corner sitting area in her office. Georgia collapsed on a small sofa, covered in exotic bird material and sprinkled with blue, red and yellow throw pillows. As usual, her subconscious noted that the development office spaces were luxuriously decorated. According to Evan, this was necessary because development office visitors were rich, potential donors.

"Our visitors are mostly members of the media or students and faculty," he explained. "They don't care if your desk is ten years old and came from Walmart. But donors care, and the development office believes you have to spend money to make money."

Marina sat next to Georgia and gave her a sympathetic hug. Then she listened in silence as Georgia repeated the conversation she'd had with Evan.

"I can't believe Evan would go along with this," Marina said.

Georgia stood up and paced in front of Marina's window, which overlooked Tolbert Gate and downtown Southern Pines. "Maybe he doesn't have much choice," she answered slowly.

Marina frowned and curled a tendril of blond hair around her finger. "You think it's a directive from the president?"

"I'm sure of it. Evan was visibly upset when he told me the news." Georgia turned away from the window to face Marina. "I always

29

thought that if a person stayed away from office politics, was loyal and did a great job, she would be rewarded."

"Yeah, like Jack McConnell? And Bob Kelly?"

Jack McConnell, vice president of development when President Van Horne took over, was told almost immediately that his contract would not be renewed. Fortunately for Jack, he had been contacted by a headhunter about a position as president of a small private institution in Arkansas.

Then there was Bob Kelly, a loyal, hardworking associate vice president of development for eighteen years. Van Horne's new vice president of development, Walter Sigman, planned to get rid of Kelly and hire a younger assistant loyal to him, but he quickly realized Bob was a walking encyclopedia on GCU history and facts. A good old boy very much respected and admired by the alumni. Someone who could be really useful to the new regime. So Kelly was "kicked upstairs" and named personal assistant to Van Horne. Although the press release read like Kelly was promoted, he merely received a new title and was stripped of any responsibilities.

Marina, who had been donor relations coordinator for nine years, bent over backwards to help Walter—the "new kid on the block." Walter was so impressed with Marina and her popularity with the alumni that he named her assistant vice president. "Not *associate* vice president," Marina told Georgia, "because they couldn't see paying a woman that much money."

Georgia sighed loudly. "Guess it's a good thing I was promoted from assistant vice president to associate vice president *before* the new president arrived on campus."

Marina nodded. "Absolutely. In case you haven't noticed, President Van Horne has replaced all of the older administrative staffers—we're talking vice presidents, deans and directors—with former colleagues and friends who are thankful and loyal."

"Don't you think I know that, Marina?" Georgia pounded the arm of the sofa with her fist. "I just figured that since the president and Evan seemed to hit it off, his job was safe."

"Do you still plan to apply for the vice president position?"

Marina asked.

"What do you think?" Sometimes Georgia wondered if Marina thought about what she was asking or if she just blurted out the question first.

"Well, bite my head off, Georgia!"

Georgia sighed, again. She knew her best friend meant well. "I'm sorry, Marina, but you know me better than anyone. Of course I will apply."

"Won't it be a waste of time and energy?"

"That's what Van Horne is hoping I'll think."

Marina's eyes narrowed. "Huh?"

Georgia put her hand on Marina's shoulder. "Think about it. If I bow out of the picture, it will certainly make things easier for him. Right?"

"Yes."

"I know every person on that committee. Not only am I more than qualified for that job, but I deserve it. I've worked hard for that position, and I'm going to get it."

Marina tugged nervously on a bottle-blonde curl. "I hate to say this, but I don't think you stand a chance."

Marina could be so aggravating sometimes, Georgia thought. This whole matter was simply infuriating. She inhaled deeply and exhaled loudly, her shoulders lifting and falling with her breath. "I want this job. I am **not** a quitter." She looked pointedly at Marina. "I refuse to hand over the job to some jerk friend of the president without a fight."

# Chapter Four

Almost 900 hundred miles away at Gabriel College in Huntsville, New York, Carl Overstreet sat in front of his computer monitor and glared at the report he was writing for the college trustees. After he reread it for the third time, he highlighted the paragraphs and angrily jabbed his finger a dozen times on the delete key. He wanted to bang his head against the monitor, but settled for slamming shut his desk drawer. He furrowed his brow and grimaced. "Do I ever need a vacation!" He groaned and smacked his forehead with the heel of his right hand. "This job is killing me!"

But he knew a vacation near the end of spring semester was out of the question. Besides, he had taken two weeks off last month. Supposedly, he used the time to write a presentation paper for an upcoming conference. In actuality, he spent most of his time drinking excellent Scotch and sleeping wherever he fell. He thought the time off would rejuvenate him, but the break only made it more difficult for him to return to work.

Carl was showing signs of stress and depression. He knew that because he had clipped the AP article from the *Washington Post* that listed the symptoms and taped it to his bathroom mirror. He had trouble sleeping at night, he could barely drag himself out of bed in the mornings, he avoided his friends and he'd lost interest in everything that he used to enjoy: fishing trips, sailing, scuba diving, good science fiction movies and gourmet cooking.

He didn't care how he looked any more or whose head he bit off. His suits were rumpled, his ties eschewed, his shoes in need of polishing, his hair creeping down over his collar, and some mornings he didn't even bother to shave. His bluish-green eyes—one of his best features—were nearly always bloodshot these days, and lately he swore the color was turning blah.

He ran the fingers of his left hand through his black, wavy hair and sighed. The sudden ringing of the phone startled him. Carl snatched the receiver from its cradle, nearly sending the whole thing to the floor.

"What is it now?" he growled.

"You have a phone call," began the hesitant voice of his secretary.

"I told you I don't want to talk to anyone!" he shouted.

"But Mr. Overstreet, he said he was **the** president of Georgia Central University," she explained.

"I don't care if he's the President of the United States, I ... wait ... did you say Georgia Central University? Paul Van Horne?"

"Yes, sir, that was the name he gave—Paul Van Horne."

"Well, well, well," he paused, deep in thought. How many years had it been since he and Paul had talked? Was it at that higher education conference in Phoenix? No, since then they'd seen each other at that alumni seminar at Princeton. Still, it had to have been at least two years ago. "Ok, I'll talk to him," he said in a softer, calmer voice.

Carl and Paul first met at Princeton when they both pledged the same fraternity. He smiled as memories of the chapter initiation flashed through his mind. And thoughts of Elena. He hadn't seen her since the wedding. He had been the best man. "After all," Paul had told him when he hesitated, "you introduced us; you're partially responsible for the outcome."

Yes, he had introduced Paul to Elena, he remembered. But he had never suspected that they would fall in love with each other. Otherwise, he wouldn't have done it, since he and Elena had been good friends working together on the *Princetonian* student paper at Princeton.

Carl had loved Elena, too, but he was afraid to tell her. Afraid that she would reject him. Instead, he found enormous enjoyment just sitting beside her in the newsroom, studying the way her lips moved up and down, as she concentrated on a story she was writing.

Afterwards they would go out to Nomad's for pizza and beer. It was there that he proudly introduced her to his best friend Paul. Paul wanted her as soon as he saw her, and whatever Paul wanted, Paul got. Not long after they met, Elena joined Paul's campaign for Student Government president—something else Paul wanted—and the day after Paul was elected, they announced their engagement.

Elena and Paul told him right away. It was as though the World Heavyweight Boxing Champion had belted him in the stomach. For what seemed like minutes, he couldn't breathe and he thought he'd died. Then he felt life flowing back. He smiled at them both and mumbled the heartiest "congratulations" a man with a broken heart could muster. When Elena pointed out how pale he looked, he said he thought he was catching a stomach bug and hurried back to the residence hall. He couldn't compete with Paul, the eternal winner.

"Hello, Carl," thundered Paul Van Horne's voice in his ear.

"Paul! How are you?" asked Carl.

"Couldn't be better. I'm in the prime of life and everything's going my way—this week, anyway."

"Maybe so, but I'm smarter, better looking, and I can still drink you under the table," boasted Carl.

"Well, I'll at least admit you can outdrink me, but the ballots are still out on who's smarter and more handsome."

Both men laughed. It was a nice feeling to be able to laugh, again, thought Carl. It really felt good. He and Paul had had some great times together.

"How does Elena like Georgia?" he asked. "Are you above or below the gnat line?"

"We are below the gnat line, and Elena is steeling herself for the hot, humid summer. How is the public relations business? Let's see, you've been PR director there for how long? Ten years?"

"Eleven."

"I'm surprised you've stayed there that long. A small shop couldn't offer you much excitement."

"It's a comfortable life," replied Carl, but not the lowly life that would have been acceptable to you, he thought. "To be honest, Paul, when I heard you'd gone to Georgia Central, I couldn't believe it. That governor and those Georgia legislators surely won't give a northerner like yourself enough money to buy pig slop, much less enough funding to build a first-class university."

"First of all, Carl, we don't feed our pigs slop. These are valuable research animals and they eat better than we do. Secondly, all I'm trying to do my first year is move in the right men—some real shakers—to help me accomplish my goals. The money will follow."

Carl was instantly on the alert. "Oh? Just what shakers have you brought in so far?"

"Do you remember Walter Sigman?"

"Didn't he head up your bicentennial campaign when you were president of the Rothschild Institute?"

"Yes, that's the man. He brought in nearly $150 million in nine months."

"Wasn't that one of the reasons the Georgia State Board of Regents hired you? They want Georgia Central to get the big bucks and play ball with the big boys?"

Paul laughed. "You always get straight to the point, don't you, Carl. You haven't changed."

"Are you disappointed that I haven't changed?"

"Not in the least, my old friend. That's why I want you to join my team. I need somebody who can play hardball with the media."

"You mean someone who can get you positive press to make Sigman's job easier?"

"And faster. The regents have given me a clear-cut deadline for the university to show signs of becoming prosperous and prominent."

"Or you'll be a president looking for a new home?"

"Exactly."

"Just how much prosperity are they expecting from you?"

"We're right in the middle of a capital campaign with a $1-billion goal, and they are expecting at least $500 million to come in before year's end."

Carl let out a whistle. "They really have high expectations for you, Paul. How is the campaign progressing at this point?"

"Not as well as I'd hoped. These good old Southern boys are trying my patience. They smile at you, shake your hand and pound you affectionately on the back, but behind that drawl and friendly veneer is a concrete wall two feet thick. I'm just trying to bring in as many powerful jackhammers as I can. So what do you say, Carl? Are you interested?"

Carl swiveled around in his seat to look out his window at the campus. From his office on the fourth floor, he could see the lake that separated the residence and dining halls from the classrooms, administrative offices and library. He took a deep breath and let it out slowly. This was opportunity knocking on his door. This was his chance to break loose from Gabriel College before it broke him. But I mustn't seem too eager, he told himself.

"Carl? Are you there?"

"Sorry, Paul. I was just thinking. Are you saying I can have the job, if I want it?"

"That's exactly what I'm saying."

Carl watched as two local fishermen headed their small boat toward the favorite fishing spot. He wished he were out there with them. He could almost feel the sun on his back, the water spray on his face and the rod in his hand. "What about a selection committee?"

"What about it? The committee is placing advertisements in the *Chronicle* and the usual headhunter agencies across the country. Finalists will be interviewed the end of May, I will make my choice the first of June and you can start July 1."

"What if I'm not a finalist? And what about the board of regents, don't they have to approve your choice?"

"First of all, it doesn't matter if you aren't one of the finalists. Secondly, the board of regents is allowing me to write my own ticket. So what do you say?"

Carl wanted to scream "yes" immediately, but he knew it was important not to seem desperate. "Well, Paul, you've caught me off guard. Frankly, I think I need more information before I can make a decision. Could you send me some details—marching orders—exactly what you expect a new vice president to accomplish?"

"I'll send it out of here overnight. I'll expect to hear back from you in a few days. Any questions, just give me a call."

"It was good hearing from you, Paul. Tell Elena `hello' for me."

Carl replaced the receiver and smiled a satisfied smile. He watched three students expressing themselves with disgusting purple paint on the "graffiti" wall, the only place on campus where they could legally do so. "If you're at the bottom of the heap, the next step has to be up," he mumbled, nodding his head slightly in agreement as he read the freshly painted message.

After feelings of euphoria passed, doubts began to surface in Carl's mind. Could the director of a small PR shop at a private college be happy and successful as vice president of a large shop at a large public research university? Was he man enough for the job? Would the regents really let Paul hire him? And knowing what a demanding person Paul was, should he accept the offer?

Goodness knows he was sick of his job at Gabriel. The challenge, the excitement, the thrill were gone. It became more and more difficult each day to get out of bed and come to work. He felt stagnant and burned out. Then when he arrived at the office, he had to walk past that odiously cheerful secretary. "Good morning, Mr. Overstreet. How are we today, Mr. Overstreet? Isn't it just a perfect day, Mr. Overstreet?" Just once, couldn't he come in and discover that she was having a bad day? Couldn't she wake up one morning and get soap in her eyes or drop her toothbrush in the toilet or put her big toe through a new pair of pantyhose?

If he were faculty, he could take a one-year sabbatical or get a Fulbright and spend three or even six months in the south of France or Rio de Janeiro. And even when they're teaching, everyone knows professors are only on campus for a few hours. Professors have it so great, he thought. They get all that time off between semesters, plus the entire summer. And they just bitch all the time. "What a bunch of spoiled wimps!" he said out loud.

So was he going to Georgia or not? Through the window, Carl watched the students pick up their paint and brushes and leave the graffiti wall. He leaned forward in his chair and strained to make out the crooked painted letters in their final piece of work: "Should a drowning rat seek refuge on a burning log?"

He swiveled his chair around to face his desk and reached for the phone. Randall Stewart answered on the third ring.

"Stewart and Associates," announced a deep bass voice with professional enunciation.

"Your new personal assistant quit already?" asked Carl, recognizing Randall's voice. Carl and Randall had been good friends since the summer Carl had been the student intern at the *Norfolk Times Dispatch*. Randall, the education reporter at the time, kept Carl away from the managing editor's wrath.

When Randall left the newspaper to manage the news bureau at Gabriel College, Carl kept in touch. In less than two years, Randall was promoted to public relations director. After Randall left Gabriel to join a national educational consulting firm, he pushed Carl for the job. Three years ago, Randall resigned from the consulting firm to start his own educational consulting business.

"Carl, is that you? You worthless good for nothing! I thought you were going to call me as soon as you got back into town."

"Hey, man, this is your call." They both laughed. "Seriously, Randy, I've been meaning to call sooner, but you know how things pile up when you're out of the office."

"I know. My personal assistant will be sorry she decided to take a two-week cruise. It will take her a month to locate the top of her desk. How was your vacation? I bet you didn't leave your apartment."

"Well, you lose, 'cause I had to go out to get more Scotch."

Randy laughed. "The time off must have helped some, Carl. You sound almost upbeat."

"That's because I've been offered a job."

"Congratulations. I didn't know you'd applied for anything since February."

"I haven't."

"A headhunter?"

Carl sighed. "Randy, this has to be confidential. Just between you and me." Briefly he told Randall about his conversation with Paul Van

Horne.

"This is what you've been looking for, isn't it? A chance to get away from Gabriel? Something more challenging?"

"It sounds like what I want, but I have to be certain. Since you've worked with college PR shops all over the United States, I was hoping you might know someone at Georgia Central University or maybe a person with inside connections."

"Have you met my partner April Pecard?"

"You don't remember the World Series party at your place when you tried to fix us up?"

Randall chuckled. "Now that you mention it, I think I might remember something."

"Guess it's difficult to remember since you unsuccessfully try to fix me up with every single woman you meet or hear about." And if I had $50 for every woman you tried to fix me up with, he thought, I could have retired from Gabriel a long time ago. Randall had introduced him to a number of attractive and intelligent women. But in the end, he always ended up comparing them to Elena, and they just couldn't measure up.

"Yeah, Carl, seems like I'd learn. Anyway, she handles the West Macon College account and is familiar with a good number of public institutions in Georgia. Why don't I talk to her and get back to you?"

"Fine, as long as I don't have to eat dinner with her to get the information."

"Carl, she shares the same positive feelings about you."

Carl hung up the phone and smiled. Maybe this wouldn't be a bad day after all, he thought. Then he picked up a black felt-tip marker and carefully penned his name in graceful cursive: Carl H. Overstreet, Vice President of Public Relations, Georgia Central University. Yeah, he thought, he would do it. Living in the same town with Elena would be an added bonus.

# Chapter Five

Since her fateful meeting with Evan weeks earlier, Georgia had been too busy preparing for battle to notice signs that summer had arrived: students in shorts lying under the trees between classes, flowers blooming in the Founders Garden, seniors picking up graduation caps and gowns, a proliferation of hometown releases about scholarships and awards, and bleary-eyed faculty with stacks of term papers to grade.

The fall-out from the Wittick fiasco was still in the news. The Mu Rho fraternity brothers, who helped plan the hazing event that left Senator Wittick's grandson in a coma, were brought before the GCU Student Judiciary Board and Discipline Committee. The board and committee suspended three of the fraternity brothers from the university and sentenced each to 120 hours of community service for violating GCU rules. The remaining fraternity brothers were put on four years of probation, and the fraternity house was closed for five years.

Even though Sherrod Wittick V had regained consciousness and was breathing on his own, he was unable to communicate or walk. His doctors were cautiously optimistic, but still concerned about long-term brain damage. Now that he was stabilized, the Wittick family planned as soon as possible to send him to the Shepherd Center in Atlanta, which was known for its innovative brand of neurorehabilitation.

During their hearing before the board and committee, the three fraternity brothers pleaded guilty to locking the senator's grandson and two others in a closet with a fifth of Johnnie Walker, a six-pack of Heineken and a gallon of cheap red wine. To prove their manhood and their worthiness to be a Mu Rho, the pledges were told to consume it all in 90 minutes. Two of the pledges left the closet and threw up, but Sherrod Wittick was carried out unconscious.

The day after the university released the decision of the judiciary board and committee, Senator Wittick phoned President Van Horne on his private line. Paul put down his copy of the *Chronicle* and picked up the receiver. "Paul Van Horne here."

"This is Senator Wittick."

"Senator, how are you and your family doing? I hear that your grandson has regained consciousness and will soon be going through rehab at the Shepherd Center. If anyone can help him recover, it will be them."

"We are hoping for the best, but only time will tell. We have been cautioned that progress will be painfully slow." The senator paused. "Listen, I read in the morning paper that those Mu Rho boys have been suspended from the university."

"Yes, that's correct, senator, and they'll be doing community service, too."

The senator cleared his throat. "I'm afraid that's not near enough punishment for what they did to my grandson."

"But that's what the judiciary board decided, senator. I have no control over their decisions."

"Maybe not, Van Horne, but you certainly could have used your influence beforehand to let them know you expected them to throw the book at those boys."

"Getting kicked out of the university is pretty harsh, senator."

"No, being left brain-damaged after a fraternity hazing is pretty harsh. You listen to me, you better get on the phone right this minute and talk to the district attorney. Tell him you want those boys indicted by a grand jury for what they did to my grandson. And you do it now, you hear me?" The phone banged loudly in Van Horne's ear as the senator slammed down the receiver.

Over the next few days, Senator Wittick began calling in favors and applying pressure to ensure that the students responsible for injuring his grandson would be severely punished. Like Van Horne, the senator always expected to get what he wanted. Two weeks later, the grand jury indicted all three on aggravated assault charges. As part of a negotiated plea deal agreement, the three defendants pled guilty to charges that they contributed to the near death of a fraternity pledge during a hazing incident. In exchange, they were sentenced to five years of probation and 200 hours of community service. Van Horne fully expected to hear from the senator, but no phone call was forthcoming. He turned his full attention to bringing in more money for the GCU coffers.

• • • • •

The number one new public relations crisis for May revolved around the senior class hiring a popular rock band to perform at a pre-graduation concert. They wanted to hold the concert in the football stadium because the university's performing arts theater was too small and the acoustics in the basketball dome were abominable. The head of physical plant and the athletic director both were adamant that the concert would not take place in the stadium because the newly installed, expensive sod would get trampled. Meanwhile, the press had gotten hold of the story—no doubt a few seniors had slipped word to a reporter or two—and the president would soon be meeting with the vice president of auxiliary services to work something out.

Thankful that she could pass the buck on that problem, Georgia picked up her purse and crossed to her office door, almost knocking over Richard Henry, her media coordinator.

"Richard, I can't talk now, I have an appointment."

Richard frowned. "There's a problem," he started.

Georgia walked by him. "It'll have to wait until I get back." Richard always had a problem. Anything he couldn't figure out on his own in two minutes, he always brought to her.

"When are you coming back?" he asked, almost with a whine.

"Richard, I don't know. If it's a real emergency—say the chemistry lab blew up, again, or a sorority has kidnapped the football team—go see Evan."

As she turned the corner, Georgia saw Richard enter Latifa's office. That's right, she said to herself, run tattle to Latifa. Richard had been nothing but a pain since the day she'd hired him. Correction, the day Evan hired him. Richard had worked in media relations in the governor's election campaign. After the election, he needed a job and Evan owed someone in the political arena a very big favor. Although Richard was occasionally competent, Georgia had managed to build up quite a file on him and hoped to fire him soon.

Georgia stopped at Sandra's desk. "I'll be back in about an hour or so," she told her. "Can you keep the wolves from my door until I return?"

"You mean Richard or Evan?"

"Both!"

"You and Evan need to make up or something. Tongues are wagging."

"That doesn't bother me," Georgia said, walking away. She was still furious with Evan for giving in to Van Horne's demands. Deep down, she realized it was all part of how "the good old boys" played the game. Evan was only abiding by the rules. It didn't matter if the rules were fair or not. Why couldn't she rewrite the rules and win the game anyway?

• • • • •

Not even bothering to knock, Richard opened Latifa's door and barged in. Latifa was sitting at her desk, her eyes closed, oohing and aahing, as her student worker Wiley Moore skillfully kneaded and massaged her back and shoulders. Wiley jumped in surprise as the door opened. Latifa opened her eyes wide then closed them into narrow slits.

"What do you mean by barging into my office without so much as knocking?" asked an angry Latifa. "I might have been in here naked or something."

"In that case, my lovely, you would have locked the door,"

retorted Richard. "Wiley, why don't you come back later?"

Wiley, just one of several student workers in the office, dropped his hands and headed for the door. Richard noted the bulging muscles extruding from the sleeves of his very tight Mickey Mouse T-shirt and thought it was a waste on a heterosexual male.

"You come right back here, Wiley," screeched Latifa. "Mr. Henry is leaving."

"No, Mr. Henry is staying right here," Richard said angrily.

"I'm busy."

"I see how busy you are."

"Wiley and I were discussing his work assignment."

"Which is?"

"None of your business. Now get out of here."

Richard turned to leave. "I guess I'll just have to tell someone else what I found out."

Latifa sat up straight in her chair, her eyes widening. "What did you find out?" She rubbed her hands together in anticipation, but Richard nodded silently in Wiley's direction. Latifa sighed. "Okay, Wiley, you can go now." She reached into her purse and handed Wiley a few bills. "Thanks for your good work." Wiley smiled, gave Richard a wary glance and left, shutting the door quietly behind him.

"Your behavior is disgusting, Latifa."

"What're you talking about? He was only getting a kink out of my back."

"Of course, and when is he coming over for dinner?"

"You're just jealous because he wouldn't let you come on to him. So shut your mouth and sit down. If you came in here to spill your guts, do it. I'm a busy woman."

Latifa was the broadcast editor and the office gossip. Anything she heard would be personally broadcast throughout campus in a matter of minutes. Richard mentally stored office gossip for later use in his struggle to rise to his highest level of incompetence. When it served his purpose, he shared what he learned with Latifa. He would use any means necessary to further his personal game plan. If he had to use someone's head as a foothold on the promotion ladder, that was just too bad. He was currently championing Georgia to become the next vice president, but only because he had designs on her present position.

Richard reached inside his coat pocket and pulled out a folded piece of paper. "Check out this list, babe," he said, handing it to her.

She snatched it from his hand. "What is it?"

"A list of applicants for the vice president of public relations' position," he replied gleefully.

"How did you get this?" she asked, because she was impressed that he had been able to get it so soon after the application deadline.

"It's better that you don't know. I also heard that the five finalists will be on campus in two weeks and the new vice president will take over July 1."

"Oh, goody!" Latifa unfolded the sheet of paper and began to read. "Who are these people? I don't know any of them! Wait, here's Georgia. Henry Carmody?" She brushed the top of her 2-inch-long macho haircut with the palm of her right hand. Her long fuchsia-polished nails were a bright contrast to her "silver smoke" dye job.

"Don't you know who he is?" Richard asked with a cocky grin on his face.

"Not that weirdo in Extension who writes the killer bird stories!?"

"Yep, he's the one."

"That's a laugh! He has a master's degree in home economics. What does he know about running a public relations office?"

"He has been writing press releases and promoting activities and research in the Office of Extension for more than 20 years."

Latifa puckered her lips. "That's true. That would make him a stronger candidate. Sometimes we don't give those writers and editors in Extension enough credit."

"Aw, come on. He doesn't have a chance. Looks like Georgia is the leading candidate to me," he said.

"I don't know," said Latifa thoughtfully. "Rumors are out there about an outside person coming in. I wouldn't bet my career on Georgia just yet."

"Stuff it, Latifa," said an irritated Richard.

45

Latifa giggled and continued to read down the list. "Wait, here's a director of public relations at Gabriel College in Huntsville, New York. Someone named Carl Overstreet."

"Naw, that's a small private school. It might be an elite private school, but give me a break. GCU is a big institution. He couldn't handle it," said Richard with finality. "There's no way the committee would even consider him."

• • • • •

Before she turned down the gravel road, Georgia compared the house number on the mailbox with what she had written on the back of an envelope. As many times as she had driven down the highway on her way to Macon, she had never noticed the driveway. Strange, she thought, that a psychologist would choose to see clients away from town. She couldn't believe she was actually paying money to see one, but Marina insisted she needed to talk to someone.

Reluctantly, Georgia made an appointment to meet with Roxanne Zeagler. Normally a positive, cheerful person, lately Georgia felt like she was scraping an emotional bottom. Marina said she was depressed. Considering the possibility—her life and career were up in the air—she hoped that Dr. Zeagler would be able to help her before her interview with the selection committee.

The curvy drive wound around elegant old live oak trees and towering pines before ending in front of a weathered wood-frame cottage, perched on a sloping backyard that ended at the river. A note on the front door told Georgia to follow the path down to the gazebo, which was halfway down the hill.

Dr. Zeagler, a cherub-faced middle-aged woman with pale blonde hair in waves around her shoulders, greeted Georgia warmly and offered her a seat in a white wicker rocker that faced the river. Georgia leaned back into soft, cozy cushions. Slowly, she began to relax and enjoy the tranquil setting. She was pretty sure she could feel her blood pressure drop and her heart rate slow down. She actually yawned. Yes, now Georgia understood why the psychologist preferred this setting to a clinical, sterile office.

Dr. Zeagler handed Georgia a cup of steaming tea. She brought the cup up to her face and inhaled the fruity smell before sipping. The flavors were a mix of strawberry or kiwi and possibly mango. "This is very good," Georgia said, taking another sip and rocking back. "I think I could sit here forever."

"Yes, that's what most of my clients say. Unfortunately, when your hour is up, you must leave." She smiled. "Now why don't you tell me why you're here?"

Georgia sighed. She wasn't sure if she could put it into words. "I just don't feel happy any more." Her eyes began to sting. A tear rolled down her cheek and startled her. Had her life become so bad that she was crying in front of a complete stranger?

Dr. Zeagler smiled sympathetically and handed her a tissue box decorated with butterflies. "It's all right, Georgia. This is a place where you can safely let it all out."

Georgia nodded, sniffed and wiped her eyes. "I'm sorry. Normally, I'm a very positive person," she continued, pausing to clear her throat. "I'm usually an upbeat person." She swallowed hard and sighed. "One of my friends thought you might be able to help me."

"Why do you think you're unhappy? Has something happened in your life? Some major change or incident?"

Suddenly, Georgia felt a lump rising in her throat, again, and the tears ran down her cheeks uncontrollably. "Oh, I'm so sorry," she cried.

"Don't apologize, Georgia. Go right ahead and cry. This is a safe place to let loose, and I have several more boxes of tissue."

Georgia blew her nose and laughed weakly. "I'm okay," she said and sniffed.

"Can you tell me why you're unhappy?"

"I'll try." She paused to compose herself. "I've worked very hard for many years to get where I am today," she explained in a near whisper.

"I see. And exactly where are you?"

"I'm associate vice president of the Georgia Central University

Office of Public Relations."

"Yes, that does sound like an important job. So what is it about your job that makes you unhappy?"

Georgia sniffed and wiped her nose. "My boss, the vice president, has been my mentor since I first went to work in the public relations office as a beginning news writer. He's given me one promotion after another and good raises. He told me when he retired, I could have his job. But now that he's finally retiring . . ." She fought back a sob. "He says I won't be promoted into the position after all."

Roxanne frowned and looked very sympathetic. "That makes you unhappy—that you won't get the promotion?"

"Yes," she said, nearly inaudible.

"Does he have someone else in mind?"

Georgia shook her head. "The new president wants to hire a personal friend. I saw the list of five finalists this morning," she said, leaning back in the rocker.

"You're one of the five, of course?"

"Yes."

"And the other four?"

"Oh, there's an associate dean of outreach in Extension Service here on campus; a corporate PR type from Chicago; a senior development person at Stanford; and the director of public relations at a small private college in New York," replied Georgia, pulling a folded paper out of her purse.

"Let me guess. Either the corporate PR individual from Chicago or the senior development person at Stanford? "

"Actually, I'm guessing not either of those." Georgia unfolded the paper and put on her reading glasses. "I think it's Carl Overstreet, PR director at Gabriel College. I jotted down some information from his resume. He graduated from Princeton the same year as the president and they were members of the same fraternity." She passed the sheet to Roxanne.

Roxanne quickly looked down at the notes. "Too many coincidences, right?"

"Right."

"So you don't really want the position?"

"But I do!"

Roxanne laughed. "Good for you!"

"But, don't you understand? I'm not going to get it. I'm just going through the motions."

"When is your interview with the committee?"

"May 16. I plan to present such an impressive strategic game plan that they'll give me a standing ovation."

• • • • •

With a fine-point red Sharpie, Carl Overstreet circled the date on his calendar. May 18 was the day he would face the selection committee for the vice president's position at Georgia Central University. He would leave May 17 and fly to Atlanta, where he would change planes for the short hop to Macon. Maria Eddings, the selection committee chair, said a graduate student would pick him up at that airport, so he wouldn't have to take the shuttle to Southern Pines.

This would be his first real trip to Georgia. Oh, sure, he had changed planes many times in Atlanta and spent hours in departure waiting areas—who hadn't? Once, he nearly left the airport with an exotic dancer for what had promised to be an interesting evening in Buckhead. Fortunately, he'd been saved from his drunken self by the early arrival of his connecting flight.

He pushed away from his desk and tilted his chair backwards, rocking slightly as he thought about what he liked about Atlanta. It had to be the green trees with skyscrapers showing between the leaves and that huge piece of gray granite looking very out of place. What did they call it? Stone Mountain? Maybe after he moved to Georgia he would climb to the top and see the view.

The ringing of his phone interrupted his thoughts. "Yes, Miss Carson?" he politely asked his secretary. He smiled as she paused before answering. He was sure she could not believe how pleasant he talked and acted lately. If she only knew he was happy because escape from Gabriel College was within his reach.

"Randall Stewart would like to speak to you."

"Thank you, Miss Carson." Carl wheeled closer to his desk and located a pad and pen. "Randy, my friend. So good to hear from you. Do you have something for me?"

"Hello, Carl. I don't have much, but what I have is good stuff, I think."

"Anything is better than nothing. What did you find out?"

"Fortunately for you, I caught April on her way down to West Macon College to talk to some professor about promoting his AIDS research in Washington. So while she was in Georgia, she made a few phone calls."

"Don't stop now. Keep talking and I'll jot down a few notes," said Carl, his pen poised.

"Okay, Carl, here's what I have. The whole university has been run by some good old Southern boys for a long, long time. Now your friend Paul Van Horne has come in and is trying to bring in some new blood to liven up the place."

"What about the public relations office?"

"I'm coming to that. Hang on. The office has been run forever by a powerful and popular man named Evan Bradshaw. The man is 72 years old. He's being nudged into retirement."

Carl felt relieved. "Well, if he's old enough to retire anyway, I guess I don't feel too bad."

"Don't get too happy, there's more. Bradshaw has been mentoring and grooming someone to follow in his footsteps."

"What's his name?" Carl frowned as he asked.

"Her name is Georgia Davis"

"A woman?"

"Yes, a well-liked and respected woman with a master's degree in media relations from Georgia Central. She's a hard worker, very reliable and dependable. April also heard, but could not confirm, that Miss Davis may finish her PhD in June."

"OK, Randy, I get the picture."

"Conscientious, witty, charming, beautiful, smart, sociable, intelligent."

"Randy, that's enough. Thank you."

"You're not getting worried, are you?"

"No, the job is mine, if I want it."

"You sound pretty confident and cocky."

"You don't know the half of it. I'm going to blow that committee out of the water. They won't even remember old Georgia-what's-her-name by the time I get through with them."

# Chapter Six

The night before her interview, Georgia and Marina met for dinner at Ruby Tuesday's at the mall. Marina ordered the house salad topped with stir-fried shrimp. Georgia selected the prime rib and baked potato. They split a pitcher of margaritas made with Avion Silver Tequila and fresh strawberries.

Georgia's adrenaline was pumping, but she was too nervous to eat much of anything. She knew she would not be able to sleep tonight. She asked Marina to join her for dinner because she knew if she ate dinner at home, her mother would drive her up the wall with her "how-to-have-a-successful job interview." Although Marina accepted the invitation, Georgia felt some reluctance on her part. Like maybe Marina had other things on her mind and only agreed out of loyalty and friendship.

Georgia took a sip of her drink, licked some of the salt from the glass rim and carefully studied her friend. Marina sat with her elbows on the table, chin in hands, while she absently stirred her drink with her finger. Georgia waved her hand in front of her face. "Marina, Marina, where are you? Come back to Earth." Startled, Marina's elbow slipped and her chin nearly dropped to the table. "Marina, what is going on with you? You're not your cheery little self."

Marina shrugged and looked up. "Sorry, Georgia. I'm just tired. It's really been a bear of a day. Alligators up to my chin. You know how that is?"

Boy oh boy, did Georgia ever know about alligators; however, she knew the development business could be rough. Marina was constantly going out of town to visit prospective donors and tell them how badly the university needed their money for scholarships, research and new buildings on campus. Not to mention the thousands and thousands of dollars for gifts, parties and receptions for donors and prospective donors. How many times had she heard Marina say, "You have to spend money to make money"?

Tonight her bubbly friend's butt was really dragging. "How did your trip to Columbus turn out?" Georgia asked in an effort to get Marina to talk. "Did you sign that old alumnus up for a few million?"

Marina leaned forward, her chin propped on both hands. "That old alumnus was Edward Ansley Liverpool."

"Yes, of course, he's on our Board of Trustees. I met him last year at the board's annual fall meeting."

Marina nodded. "Yes, that's him. One of the richest, most eligible widowed bachelors in the state," she said quietly.

Georgia frowned. "That's right, I remember that his wife died of a massive coronary about two years ago. He wanted to donate money to build a new library to be named after her. But something happened."

"The legislature wouldn't provide matching funds, so he took his money back and gave it to a university in Michigan." Marina took her elbows off the table to make room for shrimp salad.

"If he's the one I'm thinking of, he's kind of a lech, right?"

Marina looked up from her plate with a start. "Why do you think that?"

Georgia chewed thoughtfully on a bite of her prime rib. "Well, probably because he pinched my rear end, and I'm pretty sure he isn't Italian." Marina raised a questioning eyebrow. "But the room was very crowded. If it wasn't him, then it was most likely Luther Dobbs, who has been retired for 20 years. Highly unlikely it was Luther. Rumor has it he's gay."

"My money would be on Mr. Liverpool," said Marina, as she took more than a little bit of interest in a piece of shrimp.

Georgia shook her finger at Marina. "Don't you be tight-lipped with me, my friend. What do you know? Did he pinch you, too?"

Marina dropped a half-eaten piece of shrimp. "I wish he'd done something that cut and dried," she said. "Then I would know if I should be concerned."

"Tell me what he did and I'll tell you."

She shrugged. "He kept telling me how pretty I was, over and over. It made me uncomfortable."

"You are pretty, but you're right, he shouldn't keep telling you that—unless he's someone who keeps repeating themselves. Anything else?"

"He kept saying he loved my long legs and—wait, I'm not finished," she said as Georgia opened her mouth to interrupt. "He kept playing with my hair. He'd brush it away from my face with his hands and he'd curl a piece around his finger and these warning bells kept going off in my head and my stomach just twisted into one big knot."

"Maybe he's just a very lonely old gentleman?"

"When I was leaving, he embraced me."

"And extraordinarily friendly?"

"And grabbed my buttocks with both hands."

"Or your common every day dirty old man?"

Marina laughed. "I don't know what he is, but I'm not going back to see him, no matter what Walter says and no matter how much money he wants to leave the university."

"Not an unwise decision," Georgia agreed.

Marina picked up her drink. "Now I want to propose a toast to my 'bestest buddy'—Georgia Davis, future vice president of the Office of Public Relations."

Georgia clinked her glass to Marina's. "Thank you, Marina. Let's hope I can pull it off."

# Chapter Seven

Georgia despised multi-person interviews. They made her terribly uncomfortable. She took a deep breath and let it out slowly, just like Roxanne had told her in their last session: "Smile big, don't sweat and never let them know you're scared."

Georgia smiled what she hoped was a truly brilliant and confident smile and wiped a few tiny beads of perspiration from her upper lip. I am *not* scared, she told herself. I am petrified. I will *not* be able to say a word. Taking a deep breath and slowly exhaling, she looked at the face of each committee member. Even though she knew all of them and several of them quite well, they suddenly seemed like strangers to her.

Maria Eddings flashed a smile of encouragement in her direction. "Good morning, Georgia. The board has reviewed your application materials, and we're very impressed with your public relations planning strategy. We know that a whole lot of thought and work went into it. Perhaps, in your own words, you could tell us exactly what you would do first if you were chosen for the position."

Georgia felt her confidence surging and the adrenaline flowing. "Since I've been working in this office as associate vice president for more than ten years, I obviously already have a good idea of what's going on around here."

The committee members nodded in agreement. "That's definitely one of your pluses, Georgia," said Maria.

"But it could also be a minus," brought out Edgar Stephens, the new journalism school dean.

"I think it's positive, because I won't have to sit back and study the situation before making any changes to improve the office," said an undaunted Georgia. "First of all, I want to look at other university and college public relations shops. Find out how they operate, what works for them, what they'd like to change. Just from reading *Currents* and some of the other professional journals, and from talking to public relations administrators at state and regional conferences, I already know that I want to make a push for better media relations, especially at the national level. I want to make regular media trips to Washington and New York. I want to introduce more of our experts to the media. Then when a crisis comes up, our expert in that particular area will be the one they call and quote in the news."

Maria Eddings jotted down a note. "Your ideas are excellent, Georgia. Now let's talk about your dissertation—"Enhancing Media Connections at Universities in Times of Normalcy and Crisis."

"Where do you stand on that? When will you be finished?"

Georgia leaned back in her chair and took a deep breath before continuing. "I have completed my coursework, and my dissertation has been approved. Let me briefly tell you about my research results, which are scheduled to be published in the winter issue of *The Public Relations Journal*." The committee members, even Edgar Stephens, leaned forward in anticipation. Yes, marveled Georgia, I have their attention and they like what I'm saying.

# Chapter Eight

Carl felt drained when his meeting with the selection committee was over. Where was all that Southern charm and hospitality he'd heard so much about? It was definitely missing here and that made him extremely cranky and wanting a sip of Scotch. If he hadn't known the job was his, he'd have thought someone else had already been hired. Half the committee members seemed disinterested in what he had to say. The rest of them were borderline hostile. At least two of them were scrolling through messages on their cell phones. And he couldn't believe the little jerk who asked him why he didn't have a master's degree. What was his name? Dick Trumbull? Just you wait Dicky, buddy, he thought to himself. When he was on the job, the first thing he'd do was find out exactly who Dick Trumbull was and make his life miserable!

After a reception with key faculty members and top administrators from around campus, Carl was escorted to see the public relations office and meet some of the staff members. By the time he entered the front door, his smile had disappeared, a migraine was kicking in and he had an urge to break something. He suddenly felt a strong need for a double Scotch, but that would have to wait. In order to keep his temper in check, Carl bit his tongue and just grunted when introduced to individual staff members. Fortunately, most everyone was out of the building. Carl was disappointed that he did not get to meet the infamous Georgia Davis, but he knew there would be plenty of time to face off with her later.

• • • • •

A week after interviewing Carl Overstreet, the selection committee presented Paul Van Horne with one name and one name only: Georgia Davis. Four days later, Van Horne announced that Carl Overstreet, director of public relations at Gabriel College, would be the new vice president of the GCU Office of Public Relations. The State Board of Regents unanimously approved his choice.

# Chapter Nine

Georgia didn't find out that Carl Overstreet had the job until three days after graduation. Tuesday morning began as a normal day. *USA Today* and *People* magazine had both called about sending reporters down to interview one of the sociology professors, Robert Wainsley. Although Evan and Richard Henry thought it was a waste of time to pitch Wainsley's research results on gender differences to the media, Georgia had called her contacts anyway.

When Wainsley first called her about his research, it was 5 o'clock on Friday. She was packing up paperwork to take home, when Sandra stuck her head in the doorway. "Line three is for you."

"Who is it?" she asked, ducking under her desk for her purse.

"Professor Wainsley."

Georgia stood up to leave. "Sandra, will you please tell him I'll call him back on Monday?"

"No," said Sandra emphatically. Georgia was so dumbfounded that she fell backwards into her chair. Sandra came into the office and shut the door. "You need to speak to him. The poor man asked to speak to Richard, but Richard said he was right in the middle of sending out an important news release. Please talk to Dr. Wainsley. He just finished his two-year long study and he's very enthused."

Georgia dropped her bag and purse on the floor and sighed. "Okay, Sandra, I'll talk to him. Just for you."

Sandra smiled. "Thank you, Georgia. I know you'll be glad you did. Line three."

Georgia picked up the receiver and pressed line three. "Good evening, Dr. Wainsley, this is Georgia Davis. I hear you've finished your study on gender differences." Patiently, Georgia listened to

Wainsley. His enthusiasm was infectious. His research results indicated that gender differences were learned from parents, siblings, friends and teachers. Georgia took copious notes. An hour later, she was calling the media. Editors and reporters loved it and wanted to know more. CNN said they would send down a team from Atlanta Saturday for a segment to be shown Monday. The *Chronicle* promised a feature on page one. The Associated Press asked to be sent information electronically before they made a decision.

Georgia was still congratulating herself when Sandra returned to her door. "Sandra, thank you for insisting I speak to Dr. Wainsley. Now go home! The weekend is here." Sandra nodded, but didn't turn to leave. "Is something wrong, Sandra?"

She hesitated before responding softly. "Evan would like you to meet him in his office immediately."

Georgia sighed. The last thing she wanted to do was meet with Evan. Surely he didn't want to meet with her, either. Since the day he told her he was retiring, they had only met twice and then only briefly about important office matters.

"Do you know why he wants to see me?" she asked.

"I think the president and the cabinet reached a decision on the Showtime fiasco."

It's about time, Georgia thought. That woman producer had been on her back for a week. Showtime wanted to shoot a number of scenes on campus for an upcoming movie. Paul had been dragging his feet on a decision. Scott Russell, dean of the College of the Performing Arts, had been pushing for the president to give the go-ahead. Showtime had promised to hire MFA acting students and tech majors to work in various capacities, from acting extras to technical support.

"That's good," said Georgia. "Tell Evan I'll be right there."

Evan was sitting behind his desk when she entered his office. "Georgia, thanks for coming right away. Have a seat."

Georgia avoided the sofa and sat in the straight-back chair closer to his desk. She'd read somewhere in one of her "how to be successful on the job" or "how to get control of power in the office" books that the sofa should be avoided at all costs.

He smiled at her. It looked forced, but maybe she was imagining it. "You look happy today. Something must be going your way?" he asked.

"I've been pitching the results of Wainsley's research on gender differences. The press is going crazy. Even *People* and *USA Today* have scheduled interviews," she said, trying not to gloat.

"Well, well, well, Georgia. Another coup for you. Congratulations. Good job!"

"Thank you. So what's the decision on Showtime?"

"The president's cabinet doesn't like the script. They say, `No, thank you.'"

Georgia grimaced. "That won't make Dean Russell happy. He thinks his students need that kind of experience to make them more marketable after graduation," she pointed out. "Georgia is becoming known as the East Coast Hollywood. More and more studios are being built in the state. Our students need the experience to get jobs in the industry."

"I know, but Paul is very concerned about our image. He doesn't want Georgia Central perceived as a party school."

"But Evan, it's only a movie. There's no sex, no drugs, no violence. I don't understand. And Showtime says they'll give $50,000 to the general scholarship fund." Georgia didn't really care if Showtime was allowed to shoot on campus or not, but she wasn't going to let Evan off that lightly since she was still slightly annoyed with him.

"It does have drinking and some nudity," Evan said defensively.

"If the script didn't have that, it'd be a 'G' movie and little kids wouldn't want to watch it—unless it was 'Mutant Ninja Turtles Go to College.' But if the cabinet is against it, then that's that," she replied, rising from her seat.

Evan sighed and motioned with his hand. "Don't go yet," he said. "I have something else to tell you."

Georgia dropped back into the chair. "What is it, Evan?" she asked softly, but she knew what it was. He was going to tell her that she didn't get the job. He was going to say "I told you so."

Evan ran his right index finger up and down the bridge of his nose and sighed, again. "The—uh—selection committee gave their recommendation to Paul."

She leaned forward. "And?"

"The committee picked you."

Georgia jumped out of her seat. "Fantastic!" she exclaimed. "When will the president make the announcement?"

"He just called with his decision so I could alert the media. The new vice president is Carl Overstreet from Gabriel College. It's already been approved by the Board of Regents."

Georgia's heart dropped to her feet; her lungs suddenly stopped functioning; and her knees threatened to give way beneath her. Far off she heard a voice and wondered if it were hers. "But he wasn't a finalist."

"I know, but he's the president's choice," Evan said wearily. He stood up as Georgia swayed. "Georgia, are you all right?" He hurried around his desk and grabbed her elbow, but she pulled back from his grasp. "Maybe you should sit back down."

She stood as straight as she could and tried to look under control. "I'm just fine, thank you." At least I think I am, she thought. "If that's all the good news you have, then I have work to do." Good Girl, she told herself as she started for the door. I am not going to lose my temper. I am not going to become hysterical. And I will not throw up or pass out.

"Georgia, I know you're hurt and angry, and I'm sorry it turned out this way," Evan said. "I did warn you."

Georgia did not stop or give him a glance. She turned the knob, opened the door and walked out. What do you do when your life's goal gets axed, she asked herself? Why head to Tara to lick your wounds, of course.

•  •  •  •  •

Local reporter Norman Brewster was waiting in Georgia's office. He was leaning back in her chair, his feet propped on her desk, hands behind his head. When Georgia walked in, he jerked his feet to the floor and sat up straight in her chair. "Ahhhh, methinks my lady has also heard the news," he said, his face expressionless.

Georgia was not surprised to see Norman in her office. He had an uncanny ability of finding out campus news quickly from a large number of reliable, confidential academic sources. Usually, the news did not directly involve her. "I can't talk to you right now, Norman. Please leave."

Norman stood up and rushed to her side. "I'm sorry, Georgia." he said soothingly, putting his arms around her. "I know how badly you wanted the job."

With the anger and aching sorrow filling her to the bursting point, the thought of falling into Norman's strong arms for comfort appealed to her on some level, but she was stronger than that ... and she knew there would be dangerous consequences to deal with later if she caved in now. She pushed him away and pointed to the door. "Go, Norman," she said as loudly and firmly as she could. He looked at her, hesitating. "Go. Now!"

He paused in the doorway. "All right, I'll leave, but if you need a strong shoulder or a few consoling words, call and I'll be back."

• • • • •

When Marina arrived at Georgia's front door, a grim-faced Eula Mae immediately opened it and ushered her into the living room. A dejected Georgia sat on the sofa, pouring what was left of a bottle of white wine into an empty glass. Not looking up, she asked hoarsely, "Who told you?"

Marina leaned over and gave her a sympathy hug.

Eula Mae nodded at Marina and quietly left the room.

"No one really told me," Marina answered. "I merely put two and two together."

"Let me guess, Evan called to see if I was in your office?" Georgia gulped down half the wine in the glass.

"Actually, it was Richard."

"Richard?" Georgia banged her glass on the table. "What did that twit want?"

"He was trying to get out a news release about the new vice president before the weekend, and he wanted to ask you a question. As soon as I heard it was the Gabriel College guy, I reasoned if you weren't in my office, you had to be at home."

Georgia leaned back on the sofa and briefly closed her eyes and massaged her forehead with her fingers. "What's so maddening is that he wasn't even recommended by the selection committee."

"Evan did try to warn you. You knew it was a done deal from the beginning," said Marina, patting Georgia's shoulder soothingly.

"I just didn't want to believe Evan," Georgia said. "I wanted to believe there might be justice and fairness in the world. I'm an associate vice president of a major research university. He's the director of a small private college. I've just earned my PhD in public relations. He only has a bachelor's degree. Did the president hire him because he's equipped with male genitalia?" The vehemence of her own words surprised even Georgia.

"Oh, Georgia," whispered Marina, giving her shoulder a squeeze. "You know the real reason the president hired him is because he knows the man. They were college friends. Fraternity brothers. He trusts him to do what he wants."

"But I could do that. I'm loyal and trustworthy."

Marina gave Georgia a hug. "I know that, but he couldn't take the chance. Besides, it's like you said—you're missing what is of the utmost importance here."

Georgia shook her head and held out her hands in question. "What's that?"

"A penis and testicles, and there's nothing you can do about that."

•  •  •  •  •

In the public relations office, media relations coordinator Richard Henry finally finished the news release. After Evan sanctioned it, he faxed it to the President's Office for Van Horne's approval. It was the first time that Richard had been asked to write a quote for the president and it made him nervous, although he knew Georgia did it frequently. In fact, Georgia and Evan often wrote the president's speeches.

As he waited for the signal to send out the release, Latifa sashayed through his door. Normally Richard got excited when Latifa came to see him. Her appearance usually indicated that something juicy was going on in the office or on campus and he was fixing to get the lowdown. But this afternoon he was too worried about the Overstreet news release to get enthusiastic over any gossip.

"Latifa, I don't have time. Why aren't you on your way out of town with your boy toy?" started Richard before she could open her mouth.

"I don't care about your time, slime-breath, and who I go out of town with is none of your business," interrupted Latifa, shutting the door behind her.

"Latifa, don't close the door. What are you doing?" Richard rose from his seat.

Latifa stopped at his desk and leaned over as far as she could. "What's this about Georgia not getting the vice president's job?"

Resigned, Richard collapsed in his chair. "Carl Overstreet got the appointment."

She shook her long finger under his nose. Her two-inch-long fiery-red nail nearly brushed his upper lip. "And why didn't you come tell me as soon as you knew? Why did I have to hear it from Clarisse?"

Richard shivered, completely fascinated by exposed cleavage undulating in front of his face. He was suddenly reminded of old rumors circulating about Latifa and half a dozen fraternity guys at Panama City during spring break.

"Richard!" Her voice was shrill and rising.

He cringed. "Geez, Latifa, I just didn't have time."

"That's your excuse? You didn't have time?" Latifa straightened up and looked at him with loathing.

"Latifa," he nearly whined her name. How he hated it when she had the upper hand.

She turned her back to him, one hand resting on her right hip, the other tugging impatiently on a short piece of silver hair behind her left ear. "I'm listening, Richard." She glanced at him over her shoulder.

"I have been chained to this computer all day. I didn't even get lunch." He lowered his voice. "And when I wasn't writing, I was thinking about Georgia not getting promoted."

Latifa whirled around to face him. "Since when have you ever been concerned about her feelings or anybody else's?"

Richard jumped to his feet, a red flush creeping out of his shirt collar and spreading up his neck. "Because if she doesn't get promoted, I don't get promoted."

Latifa's eyes widened, then narrowed. She paused for a few seconds before she spoke. "I understand, Richard, and you are forgiven, Sugar—this time."

Richard watched as she crossed to the door. The fabric of her tight-fitting dress clung to her body curves and accented every muscle movement. "I hate to gossip and run, but Wiley—the dear boy—is waiting on me for inspiration." As she left his office, she puckered her lips and kissed the air in his direction.

• • • • •

While Richard worried about media reaction to his press release, Georgia and Marina ate the canned chicken noodle soup that Eula Mae had heated up for them. She served it with Ritz crackers and iced tea. Although Georgia protested futilely to her mother that she wasn't hungry, she felt better by the time she finished the last spoonful. Georgia decided it was good that she had a great friend like Marina, who would take time to comfort a hurting comrade, and a mother, who stubbornly refused to let her daughter starve to death.

When Eula Mae slipped out of the kitchen to watch the news, Georgia glanced at Marina and smiled, and noticed for the first time the troubled expression on Marina's face. She reached out to Marina and patted her hand. "It's okay, Marina. I'm going to be all right. You can stop worrying now."

Marina looked over at her, smiled a sad smile and nodded. "I know," she responded quietly.

"Are you all right?" Georgia asked her friend.

"Sure, I'm fine," she answered, quickly wiping away a tear from her cheek.

Georgia moved over to Marina for a closer look. "No, I don't think so. I've been so caught up in my own problems, I didn't notice you were hurting, too. What's wrong?"

"Nothing." The word came out in a half whimper.

"Don't do this to me. Do I have to guess the worst? You've been fired?" Marina shook her head. "You're pregnant?" She shook her head, again. "You have herpes? Worse? You're dying of brain cancer?"

"Please, no more. It isn't as bad as it seems," Marina said.

"How do I know? You haven't confided in me yet."

"You do know a little," admitted Marina. "Remember earlier this semester I told you about visiting Mr. Liverpool?"

"Edward Ansley Liverpool? Board of Trustees Liverpool? Billions-of-dollars Liverpool? Prospective donor Liverpool?"

"Yeah, all of the above."

Georgia wrinkled her brow in thought. "Marina, I thought you weren't ever going back to see him?"

"I wasn't, but he specifically asked for me. He wanted me to explain about making the university a beneficiary in his will. I was afraid Walter would think it was silly to fuss because an old man paid me a few compliments," confessed Marina.

Georgia shook her head. "So you went back. He didn't try anything, did he?"

"No, but he ... Well, he made me ... I sort of felt ... Maybe I'm making a mountain out of a mole hill."

"You are making me crazy," blurted out Georgia. "Tell me what he did."

"Okay," Marina said and took a deep breath. "Well, to play it safe, I took Larry Ingle, my student intern."

"Yes, that was a good move," Georgia reasoned.

"But Mr. Liverpool sent Larry to his office to find something. As soon as Larry was gone, he gave me a hug and said something like, `I bet you drive all the young men wild,' and I pulled away from him."

"You are kidding? Did you tell him to stop?"

"Yes, but maybe I said it too nicely. I didn't want to offend him, since the university could use the money. But he just laughed and told me I looked cuter when I blushed. Then he grabbed me, again, and kissed me on the mouth. I tried to pull back and get away, but he was too strong. I finally just jabbed him in the ribs as hard as I could."

"I bet that stopped him!"

"No, he just laughed and said, `I love a feisty woman,' then he pushed me up against the door and kissed me so hard I bit myself, see?" Marina pulled down her lower lip to show Georgia. "Fortunately, Larry came back then. I said I didn't feel well and we left. When he shut the door behind us, I could hear him laughing on the other side."

Georgia sputtered. "Men! Some of them can really act like jerks!"

"I know, and you haven't heard it all. Mr. Liverpool called Walter this morning and told him he was very impressed with me and that thanks to my explanation of financial needs, I convinced him not only to leave the university $40 million in his will, but he's giving us $5 million now for scholarship funds."

"What? I guess that's his way of apologizing."

"I don't think so. I think it's a bribe."

"What do you mean?"

"He wants to give the check to me personally and to show his gratitude, he wants to fly me in his private jet to Savannah, so he can wine and dine me on his yacht."

"Unbelievable! And Walter agreed to this?"

"He and the president are so excited that they're already drawing up the papers for the Edward Ansley Liverpool Scholarship Fund."

"When are you going to tell Walter you can't go?"

"How can I? What do you think Walter would say if I told him his hot new donor was a dirty, horny old man and I wasn't going? It would be Mr. Liverpool's word against mine. Who do you think Walter would believe, me or old money bags?"

"You have a point, but you know you can't go."

"What else can I do?"

"Let's think about this. We can find a solution." Georgia gave Marina a smile of confidence. First things first. She would worry about Carl Overstreet later.

· · · · ·

After Marina left, Georgia made her way to her bedroom and quietly shut the door. A few seconds later, she heard a knock. She knew who it was, but she did not want to deal with her mother or anyone else. She only wanted to take a long shower and go to bed.

Eula Mae continued to knock. "Georgia, let me in. This is your mother. The only mother you have."

Georgia sat on the side of her bed and fell over backwards.

Eula Mae knocked, again. "Georgia, this is your mother who carried you in her womb for nine very long months and endured 32 hours of extremely painful labor."

Georgia dragged herself off the bed and opened the door. "Mom, please, I've had a very rough day. I only want to shower and go to bed."

Eula Mae, already dressed in her Star Wars nightie, sashayed past her daughter and sat on the bed. "Is it true what I heard on the news? That the selection committee recommended you for the vice president's job, but that the new president gave the position to some unqualified male? A former fraternity buddy? What happened?"

Georgia sat next to her mother on the bed. "Mom, you don't believe everything you hear on television, do you?"

"If I hear it from that hunk of an anchorman on Channel 7, then yes, I do. Are you telling me the president didn't give your job away to somebody else?"

Georgia sighed. "Okay, Mom, yes, it's true," she reluctantly admitted.

"And all those nice folks on the selection committee really did recommend you to the president?"

"Yes," Georgia said, "but it was only their recommendation. The president can choose whoever he wants. After all, he runs the university as he sees fit."

Eula Mae paused a moment before she replied. "Hmph! Well, you sound okay considering you've been shanghaied and stabbed in the back."

"Mom, how many times growing up did you tell me that life is not fair? Obviously, you were right. I'm accepting what you taught me and I'm moving on."

Eula Mae laughed. "Okay, okay, I deserve that. Sweetheart, I'm sorry it's turned out badly for you. I know you've been working hard for that vice president's position for years. Is there anything I can do? Aside from rolling the president's yard and egging his windows?"

"Thank you, Mom, but I'm going to be okay. Disappointed, angry, totally pissed off, but it is what it is. If Hilary Clinton can survive her big loss with the entire world watching, then I can survive this one."

"Here, let me give you a warm fuzzy." Eula Mae wrapped her arms around her daughter and gave her a big hug. "And tomorrow I will clean the entire house and cook us both a nice hot meal."

Georgia couldn't help but laugh. Her mother had never even cleaned her own home. A cleaning service did. And her idea of cooking a hot meal was re-heating restaurant leftovers in the microwave. "Thanks, Mom. I appreciate it, but that's not necessary. Don't worry about me. This is something I have to handle by myself. You and Dad raised me to be strong and to stand up for myself, didn't you?"

"That we did and I think we did a good job."

"Yes, I think so, too." No one would ever have called her parents over-protective. They were not helicopter parents, either. There were always choices and options growing up. She always suffered the consequences when she chose wrongly. She still remembered the time in sixth grade when she spent her monthly budget money at the mall. This money was supposed to pay for her school lunches and other necessary items. When she asked for more money for lunch, her parents refused. She suffered the consequences. Every day for three weeks, she had to make a P&J sandwich for lunch. A valuable lesson learned.

Eula Mae reached over and gave Georgia another hug. "Want me to start bad-mouthing the president to my friends?"

Georgia patted her mother's back. "Thank you, Mom, but that won't be necessary. I have a feeling he's expecting that already. My friends at the university will be doing enough of it without help from you."

"What are your plans? Are you thinking about looking for another PR position somewhere else?"

"The idea has crossed my mind, but I'd have to be willing to move, and that would mean uprooting you, again." Georgia remembered the effort involved with moving her mom from Florida to Georgia—selling the condo, getting rid of all the stuff her parents had accumulated over the years, settling her mother into a new life and finding a new dentist and doctors willing to take a Medicare patient.

"Georgia, your career is what's important. You have sacrificed a lot for it."

Yes, thought Georgia, that she had. Here it comes. She knew what was coming next.

Eula Mae paused briefly and took a deep breath. "If you weren't so passionate about your career ... if you didn't love your work ... if it wasn't the reason you get up every morning."

"I know, Mom, if it weren't for this job, I could be happily married and you could have grandchildren to spoil." How many times had she heard this from her mother? Too many to count.

Eula Mae spread her hands on the duvet and chuckled softly. "I did it, again, didn't I?"

Georgia sighed and nodded.

"I'm sorry, Sweetheart."

Georgia pulled her mother up off the bed. "It's all right, Mom. I understand. Look, it's been a long day and tomorrow will probably be worse. I need to try and get some asleep."

Eula Mae ambled towards the door. "Of course, dear. Try and get a good night's sleep."

"I'll do my best. Please don't worry about me. I'll be okay. But promise me something."

"What's that, dear?"

"When you start talking to your friends, please don't talk ugly about my new boss."

"Why not?"

"Because I need to keep my job until I have another one."

"I see ... All right, no bad words will pass from my lips regarding some warty toad of a loser who's stealing your job."

"Mom!" Georgia sighed, again, and nudged her toward the door. "Good night, Mom, I love you!"

"Good night, Georgia. Love you, too!"

• • • • •

Besides her mother and Marina, Georgia refused to discuss Carl Overstreet with anyone until her weekly visit with Roxanne Zeagler. She had remained so cheerful and optimistic at work that, except for Evan, everyone in the office seemed to believe she hadn't really wanted the vice president's job after all. But Roxanne knew otherwise.

"I'm not surprised you didn't get the position," said Roxanne to Georgia after she arrived for her appointment. "But I know you're upset."

"My only consolation was that the press was very critical of Paul's decision not to go along with the selection committee's choice," said Georgia.

"That was a good editorial, too."

"The one about the president slapping the committee in the face?"

"And how their time and effort had been wasted for nothing." Roxanne shook her head. "It really is a dog-eat-dog world out there, Georgia. The president wanted a man in that position—his man."

"I thought that hiring and promotion practices were changing, but now I'm not sure," said Georgia. "I've never considered myself a feminist. I thought if you worked hard and were competent that you could be anything you wanted to be. Equal opportunity for all."

"And now you believe that's not true?"

"I know it's not true," said Georgia with finality. "It doesn't matter how hard you work or how good you are or how many degrees you have. What counts is who you know and whose rear end you're kissing."

Roxanne suppressed a smile. "Do I detect a note of cynicism today?"

Georgia shook her head. "No, I'm just facing up to reality. What do you think I should do now?"

"Since you are calm and you aren't talking suicide or self-torture, I think you probably know what you need to do."

"In the morning, I plan to pay a visit to Rodney Feldman, the equal opportunity officer."

"That could be risky, especially if he's one of the new president's hires," Roxanne pointed out.

"Not Rodney. He was hired under the last president and is a fine Southern gentleman. Don't worry, I don't plan to file a grievance. I just want to find out my options."

"All right, as long as this is only a fact-finding mission. What else?"

"Well, I guess I'll update my resume and start networking. I'll call all of my friends and acquaintances, especially my PR colleagues at other academic institutions, and let them know that I'm looking."

"Very good. In the meantime, strive to be a good team player. When Carl Overstreet arrives, bend over backwards to help him settle into his job. Don't give him a chance to call you a bad loser. If you can impress him in this way, you will have an ally instead of an adversary should he talk to a prospective employer."

Yes, I'll be a team player, thought Georgia. He'll never know how much I hate his guts. And I'll be there the day he falls on his face.

• • • • •

Rodney Feldman welcomed Georgia into his office and shook her hand enthusiastically, but—at least she thought—nervously. Before she could start asking him questions, Feldman opened his wallet and started pulling out photos of his new grandson. Then he told her about his youngest son Phil, who was flying fighter planes for the Navy in the Middle East; his only daughter Meg, who was trying to make it as an actress in Atlanta and had finished her fourth acting role in a cable TV commercial; and his oldest son Luke, who had graduated from Emory University Law School in Decatur. Twenty minutes later, he walked over and shut his office door. "I guess I know why you're here," he said, sitting down behind his well-worn faux-oak desk. "I wasn't surprised when I heard what happened."

"You and Evan." An uncomfortable silence settled between them for a minute, then Georgia spoke. "The reason I'm here, Rodney, is to find out about my rights and how the grievance process works."

Feldman frowned and chased a paper clip around the top of his desk with his finger. He stopped and looked directly at Georgia. "Trust me, Georgia, you don't want to file a grievance."

"I didn't say I wanted to file, Rodney. I only need to know how it works."

Rodney cleared his throat. "It's a long drawn-out process for university employees. The administration has made it as complicated as they possibly can in order to dissuade anyone from filing frivolously. First, you would have to draw up a formal grievance letter, naming names and putting down allegations. Each individual named receives a copy of this letter and has an opportunity to respond. You must arrange for faculty and staff members to agree to serve on the grievance committee. No lawyers are permitted. Before the grievance session, you must submit a list of possible witnesses to be called. During the session you call and question the witnesses and you testify before the committee. The other side gets to question you and your witnesses. The whole process can eat you up inside and out and leave you an emotional wreck." He paused and looked at her expectantly.

Georgia's shoulders sagged. "I didn't realize that."

"Most folks don't." Feldman pushed back his chair and stood up. He walked around his desk and sat down in the chair next to her.

"Look, Georgia, I'm not saying you don't have a case. After all, the selection committee did recommend you. You have better job experience, you have him beat education-wise and the winning applicant is a man. On the other hand, there is no law that says the president has to hire the person a selection committee recommends; and maybe Van Horne hired Overstreet for reasons unknown to us.

"My advice is to wait until after Carl Overstreet arrives. He might prove to be a real go-getter. Maybe someone you will enjoy working with. Six months from now—if you still want to do it—you could file a grievance."

Georgia looked down at her hands in her lap for a few seconds, then she looked up at Feldman. "I don't want to file a grievance against my alma mater, Rodney. I need to get back to my office. You told me everything I came here to find out. Thank you for the information." She stood and held out her hand.

Feldman stood and shook her hand. He watched her walk to the door. "Georgia?"

She turned. "Yes?"

"Just between you and me, if worse comes to worst, you could always skip the grievance process, get a lawyer and sue. Loyalty to your alma mater be damned."

• • • • •

Evan Bradshaw and Carl Overstreet both had their farewell parties on June 24.

Evan's dinner was held in the Holiday Inn ballroom in downtown Southern Pines. Nearly 300 guests paid $50 each to eat prime rib and pay tribute to a man who had once wielded great power at the university and with the media. An entertainer from Atlanta presented a humorous look at Evan's life at the university; the GCU Office of Public Relations staff presented him with an engraved Seiko watch; President Paul Van Horne gave him a plaque; Sandra Gibson cried into a pink hanky with red lace until she got the hiccups; and Evan drank so much cabernet sauvignon, Georgia insisted on driving him home.

• • • • •

Neither Evan nor Georgia spoke during the short drive to his townhouse, which he'd purchased after his wife died, when he decided to downsize. It was close enough to the university that Evan could walk to the office on days when the temperature was below 80 degrees and the humidity breathable.

Georgia pulled up to the front door and started to get out of the car, but Evan grabbed her wrist. "Where are you going?" he asked.

"To help you to the door," she answered.

"You saying I'm drunk?" he asked indignantly.

"Of course not. I merely thought you might need someone to hold your presents while you opened the door," she lied.

"That's good, since I only let you drive me home 'cause I couldn't remember where I parked my car," he said, sounding like his tongue was fat and numb.

Georgia walked around the car to the passenger side. Although she had been to a lot of social functions—receptions, dinners, cocktail parties—over the years, this was the first time she'd ever seen Evan tipsy. She opened the door on his side and offered him a hand, which he refused. Stepping back, she watched him slowly ease himself out and stand up unsteadily. He took one step toward the house and lost his balance. Georgia grabbed his elbow and he didn't complain. With a shopping bag full of gifts and mementos in her other hand, she walked with Evan up to his front door.

Unable to find the key hole, Evan gave Georgia his key. Making sure Evan was leaning against the porch railing for support, she dropped his "goodie bag" and opened the door. After depositing his bag on a chair in the living room, she turned and helped her now ex-boss through the doorway. She guided him over to his overstuffed recliner and gently sat him down. She heard him sigh softly and saw his eyes close. "Good night, Evan." She turned to go.

"Georgia," he called after her. She stopped and turned. He reached out his hand towards her. "We were a good team, weren't we?"

Georgia walked back to him, squeezed his hand and kissed him on his forehead. "Yes, Evan, we were the best."

He smiled a crooked smile, nodded his head in agreement and closed his eyes. Before she shut the front door behind her, he was asleep.

• • • • •

The public relations office staff took Carl to lunch at Lilly's, the local blue-plate special restaurant. He had roast beef and gravy with potatoes, carrots and green beans. His happy secretary chirruped and cooed throughout the meal. The office gave him a goody basket: gnat spray, suntan lotion, sun glasses, a book titled *How to Speak South Georgian*, a peanut watch and a framed, autographed group photo.

Carl wiped the gravy off his mouth and looked around the small private dining room at the staffers and colleagues who came to bid him adieu. He wasn't the sentimental type, but he was surprised to see about two dozen smiling faces looking up at him expectantly.

"Thank you, everyone, for showing up today. Either my secretary guilted you into being here or you came to make sure I really am leaving." Everyone laughed loudly.

"I won't believe it until I see you walk out the office door with your PRSA award plaques under one arm and your Star War posters under the other," yelled the public relations office photographer.

"Yeah, you cost me 20 dollars," said Eric Jones, the office's science writer for 18 years. "I bet Sam that I would retire before you ever left Gabriel."

Carl smiled. He had inherited Eric when Randall Stewart left the director's position to him. Anytime Carl annoyed Eric, he would threaten to quit, but he never did. He came close one hot, humid summer day, after Carl sent him into the deep woods to take photos of an archeological dig. When he returned, half-eaten alive with chiggers, Eric said that was it. He had put in over 10 years. He was quitting to open his own photography studio. He changed his mind after Carl gave him three days off and sent him a case of his favorite craft beer.

"Sorry about that Eric, but Sam offered me 20 bucks if I would leave." The group laughed, again. Yes, he thought, even though his last year at Gabriel had been boring and depressing, most of his time there had been good. He would be taking a lot of special memories with him when he moved to Georgia.

Carl couldn't wait to start work at Georgia Central University on July 1. But the best news was that he would be dining with Paul and Elena very soon. In anticipation of their reunion, he started working out and trying to lose a few pounds. He even bought new clothes for the occasion.

When Paul called to let him know the State Board of Regents had approved his appointment, he advised Carl that it came with some reservations. Although the press was critical of how Carl had been hired over the selection committee's choice—Georgia Davis—he said the uproar seemed to be calming down. But Paul warned him that it wouldn't be smooth sailing for him. Carl prepared himself for the worst.

# Chapter Ten

Evan spent his last week at GCU going through files, packing up his books and papers, and sending out letters and memos. On his last day, he took a box into Georgia's office unannounced. Georgia was trying to get out a news release on a new surgical technique that had been developed by one of the research professors in the Clark College of Medicine. But she was finding it difficult to concentrate after sending Marina to talk to Lynn Howington in the Equal Employment Opportunity Commission office on campus. She was expecting her to phone any second.

Evan walked in and put his box on Georgia's desk. "Is this a bad time?" he asked her. "I could come back to campus for homecoming."

Georgia smiled. She was glad Evan seemed to be in a good mood. "No, I have a few minutes for you. Please sit down."

"Thanks, but I still have a few more boxes to clear out of my office. How would it look for the new vice president to show up and find his office filled with my personal belongings?" He reached down into his box and pulled out a potted plant and a spray bottle.

Georgia looked at the plant curiously. "Is that an orchid?"

"Yes, a *Cattleya bowringiana*," he said proudly. "I grew it in my window green house and I want you to have it."

"You know I'm no good with plants," she protested, looking at the large thick green leaves.

"All you have to do is spray it and keep it in the sun and one day a new bud will pop open with a gorgeous bloom."

Georgia followed Evan over to her sunny window where he placed the orchid on the wide sill. "Evan, I'm touched."

He looked at her and smiled. "You should be. I don't grow orchids for all the ladies. Only a few special ones."

"Thank you, Evan. Thank you, very much."

"Now when I'm vegetating in front of my TV, I can picture you working away with my orchid blooming behind you."

"Evan, I'll miss you. I owe you big time. You taught me everything I know about public relations in academia," Georgia's throat tightened and her eyes filled with tears. Oh, no, she thought. She had promised herself there would be no blubbering.

"Don't you get sappy on me," he said gruffly, his voice touched with emotion.

"Not me, I'm glad to see you go. Good riddance! Out with the old and in with the new."

They both laughed and Georgia knew her hysterics crisis had been averted. Evan reached out to Georgia and gave her a long hug. She hugged him back fiercely. Evan would have liked the moment to last indefinitely, but he gently pushed her away.

"Okay, enough is enough, young lady" he said. "We don't want Latifa to walk by and see us in a clutch! We'd be the center of the rumor mill by lunch time." His face sobered. "Seriously, Georgia, watch your back. Overstreet will probably feel threatened by you, especially since he knows you wanted the job. Don't provoke him or do anything that will provide him an excuse to fire you before you can find another position. You are looking, aren't you?"

"Yes, I'm looking," she replied with a sigh.

"I'll be glad to write you a glowing letter of recommendation or make phone calls to a few people in your behalf. Whatever you need."

"All of the above?"

"You got it. If you ever need any advice, I know this old, retired, bored-to-death vice president who would love your company."

"Evan, I'll call." And she knew that she would.

• • • • •

Marina phoned about five minutes after Evan left Georgia's office. Even though Georgia was pulling together a list of health/medicine reporters to send her press release to, she set her work aside to hear what Marina had learned.

"Lynn talked with me briefly," began Marina, "but she thinks I should speak to Walter and tell him what happened between me and Mr. Liverpool."

"Are you still against this?" Georgia had bad feelings about this herself, but didn't see that Marina had much choice.

"I don't feel comfortable with it, no. But the worst I could do is lose my job, I guess."

"Then you'll do it?"

"I'll sleep on it."

•  •  •  •  •

That afternoon Georgia chaired the weekly staff meeting. The writers, editors, photographers and broadcasters looked at her expectantly. She wished she could tell them that she was looking for another job and that they should update their resumes, too. She didn't. Instead, she told them what she felt they needed to hear. "As you know, Carl Overstreet will officially be here tomorrow, July 1. Although I have not talked with him personally, he did send me a brief note, and I will meet with him in the morning." She paused and looked around the room.

"Do you think he'll change anything right away?" asked Delores Rinehart, the senior news writer.

"I seriously doubt it," Georgia answered. "He'll want to come in and see what's going on before he does that." At least that's what she was hoping. However, that had not been the case with the new president. Paul Van Horne had started making changes his first month in the position. "How many of you had the chance to meet him when he was in town for his interview?" she asked. Four people, including Latifa, raised a hand.

Georgia turned to Will Bryant, their chief photographer. He usually had a quick and fairly accurate take on people. Georgia had already heard negative comments about Carl from the other three. Since Will had refrained from sharing his thoughts at the time, Georgia thought he might have something positive to say. "What did you think of him, Will?"

Will shrugged. "He was okay, maybe a little stressed. He asked if I'd taken the photos in the annual report. I told him I'd taken a few. He said they were boring. He left. End of story."

Georgia cringed. Not a good first impression, she thought, especially for someone being considered for an important position. Unless he already knew he was getting the job. No, Georgia, she fussed at herself. Don't go there!

Latifa mumbled something at her end of the room and those closest to her laughed. "I met the man and, quite frankly, I think he's a total jerk," she said out loud. "I don't blame the committee for not wanting him in the job."

That was Latifa, thought Georgia. She never minced words. *Diplomacy* was one word that wasn't in her dictionary.

Dudley O'Brien, another news writer, voiced his disapproval, too. "When I introduced myself to him, he said he was familiar with my writing. Then he asked me if I thought I would ever be a good writer."

At that point, Georgia lost control of the meeting. Everyone began talking at once. Each person had something to say about the new vice president. Georgia was glad Carl Overstreet was not present to hear what they were saying or they'd all be fired on the spot. Georgia stood up, placed two fingers in her mouth and let out a shrill whistle. Suddenly, instant quiet.

"Thank you." said Georgia, as she sat down and ran her fingers through her short dark brown hair. "I realize everyone has already started forming strong feelings about Mr. Overstreet, but let's not forget that he's the one the president hired. He's the one who will be your new boss starting tomorrow." Murmurs of dissatisfaction went up around the room. "Right now you're unhappy with the president's choice. All I'm asking is for you to give him a chance. Anyone can have a bad day." She paused for a few seconds. "After all, if I can stand up and welcome him to this office, then I think all of you can, too."

She looked from face to face. A few of them looked like they wouldn't give their own mother a chance. Latifa had a big sneer on her face. Half of them looked undecided. Delores looked contemplative. Richard just sat there and scowled. Was there any hope, Georgia wondered?

"I think Georgia's right," agreed Delores, after a long period of silence in the room. "Anyone can have a bad day. Remember when Dudley's car broke down in the driving rain storm, miles from nowhere, no cell service and no one would stop to help?"

Everyone nodded.

"Definitely a bad day!" pointed out Will. "Dudley was a total cretin when he got to the office. He even snapped at Evan."

Everyone murmured in agreement. Dudley buried his face in his arms on the table.

"Then please, do me a favor," asked Georgia. "Give the man a chance to do a good job."

"I think that's the least we can do," said Dudley. "After all, if Georgia of all people can give the man a break, then we should, also."

Georgia looked around the room. Everyone seemed to be agreeing except for Richard. He appeared to have other things on his mind. Oh, well, she thought, he is the least of my worries. At least, she hoped so.

● ● ● ● ●

When Georgia locked up her office for the day and exited the building, she found Norman waiting on the wrought-iron bench outside the entrance to the building. Pretending not to see him, she continued up the sidewalk toward the parking deck. As she sprinted by the bench, Norman rose quickly and fell in behind her. He followed her all the way to her car. As she unlocked the driver's side to her Toyota, he leaned over and held the door so she couldn't open it.

"Norman!" she called out, trying to sound as irritated as she felt. "What are you doing?"

"Ahhhh, my lady."

"And you can drop the 'my lady' stuff," she interrupted him. Why Norman continued to refer to her as "my lady," Georgia did not know, unless it was just to irritate her. She thought that if she pretended not to notice, he would soon tire of the game and discontinue his fun. Unfortunately, that wasn't working.

"Ahhhh, my lady is rather testy tonight, I see."

"I wasn't until a few minutes ago," Georgia said irritably. She tried to open her door, again, but Norman continued to hold it shut. "Norman Brewster, I've had a long day, and I'm too tired for any of your juvenile games."

Norman grabbed the door handle and opened the door. Georgia nodded thankfully and slid in under the steering wheel. With a serious expression on his face, Norman crouched down between her and the door.

"What is it, Norman?" she asked with a feeling of unease.

"I've heard some negative things about this Overstreet fellow."

"Thank you, but I've gotten an earful from the public relations staff. Doesn't anyone want to give him a chance?"

"Let me just tell you what I heard."

"No, Norman, now get away from my car before I call campus security." Georgia pulled out her cell phone threateningly.

Norman stood up and backed away from the Toyota. He threw up his hands. "Fine, Georgia, just go on home and don't hear me out." Georgia turned the engine and put it into gear to back out of her spot. "Promise me one thing, Georgia." He looked directly at her with grave concern in his face.

"What?"

"Watch your back." He turned and walked away.

● ● ● ● ●

Carl went straight to Paul's office his first morning on the job. Paul welcomed his friend warmly. "Sit down, Carl. Have you been by your office, yet?"

"No, I wanted to meet with you first," said Carl, accepting a cup of coffee from Paul. He took a sip and smiled. "Just the way I like it, Paul. You remembered after all these years."

"How could anyone forget someone who has to have a fourth of a cup of cream and four grains of sugar!" Both men laughed. "How's the condo?"

"It's perfect," said Carl. "I feel lucky to have found something that decent and comfortable within walking distance of campus."

"Are you still coming for dinner tonight?"

"Unless I have to work late." But Carl knew if he had to, he would jump off a moving train to make the dinner.

"You better not. Elena has been cooking all week."

Carl smiled at the mention of her name. Something stirred deep inside. He could hardly wait to see her. "I'm looking forward to seeing Elena, again. Is she as beautiful as ever?"

"Even more so and I'm not prejudiced," Paul joked.

"Well, I still have to get through today before I can enjoy myself tonight. I read everything your office sent me—the job descriptions of everyone and a bit of personal history, plus news stories and some of the publications. Is there anything you haven't told me that I need to know before I get to work?"

Paul rocked back in his black leather chair and clasped his hands. "Georgia Davis."

"My associate vice president who applied for this job and didn't get it?"

"Evan has been grooming her for the job for at least a decade."

"I knew that before I came down for my interview, Paul."

Paul looked relieved. "Then you realize how disappointed she is at not getting the position?"

"Hey, she's a big girl. If she doesn't realize how unfair life is by now, then she has a problem and needs to look for a job elsewhere."

Paul frowned. "Don't get me wrong, Georgia Davis is quite competent. More importantly, she has a lot of loyal and powerful friends on campus and especially among the alumni."

Now it was Carl's turn to frown. "What are you saying? Treat her with kid gloves?"

"Go in with your eyes open, Carl. I want an award-winning public relations team, yes. But I'm also giving you free rein to reorganize the office in any way you choose. Be careful. A lot of people will be watching and analyzing every move you make."

A call from the State Board of Regents' office in Atlanta interrupted the meeting between Paul and Carl. "Mr. Van Horne, this is Steve Smith, assistant to Chancellor Reginald Howell. The chancellor asked me to call and let you know that the board has approved your request to form a new school, the College of Genetic and Molecular Sciences."

"Thank you, Steve. That's good news. Now I can attempt to woo that dean away from MIT. What about the request for the new building?"

"Are you talking about the performing arts center or the $50-million research center?"

"The research center, of course."

"The board is still discussing that one, sir."

"Please reiterate to the chancellor for me that we have no hope of getting the folks at Dwight Diamond International Research and Development Center to relocate their headquarters to the GCU campus, without the promise of this new research center."

"We understand that."

"The center researches, develops and manufactures small batches of experimental drugs for doctors to use in clinical trials, which could lead to future production of lifesaving drugs. What a coup for us to land this group of researchers and chemical engineers! Not only will our students, professors and researchers benefit from this, but the center's well known cancer research breakthroughs will put GCU on the world's map. Not to mention that the university could potentially make healthy financial gains from drug patents."

"The chancellor realizes the urgency of this matter, sir. The board is expected to act on the matter this week."

• • • • •

Georgia Davis was talking with Sandra Gibson outside the vice president's door when Carl Overstreet arrived at the office. Georgia, who had seen the press release photo, recognized him instantly. He was much better looking in person, she admitted to herself, but there was a melancholy look to his eyes, as though he didn't have any fun in life.

Sandra literally jumped to her feet when she saw him. "Good morning, Mr. Overstreet." She held out her hand.

"Good morning. Ms. Gibson, isn't it?" Although he acknowledged Sandra and shook her hand, his eyes were on Georgia. What an attractive woman, he thought, wondering if she worked on his staff.

Sandra noticed his gaze and nervously introduced them. "Mr. Overstreet, this is Georgia Davis, your associate vice president." Carl was momentarily caught off-balance at the mention of her name. Although he recovered quickly, Georgia noticed his reaction. "Georgia, Carl Overstreet."

Georgia extended her hand. Carl, who was now composed and in control, grasped her hand and firmly shook it. Georgia and Carl appraised each other warily, like a pitcher and a batter with the bases loaded.

"I'm glad to meet you at last, Ms. Davis."

"Same here, Mr. Overstreet. But if we're going to be working together, could we be a little bit less formal? Could we go by first names?" Georgia asked.

Carl looked at her silently for a few seconds before answering. He liked her directness. "All right, Georgia, it is." He wasn't used to such informality, but he guessed he could handle it if that's how they did it in the Deep South. He looked over to the secretary. "Will you feel comfortable calling me Carl?"

Sandra looked over at Georgia, who nodded. "Yes, Mr. Over ...

Carl, and I would like for you to call me Sandra."

"Well, now that we've settled that, I think I'll check out my office," Carl said, turning toward his door. He paused halfway and turned to face Georgia. "Notify everyone there will be a staff meeting at 1 p.m. I'll see you in my office in half an hour." Carl entered his office and shut the door behind him.

Georgia frowned at the demanding tone in his voice and the abruptness of his departure. No "please" or "thank you." He was obviously used to giving orders and having them obeyed without question. As she turned to ask Sandra to notify everyone about the staff meeting, she wondered if he had saved his well-mannered, good-behavior personality for his first day on the job.

• • • • •

Carl was hanging up the phone when Georgia knocked and entered. He didn't ask her to sit down, so she stood in front of his desk and waited. He sat in silence and stared at her. "Why are you standing there?" he finally asked.

"Because you haven't asked me to sit down," she stated matter of factly.

Carl leaned back in his chair and willed himself not to smile. "I thought you told me this office was informal? Sit down. Please."

Georgia hesitated briefly. But then she followed her own advice about giving the new vice president a chance. She sat down. He nodded his head. Was he happy that she had followed his order to sit, she wondered.

"I don't mince words. I always come straight to the point," began Carl. "In fact, people often think I'm not very diplomatic."

"Good, that will certainly save us a lot of wasted time."

Good, girl, he thought. "I understand you wanted this job."

Georgia looked him in the eye and didn't blink. "I've always wanted the job," she said, "I'd have been a fool not to have applied for it, wouldn't I?"

Excellent reply. Carl couldn't help but like her spirit. "I feel uncomfortable about that."

"You feel uncomfortable that I applied for the job or that I didn't get the job or that you know I wanted the job?"

"All of the above."

Georgia took a deep breath. She realized that what she said next would determine their working relationship. "Look, Carl, I applied for the job, I tried my best to get it, I didn't get it. Period. All that is behind me. If you are concerned that I won't be able to work with you, don't worry. I am responsible, reliable and loyal." Georgia crossed her fingers. "And I have no hard feelings."

Carl crossed his arms and stared at her in silence. Seconds passed. Just when she felt so uncomfortable she thought she'd have to say something, he glanced away from her, pushed himself up to his desk and picked up the telephone receiver. "As you leave, tell Ms. Gibson to come in here," he said and began pressing numbers.

Georgia, suddenly realizing she had been dismissed, rose from her chair. Dang it! she thought as she left his office. What an arrogant excuse for a vice president!

• • • • •

Everyone was in the conference room before 1 p.m. Talking was loud and heated until Carl walked into the room and sat at the head of the long table. "Good afternoon," he greeted everyone tersely.

After a second of hesitation, they echoed a response.

"I'm a man of few words," began Carl. Every eye in the room was riveted on him. "I have often been accused of being tactless and undiplomatic. I am. My critics say I will do anything—even fire my own mother—to improve a work situation. They're right."

Latifa elbowed Richard in the ribs. Several others gasped quietly or mumbled under their breath. Georgia shook her head slightly in disbelief. This was a new-boss pep talk to the troops?

"Dr. Van Horne hired me to take this office and turn it around. He wants a smooth-running, efficient public relations shop ASAP. I do not plan to disappoint him. You are either with me or against me. If

89

you are with me, be prepared to work harder than you ever have in your life. If you are against me, then update your resume and leave as soon as possible." Carl rose to his feet and left.

The staff members sat in stunned silence. Finally Delores turned to Georgia and asked, "This is the guy you want us to give a chance?"

The room broke up in pandemonium. Georgia looked at everyone talking agitatedly at once. Oh, yeah, she thought, Carl Overstreet is going to be a hard-sell.

•  •  •  •  •

Following the GPS instructions on his cell phone, Carl turned off a major thoroughfare on the outskirts of town. The homes in the obviously new subdivision were large, upscale properties on several acres of land. The Van Hornes' house, a Tudor-style two-story gray-stone home, was set back in the woods with a long winding drive. Carl followed the drive around to the back of the house, where wrap-around decks on the first and second floors overlooked a large lake. A gravel path led from the house to a boat dock and a mid-sized sailboat.

Carl parked next to a four-door garage. As he opened his car door, an English sheep dog ran up to him wagging its tail and barking. "Hello, fellow," he spoke to the dog soothingly and reached out his hand slowly. The dog stopped barking and sniffed his hand tentatively. Carl scratched its ears and smiled as it began nuzzling his arm. When the dog stood on its hind legs and attempted to lick his face, a female voice called from the front door. "Hamlet! Down, boy! Come here!"

Carl turned quickly and there she was—Elena! He felt his pulse quicken, just as it had so many times before when they were in college together. Her blond hair had darkened to a light brunette. She no longer wore it straight and long, but short and full around her face. Maybe she had a few wrinkles and five or ten extra pounds, but she looked better than he had remembered.

Elena left the house and came down the walk toward him. "Carl!

It's so good to see you!"

He met her halfway and picked her up off the ground in a bear-hug. She laughed melodically, just the way he remembered. His lips brushed hers before he kissed her cheek. He held her at arm's length for a better look. "You look fantastic!" he told her.

Elena grabbed his arm and led him toward the house. "That's something I always liked about you, Carl."

"What's that?" he asked. He was happy to be with her. He felt alive. He felt 20 years old, again.

"You always had something nice to say to me. No matter how bad a mood I was in or if I insulted you, you always said something positive to me and brought me out of my funk."

"Elena, please don't spread that around. You'll ruin the ogre reputation I've worked so hard over the years to perfect," said Carl.

Paul was opening a bottle of pink blush when Carl and Elena entered the kitchen, giggling like school children. Paul smiled and handed glasses to them. "How did your first day go?" he asked Carl.

"Paperwork and red tape, employee benefits, parking permit, payroll deductions. Got the picture?" Carl took a swallow of wine and winked at Elena. She smiled back.

Paul poured more wine into Carl's glass. "I meant how it went when you introduced yourself to the staff."

"I think I scared them to death. Most of them probably went home and started updating their resumes." Carl finished off his second glass of wine and held it out to Paul for a refill.

"Knowing you, I bet they did just that."

Elena, who had been slowly sipping her wine, looked concerned. "Fellows, you're talking about these staff members like you want them to leave the university," she said anxiously.

Paul sat down his glass and poured another glass for Carl. "Elena, I want to get rid of the dead wood. Sure, we'll lose a few good men and women, but the losers will be gone, too. You have to take the bad with the good."

Elena moved over and sat by Carl. "You mean you weren't kidding, you really are acting like an ogre?"

"Do you think I would have offered him the big bucks to move down here if I wanted a pussy cat?" asked Paul, as he poured Carl another glass.

Carl shifted uncomfortably beside Elena. "It's a job. Somebody has to do it. It's nothing personal, and I'm good at it," he said, wondering how the topic ever came up. Suddenly he feared that his evening was circling the drain of disaster.

Elena looked straight into Carl's eyes. "That doesn't sound like the Carl I know."

If Paul weren't around, I'd grab you and kiss you and make you wish you'd never married that man, Carl told her in his mind. "Elena, I'm an older, wiser, politically savvy Carl."

"The Carl I know is ethical, moral and just." She frowned at him.

"So is *this* Carl." Unless it involves stealing my friend's wife, he thought.

Paul roared with laughter as he filled Carl's empty glass. "I think I'll go see if the charcoal is hot enough for the steaks."

Carl watched Paul leave the room. He was alone with Elena. This was his chance to tell her what he hadn't been able to tell her 20 years ago. He downed his glass of wine and reached for Elena's hand.

"Carl, Carl, Carl." Elena put her hand to his flushed cheek. "Could you have changed so much over the years?"

Carl looked at Elena and opened his mouth to profess his love for her, but the words failed to come out. Not only that, but the room seemed to lurch and darken. He looked at Elena, who was looking at him strangely. He suddenly felt quite nauseous. Had he had too much to drink, he asked himself. Had he had lunch? He couldn't remember. Elena was speaking to him, but he couldn't hear what she was saying. He could see the alarm in her eyes—those same sultry eyes that always left him weak-kneed. He heaved and passed out.

# Chapter Eleven

It was nearly 10 o'clock when Carl made it to his office the next morning. He abhorred tardiness in his employees. He had no excuse. He had slept through the alarm and was only awakened at 9:15 when his secretary called and let the phone ring persistently until he answered. Although he'd planned to get rid of Sandra Gibson and hire a new secretary, he felt such a show of loyalty and perseverance now entitled her to a little more consideration.

Carl massaged the top of his head where his skull felt like it had been pierced with an ice pick. As he collapsed gingerly into his desk chair, Sandra came in with a cup of black coffee, a bottle of extra-strength Tylenol and a pile of phone messages. "Sir, I told everyone who asked that you were fighting a flu bug and would be late. Do you need anything else?"

"Not right now," he said, half groaning. As she left his office and shut the door, he expressed thanks for inheriting such an efficient secretary. Then he swallowed two Tylenol and sifted through his messages. Sandra had carefully printed the identification of each caller. "Bless your heart," he muttered, counting out three messages from Paul; one from Bill Swanson, head of campus police; one from Grace White, head of the student infirmary; and one from Elena.

Ah, Elena, he thought, wondering if he would ever be able to look her in the face, again. He could only remember bits and pieces of last night and none of it was pretty. He was almost sure he had thrown up all over the coffee table. Was that before or after he passed out? He buried his face in his hands. If he could just swallow the whole bottle of Tylenol and end it all, but that was too easy. His right hand trembling, he reached for the phone.

Elena answered on the first ring. At the sound of her voice, he almost hung up. He managed to get out a nearly strangled "good morning."

Elena hesitated briefly. "Carl? Is that you?" she finally asked.

"Yes," he answered hoarsely.

"Are you all right?" she asked with concern in her voice.

"I was crude ... I was rude ... and I acted deplorably," Carl said. And although he wasn't the apologetic type, he added, "And I'm very sorry." When she didn't say anything, he continued. "I did not eat any lunch, and it was stupid of me to drink so much on an empty stomach. I haven't been that drunk since ... since ... well, you know?"

"Since you drank the gallon of Purple Passion at a certain fraternity pledge party," she finished for him.

"Yes, I think you're right," he said, painfully recalling that night and his particularly glaring lapse of judgment. "I think you and Paul dragged me home that night, too." Yes, he would not forget that night—the evening Elena broke his heart, the night that he learned Elena planned to marry Paul. The mixture of vodka and grape juice didn't taste that good. He just wanted to get as much of it down as quickly as possible to numb the feelings he had for Elena. Not that he had ever stopped having feelings for her.

"I knew you'd be flogging yourself, Carl. That's why I called to tell you that everyone makes mistakes. Knowing how badly you feel physically and mentally at this moment, I certainly wouldn't chastise you for your behavior."

"You'd certainly be within your right to do that."

"I know, and if you'd been some stranger, I probably would have suggested that Paul fire you."

A knock sounded at the door and Sandra stuck in her head, hissing a message. "The president's on the line." Carl nodded.

"Carl? Are you still there? I was only joking."

"I'm sorry, Elena, but Paul is on another line and I really need to see what he wants. He's my boss, you know."

"Well, it's nice to know who comes first with you. You can finish apologizing to me later. Bye."

Carl heard her hang up. "I love you, Elena," he whispered into the receiver.

•  •  •  •  •

Georgia gave her full attention to Grace White. Grace never called over something frivolous. When the director of the infirmary was concerned enough to phone the public relations office, then the situation was either serious or showed signs of getting that way.

"Thank you for taking my call, Georgia. I left a message for Mr. Overstreet to call me back, but he hasn't and I wanted someone in your office to know what's happening here."

Georgia frowned. She detected a tone of apprehension in Grace's voice, something she had not heard since last year, when an unconscious student brought to the infirmary by friends had died of a drug overdose. "What's the problem, Grace?"

"Meningitis."

Her neck muscles tensing, Georgia asked, "Meningitis?" She needed to make sure she had heard correctly.

"Yes. Two days ago, we had a female student in here exhibiting early symptoms of meningitis."

"Viral or bacterial?" Even as she asked, Georgia tried to remember which one was the deadliest and which was the easiest to cure.

"Bacterial."

"Grace, is that good or bad?"

Georgia heard her pause and take a deep breath before responding. "Viral meningitis is usually relatively mild and clears up within a week or two."

Georgia braced herself. She knew she didn't want to hear this. "And the bad news?" She knew there had to be bad news or Grace wouldn't have called.

"Bacterial meningitis is a serious infection of the fluid in the spinal cord and the fluid that surrounds the brain. It can cause severe problems that can result in brain damage. Even death."

"But isn't it rare and hard to catch?" Georgia groped for an encouraging word from Grace, but apparently none was forthcoming.

"I'm sorry to be the bearer of bad news, Georgia, but this is serious. Very serious. Although the bacteria are spread by direct close contact with an infected person, casual contact is no problem."

"Kissing would be bad?"

"Yes."

Sharing a beer or a burger at a party?"

"That's right, but just sitting next to the person in class would not necessarily be a problem."

"Unless the infected person sneezed in your face?"

"Yes. To get infected, an individual would have to come in contact with discharges from the nose or throat of an infected person."

"Well, that's encouraging. How is the student?" Georgia grabbed a pencil and began making notes.

"She's on antibiotics and doing just fine. Fortunately, she came to us in time. As a precaution, we immunized her roommate and a boyfriend."

"Sounds like you did all the right things, Grace. Is there something else I should know?"

There was a long pause. "A student in the girl's English class came into the infirmary today."

"Oh, no, don't tell me."

"Yes, he has it, too. Georgia, I don't want to alarm you, but he was at a fraternity party last night." Georgia groaned. "He said there was a lot of shared food and drinks, and he thinks he remembers kissing more than one or two young women. This could mean trouble."

• • • • •

Carl did not want to see Georgia. He'd had enough on his mind without having to deal with her. He was still hung over, he had lost ground with Elena after last night's behavior and now Paul was on his case about some broad in development who wouldn't eat dinner with a donor so the university could get $5 million in scholarship money. Women could be such a pain, he thought, as he tried to listen to

Georgia's concerns over two students with meningitis.

"Miss Davis—Georgia," began Carl, as he wished fervently for a little Scotch. No wonder she was still unmarried. Probably not a man in the entire state could put up with all her bitching and negativity. "Why are you so agitated over two students getting meningitis? You just told me it wasn't very contagious and antibiotics clear it up."

"You just don't understand the situation," exclaimed Georgia, wondering why he didn't see this as an urgent problem.

"Exactly what don't I understand?"

"This kind of meningitis is caused by bacteria."

"I know that!" he raised his voice, but regretted it as his headache pain elevated four notches.

Georgia could see Carl was becoming agitated. He looked like he was hung over, too. She took a deep breath and tried, again. "Carl, the bacteria can be spread by kissing an infected person, by eating or drinking after an infected person or by having an infected person sneeze or cough in your face."

He slapped his hands down on the table. "So? A few students come down with it, the infirmary gives them an antibiotic and they're back in class in no time. Big deal! I had mono once and missed a final exam, but I still graduated."

"This isn't mono, and we might not be talking about just a few students. We're talking about the possibility of maybe five or six more getting it."

"Five or six more?"

"Yes. And if a student comes down with bacterial meningitis and doesn't get immediate help, death can occur within a few hours." Was she the only person in the room who understood the seriousness of the situation? It was hard to tell. After all, he had looked awful even before she told him about the meningitis. Maybe he wasn't hungover. Maybe he was coming down with something himself.

Carl massaged the top of his head. "That's just a worse-case scenario," he said gruffly. The phone on his desk rang. He yanked up the receiver. "Yes?" he barked. He listened intently, looked directly at Georgia and handed her the receiver. "It's for you."

97

Georgia accepted the receiver. He didn't have to act so irritated, she thought as she put the receiver to her ear. "This is Georgia. Oh, Grace. Oh, no. Let me call you right back." She hung up the phone. "Grace has another student with signs and symptoms of bacterial meningitis. They are getting ready to do a spinal tap to make sure. If it's positive, she wants to immunize all students who might have been in contact with the three who are infected. She's already contacted the Centers for Disease Control in Atlanta. Carl, we need to get out a press release immediately, even if we decide not to hold a news conference."

Carl rolled his eyes toward the ceiling. His headache was like an axe ripping through his skull. He cursed himself and his decision to ever move to Georgia.

• • • • •

Five reporters showed up for the press conference: reporters from the student paper, the local weekly and a local AM radio station; a student stringer from the Macon daily; and Norman Brewster from the local daily, who met Georgia outside her office. "Good morning, my lady. Is there any chance you're announcing the new boy is quitting?" Brewster whispered in her ear. Georgia glared at him and continued down the hallway with him following her all the way to the staff conference room.

Carl turned the press conference over to Georgia. She was accompanied by senior writer Delores Rinehart, who would write and send a release to the wires, and Grace White. When Georgia walked up to the microphone-decorated podium, the room went silent. She tried to ignore Brewster, who grinned broadly from a front row seat and sent her a kiss with his lips.

"Thank you for taking time out of your busy schedules to come here today. We'll keep this as brief as we can. For those of you who don't know me, I'm Georgia Davis, associate vice president for the GCU Office of Public Relations. To my right is Delores Rinehart, a news writer in that same office. To my left is Grace White, head of the student infirmary, who will speak to you this morning about a serious situation developing on campus.

Grace White nervously moved to the podium and tried to lower the microphones. She stood only about 5 feet tall and had to stretch to see over the top of them. "Thank you for coming. We need your help today in getting out important information to the public—especially to faculty, staff and students at the university and to the people they come in contact with."

Georgia was relieved to see that Grace had everyone's full attention. She made the mistake of looking at Norman, who gave her a smile and winked. Quickly she turned her attention back to Grace.

"Three students have tested positive for a strain of the bacterium *Neisseria meningitidis*. This bacterium can live harmlessly in mucus membranes, but can suddenly enter the blood or spinal fluid and kill an individual within hours."

The reporter from the student paper gasped and furiously made notes. The others murmured loudly. "How did they get it?" asked Brewster.

"We don't know," explained White. "The bacterium is spread through bodily fluids, such as saliva. A person who is completely well can pass it on to another person. You could catch it by drinking or eating after someone who has been infected or if an infected person were to sneeze on you or kiss you."

"That would be a really deep kiss in which saliva was exchanged, of course?" asked Brewster.

"Yes, Mr. Brewster, that is correct." Grace then carefully explained why it was important that anyone who had been in direct contact with any of the three infected students should voluntarily come in for immunization, especially those who had close or prolonged contact with any of them. "Anyone who comes into the clinic will receive a one-shot dose of a broad-spectrum antibiotic or a drug prescription for an antibiotic to take by mouth. Are there any questions?"

The young stringer for the Macon daily waved her pen in the air. "Well, if you're concerned enough to ask students to come in for immunizations, is it safe for all of us reporters to be here on campus?"

The reporters laughed.

"Two of you are students here, right?" White asked. The students nodded. "Do either of you know the three infected students?" They shook their heads. Then I would say you have nothing to worry about, unless you attended the Sigma Iota house party this past weekend."

The reporter from the student paper nearly fell out of his chair. "Wait ... I was there!" He stood up anxiously and stepped toward the podium. "Am I at risk of getting meningitis and dying just for going to a party?"

White stepped toward the young man and touched his shoulder. "Did you drink or eat after anyone at the party?"

He rubbed his left ear. "Well, they were passing around this German drinking boot." His eyes widened. "You mean one of them drank out of it at the party?"

Grace nodded soberly. "The chance that you were infected is very, very small."

Georgia cringed as the reporters sitting on either side of him got up and moved away, laughing nervously.

The student newspaper reporter turned ashen. "Uh... what did you say were the symptoms?"

"Primarily, a high fever, headache and a stiff neck," explained Grace. "But the symptoms can include nausea, vomiting, sensitivity to light, confusion and sleepiness. By the time the disease has advanced, bruises develop under the skin and spread quickly." The reporters bent over their notepads and took detailed notes.

Brewster turned his attention away from Georgia and began taking notes. "What is the incubation period for this?" he asked.

"That's a good question, Mr. Brewster. It is commonly about three days, but can be as long as ten."

"So if we can go ten days without any more cases, then we can assume the outbreak is over?" Brewster asked.

"Yes, I think that is safe to say." White looked at every face in the room. "Please, let me emphasize that bacterial meningitis is relatively rare and usually occurs in isolated cases. Clusters of more than a few cases are uncommon. There is no need to panic."

The reporter from the weekly paper chewed his lip thoughtfully. "What about the high school students visiting campus today?"

"Yeah, that's right!" exclaimed the reporter from the student paper. "They're attending a literary magazine workshop at the student center."

A feeling of unease spread through Georgia's stomach. White stepped back to the microphones. "Those high school students stand a better chance of winning the state lottery than getting infected with meningitis," she answered.

Oh, God, prayed Georgia, please let Grace be right.

# Chapter Twelve

Latifa's door was shut and locked, but Richard knew she hadn't left her office. He could hear muffled sounds from within. He knocked louder. "Latifa, I know you're in there." He thought he could hear someone laughing. He knocked, again. "Don't make me get the master key from Sandra."

Sounds of furniture being moved could be heard through the door. Then Richard recognized Latifa's strained voice. "Dammit, this better be important," she said, as the bolt noisily snapped back. The door opened abruptly and a red-faced Wiley ran out, buttoning his shirt and tucking it into his pants as he disappeared down the hallway.

A furious Latifa loomed in the doorway, her eyes narrow slits, her white short hair literally standing up straight. She crooked a long red-nailed finger in his direction and motioned for him to come in.

Squelching any feeling of apprehension or inadequacy, Richard marched into her office. The door slammed shut behind him. She stared at him as though he were a roach in her caviar. Her red lips twitched to one side. Two large, nearly fully exposed breasts heaved with each breath and seemed in danger of tumbling out of the low-cut, black sun dress. They continued to stare at each other in silence for an undetermined amount of time.

"So, what do you want?" she asked, breaking the silence.

"What were you and Wiley doing?"

"None of your business! Speak up or get out!" She placed her hand on the door knob.

"Let's talk. Sit down."

"Don't order me around," she snapped, twisting the door knob and opening it a crack.

Richard quickly realized if he didn't change his demeanor, he would lose a possible ally. "Okay, okay," he said soothingly. "Latifa, will you please sit down, I have something most urgent and beneficial to tell you."

She closed the door and pointed a red fingernail in his direction. "Now you're talking my language, hon." She moved slowly and sensuously to her desk and sat down, her tight spandex dress hiked mid-thigh, her long, shapely legs crossed at the knees and tucked to one side. "Well, sugar, what is it?"

"Uh ... You're not particularly fond of our Mr. Overstreet, right?"

"You name me one man or woman in this office who says they like that twit and I'll prove they're lying."

"Then you wouldn't cry if he left?"

"Look, sweetheart, you're talking about the sleaze bag who got up in front of the advisory board and said my admissions office video looked like it was shot and edited by Homer Simpson. I don't care if the man gets shredded in a giant meat grinder. What did you have in mind?"

"Well, as you have so aptly shown, Mr. Overstreet has a fatalistic talent for offending people."

"Offending? Not strong enough. Try antagonizing. Try alienating. I heard Mr. Overstreet tell the CEO of Atlanta Aeronautics that Southern businessmen acted like they wore lace panties under their trousers. It's one thing to insult your staff members and send them scurrying for the want ads, but as soon as the alumni and prospective donors start feeling the sharp point of his stick in their jugular, then the university's ship is going down in swampy, alligator-infested waters."

Richard smiled triumphantly at Latifa. "Then I can count on you to help me with my plan to discredit Mr. Overstreet and get him fired?"

"Sugar, you just point me in the right direction," she said, running her small pointy tongue across her red pouty lower lip in anticipation. "As long as it won't land me in jail or get me fired. What's the plan?"

"I need to get to Georgia's computer and access her e-mail."

"That means you have to pick a time that she'll be out of the office and some way to slip past Sandra."

"That's what I need you for—to distract Sandra. Pull her away from her desk long enough for me to get into Georgia's office and send a letter to the editor of the daily paper."

"And this letter would appear to be from Georgia and would say some negative things about our new boss?"

"Exactly!"

● ● ● ● ●

Five days after the press conference with Grace White and after only a dozen students dropped by the health center to be immunized, three new meningitis cases were confirmed on campus. All three had been at the fraternity party. One of the three died. President Van Horne declared a medical emergency at the university.

In an early morning press conference—attended by local, statewide and national media—President Van Horne expressed sympathy to the friends and family of the student who had died and announced a mandatory immunization program for all students. "Students who do not get immunized will not be allowed to attend fall semester classes," he warned.

"Man, oh, man," exclaimed the student newspaper reporter as he scribbled notes.

"The Advisory Committee on Immunization Practices recommends that college freshmen living in residence halls, who are at an increased risk of getting meningococcal disease, receive the polysaccharide meningococcal vaccine," continued Van Horne. "In light of the unusually high number of meningitis cases on campus this summer, including the death of one male freshman, it is imperative that all students report this week to the health center for immunization."

Van Horne turned the microphone over to Grace White, head of the health center. "This is a very unusual and serious situation," she said. "Only about 3,000 cases of meningococcal disease occur each year in the United States. Ten to 13 percent of these patients die despite receiving antibiotics early in the illness. Of those who survive the disease, 10 percent have severe after-effects, including mental retardation, hearing loss and loss of limbs. The American College Health Association has recommended that college health services take a more proactive role in alerting students and their parents about the dangers of meningococcal disease. Two recent studies initiated by the CDC indicate that college students, especially those who live in residence halls, are at an increased risk for meningococcal disease. This and the six known cases of bacterial meningitis here on our campus, including one death, along with encouragement from the CDC, have spurred President Van Horne to require all students be vaccinated against this potentially fatal disease."

Carl stood beside the president and looked out over the reporters, photographers and television camera crew. He could feel the start of another of his famous tension headaches. He massaged the bridge of his nose slowly. Sometimes that helped ward off the headache until he could reach a bottle of Scotch, but not this time. He groaned out loud. This job was going to kill him yet.

# Chapter Thirteen

After two weeks went by with no new meningitis cases reported on campus, tensions began to ease.

Carl initiated his "Good Morning, GCU" weekly newsletter, which went out to all top administrators, deans of schools and colleges, the Board of Regents, the Board of Trustees, GCU Foundation Board members and alumni leaders. The online publication offered a weekly review of the university as portrayed by the media. It included links to reports of faculty interviewed for radio, TV or news media, GCU research covered by the press, newly published books by faculty and staff, large research grants received, any enormous donations received and the university's rankings in national studies.

"Carl, this is a fantastic idea," said Paul, waving a printout of the first weekly newsletter in the air. "Even old Oliver Betts—that sorry excuse for a genetics professor—is impressed at what the media is saying about him and his research. He told me he might even be willing now to talk to a reporter or two himself. Also, that red-bearded fellow on the Board of Trustees said he liked it. You know the one. He took offense when you told him grits were not fit for human consumption?"

Paul continued his list of people praising the newsletter, but Carl tuned him out. He had scheduled lunch with Elena and all he could think about was how to go about expressing his true feelings for her. He had it all worked out in his mind. In his version, she was always very touched. She would cry out that she had always felt the same way about him, but was afraid to tell him. Then they would fall into each other's arms and ...

"Carl? Carl, are you ok?" Carl's daydream evaporated as he suddenly realized Paul was standing in front of him shaking his shoulder. Paul laughed as Carl shook his head and looked up at Paul.

"Oh, Paul, I'm sorry. I have a million things on my mind. You understand?"

"And is one of them Elena?"

Carl's heart dropped to the heart-of-pine floor. "What do you mean?"

Paul sat down behind his desk and placed his hands behind his head. "Elena said you two were going out for lunch today, and I see it's getting close to the noon hour. I thought perhaps you were wondering if this meeting would cause you to run late?"

Carl laughed. "Hardly, I was thinking of this jerk Richard Henry in my office who keeps me agitated. If I didn't think it would end my career, I'd like to tie him to his chair and gag him."

"Not the best member of your staff?"

"Hardly. He spends a lot of time in Latifa Benedict's office with the door closed. At first I thought they had something sexual going on, but when I suggested it to my secretary, she said absolutely not. She thinks the guy is of a different sexual persuasion."

"Hmmmmm." Paul nodded. "Well, keep an eye on him. Think he's looking for another position?"

"I can only hope."

"Have your ogre tactics scared off anyone?"

"Two writers, Delores Rinehart and Dudley O'Brien, and Will Bryant, the chief photographer. Dudley, I'm not sorry to see go, but Delores is an excellent writer. Will is retiring early to spend more time doing commercial photography."

"You still plan to keep Evan's old secretary?"

"Paul, that woman is solid gold. She reads my mind. Before I can press the intercom to request something, she's placing it on my desk."

"That's good. Sandra Gibson has always seemed competent and loyal. What about Georgia Davis?"

"Nothing to complain about yet. I don't know what I would have done without her on this meningitis crisis. And at least twice I've caught her smoothing ruffled feathers after I've opened my mouth without putting my brain in gear. I'm sorry, Paul, but sometimes these fine old Southern gentlemen drive me crazy. No wonder the North won the war."

"Everything you've said sounds good, but the EOC director told me she visited their office back a few weeks ago to get information on filing a grievance. She was advised to work with you. But my advice is not to turn your back on her. In fact, I'd start looking for some way to let her go." Carl glanced down at his watch and looked pointedly at Paul. "Okay, Carl, you're dismissed. You and Elena have a good lunch. I know you have a lot to catch up on."

You don't know the half of it, Carl thought, as he exited the president's office.

● ● ● ● ●

Pedro's Taco Hut was overflowing with students when Georgia arrived. Mexican and Chinese restaurants were popular with students living on a shoestring budget because they could get lots of food for less money. Fortunately for Georgia, Marina arrived before the hungry hordes and staked out a booth in the rear of the restaurant. Stepping cautiously between packed tables and over book bags tossed on the floor, Georgia crossed the room to reach Marina.

"I ordered you a chalupa with guacamole and a Cherry Coke," said Marina, her blond curls whirling around her head as she bounced excitedly on the seat.

"Did you do it?" Georgia asked, as she sat down.

"Yes!" Marina yelled, placing a digital recorder on the tabletop. "Want to hear it?"

Georgia reached for the small black and silver recorder. It was smaller than the palm of her hand and fit easily in a pocket or small handbag. After Marina's boss laughed at her concerns about Ed Liverpool, Georgia suggested her friend meet the prospective donor for lunch. Then Marina could discuss the visit to his yacht and hopefully get something recorded that would indicate his real agenda.

"I have it set to the spot where the conversation takes on a sexual tone," said Marina, who met Liverpool in Atlanta at the City Grill. "Put this in your ear and press the forward arrow."

Georgia did as she was instructed and immediately heard Marina's melodious voice and the baritone voice of an older man. "Marina, dear," came the hoarse South Georgia drawl of rich alumnus Ed Liverpool. "I'm so glad Walter was able to convince you that I truly am a proper gentleman. I'm delighted to hear that you'll be joining me on my yacht for dinner to personally accept the $5-million check for scholarship funds."

Georgia closed her eyes and tried not to gag. Liverpool told Marina to be at Garner's Field on Friday at 3 p.m. and his private jet would "whisk" her to Savannah, where his chauffeur would meet the plane and deliver her to his yacht, *S'amuser Bien* at Thunderbolt Marina. "Then my sweet Marina, we will sail up the Intracoastal Waterway towards the Atlantic, where we will dine on deck by candlelight. After dinner it will be just the two of us, a bottle of French wine and the stars above."

Georgia cut off the audio recorder and looked at Marina. "I don't think I can take much more of this."

"Where are you?"

"Just you and me and the stars above."

"Oh, you haven't gotten to the good part yet," exclaimed Marina. "Look, I was there in person with his hand reaching under the table to squeeze my knees. You only have to listen to his sweet talk."

"Okay, okay." Georgia turned it back on. She heard Marina giggle uncomfortably in an effort to suppress a strangled gasp. "Why Mr. Liverpool, please; you must not go to any trouble on my account!" she told him. "By the way, what time do you think I will be returning to Southern Pines?" Obviously, thought Georgia, Marina was trying to steer the conversation back to the purpose of her visit. "I have a brunch meeting Saturday morning, so I can't be out too late."

"My dear, Marina, you better cancel that brunch meeting. The good times will be rolling on my yacht the entire weekend. Walter will be lucky if I get you back in time for work Monday morning."

"But, Mr. Liverpool," Marina objected.

"Uh-uh-uh! You want me to be happy, don't you?"

"Yes, of course, I do."

"That's good, because the happier you make me, the bigger that scholarship check is going to be." Georgia yanked the earpiece out and slid the recorder back to Marina. She felt a chill, and goose bumps broke out on her arms.

"Marina, that's the most disgusting, lewd, vulgar man! And to think he is so well regarded in the business world, not to mention a respected alumnus of our university!" A student waiter with green hair and a pierced eyebrow plunked down Georgia's chalupa and Marina's deluxe bean burrito on the table. "Have you talked with Walter yet?"

"I have an appointment after lunch," replied Marina as she raised the burrito to her lips.

"After he hears this recording, Walter will not allow you to meet alone with this good old boy ever again."

"I know, I know ... but there's one thing."

"But what?"

"It's just that we really could use his $5 million for scholarships."

"I know, but your virtue is worth more than any amount of scholarship money."

"I think so. I just hope Walter does, too."

• • • • •

Elena was almost 30 minutes late, but Carl wasn't surprised. When they were in school together, she had been late for everything—meals in the dining hall, classes, movies and meetings. It was just Elena. She couldn't get anywhere on time and if you wanted to be her friend, you accepted it.

Not being familiar with most of the restaurants in town, Carl let Elena choose. She said Natalie's was her favorite. He didn't realize it was French until he arrived and glanced at the menu. He asked for the corner table in front of a window that overlooked campus and sat down to wait for her. He watched the waiters in their black pants, black shoes and white dress shirts with black ties walk suave and tall around the dining room. The tables were covered with white cloths and set with what he termed "sissy" china, silver, crystal goblets and a liter glass bottle of "l'eau." Somehow he was not surprised at the absence of students.

Just as Carl glanced down at his watch for the tenth time, Elena breezed in, kissed his cheek and sat down before he could rise to his feet. "Oh, Carl, it's so good to see you with a little pink on your cheeks. I hope I didn't keep you waiting too long, but I just couldn't find a parking place. I kept driving round and round the block."

Any frustration Carl may have felt for having to wait more than half an hour, melted away when he looked at Elena. At last, here she was sitting across from him. Just the two of them without Paul. He loved how the sunlight brought out the natural blond highlights in her hair. The sound of her voice was indeed music to his ears. He sighed happily and smiled.

"Now what was that for?" she asked.

"Huh? What?" He was jolted back to reality.

"That big dopey smile, silly. What were you thinking about? It certainly wasn't about anything I was saying."

When the waiter appeared to take their drink orders, Elena ordered a glass of white zinfandel and Carl asked for Scotch on the rocks.

"So? How are you settling into your new role as the vice president 'ogre'?" she asked mischievously.

"Not too bad. Only three staff members turned in their resignations today."

Elena's smile disappeared. "That's not funny, Carl. Surely you aren't serious?"

Carl noticed that Elena's face was tensing up. He quickly decided to get their conversation moving down another track. He laughed out loud and covered her right hand with his. "Of course I'm not serious," he lied, giving her hand a gentle squeeze. "But let's not talk about boring work. Let's talk about you. I want to know what you're doing and what it's like to be the woman behind a president of a major research university." There, he thought, those should be safe topics.

Elena's face relaxed. She leaned back into her chair, pulling her hand away from Carl's and dropping it in her lap. Then she scrunched up her nose just the way she used to do in college—right before she introduced a serious topic into the discussion. She sighed and Carl held his breath. "Oh, Carl, my life is rather boring. I doubt if it would be of interest to you."

"Now, now, Elena. I don't believe for one moment that the beautiful and talented wife of a powerful university president could possibly lead a boring life." Carl leaned forward, his forearms resting on the table. "The wife of President Paul Van Horne must lead a very exciting life." He leaned closer to her, until he could smell the scent of her perfume. What was it? Joy, he thought he remembered. A very expensive perfume that her rich great-aunt had introduced to her when she graduated from high school. Reminded him of his mother's rose garden.

Elena ran her fingers along the edge of the table. "I guess 'boring' is not the correct word," she began hesitantly. "Unfulfilled, maybe?" she glanced up at him and then back down to her hands now resting on the table. "Yes, that's what I am, Carl. Quite unfulfilled."

The waiter arrived with their drinks. Carl's mind slowly processed Elena's unexpected revelation. What did it mean and how could he use it to his own benefit? He sipped his Scotch and knew the amber brown liquid would help him figure everything out.

The waiter pulled out a pen and black leather order book. "Is madam ready to order?" he politely inquired.

Elena nodded and flicked the corner of her eye with a finger. Carl's heart fluttered. Could she have brushed away a tear?

"Just the shrimp crepes and a small house salad, please," she replied softly.

"And for you, sir?"

A flustered Carl glanced quickly at the menu. How he hated French restaurants. There never was anything on the menu that "real" men would want to eat. "Oh, let me see ... I'll have the spinach salad and the salmon."

"Excellent choice, sir." The waiter bowed, collected the menus and left.

Carl and Elena sipped their drinks in silence for a few minutes. "Elena," Carl began, but Elena interrupted him.

"Oh, Carl, I'm sorry about what I said earlier in a moment of weakness. I'm just feeling a little down today." She smiled at him—a little too brightly, he thought.

"Yeah, I have those 'down' days myself," he said. That was one reason he had an ongoing intimate relationship with Scotch, he reminded himself. To keep at bay all those negative feelings of frustration, rejection and loneliness—to name a few.

Elena put down her wine glass. "Everything was different in college."

Yeah, you can say that, again, Carl mentally agreed as he took another swallow of Scotch. "We were younger then, Elena. We had big plans to conquer the world."

"Did I ever have grandiose plans," Elena said thoughtfully. "Remember, Carl? I was leaving town as soon as I graduated from Princeton. Heading off to New York City to break into the book publishing world."

Carl nodded. "That's right. I remember now. You wanted to be an editor for a big publishing house like Simon and Schuster or Random House."

"Or go to London. Remember? I applied at Dorling Kindersley publishing house."

"Yes, that's right. You bugged Professor Hargrove for a week until he mailed off a reference letter." Carl ran his finger thoughtfully around the rim of his glass. "Didn't an editor call and ask you to fly over for an interview? What happened?"

"What happened?" she asked. "What do you think happened? Paul happened."

"Yes, right."

"We got married and the rest is history. I worked at several pathetic little jobs until he finished his master's and doctoral degrees.

Now here I am—simply Mrs. Paul Van Horne." She sighed. "Being a university president's wife is bad enough, but trying as a northerner to make friends and fit in here in the Deep South, is beyond difficult."

Elena looked so sad and desolate, Carl found himself fighting for control of his emotions. All he wanted to do was sweep her up into his arms, tell her how much he loved her, how much he'd always loved her, and how if she'd only married him, she could be living the career of her dreams in London or New York City. Instead, he reached out and lightly squeezed her forearm. "Elena, I'm sorry you didn't get to have the career you wanted. You gave up a lot of your dreams to marry Paul. I understand now what you meant earlier about being unfulfilled."

"Carl, you are such a dear friend to patiently listen to me rant and rave about this. I knew I could talk to you, my dear old friend. I knew you would understand how I feel. This isn't something I can talk about with Paul. He has more important things to worry about than whether or not his wife is fulfilled."

The waiter set down their salads and another Scotch for Carl, and quickly left. Carl took two more sips of Scotch while watching Elena take dainty bites of her salad. His heart seemed to swell inside with his feelings for her. Finally, he couldn't wait any longer. "Elena, I love you," he confessed out loud.

Elena looked up at him, swallowed and smiled. "I know you do, Carl," she said quietly. "I've always known. When we were in school, you followed me around everywhere I went. You were always ready to help me when I needed it and to console me when things went wrong. I kept waiting on you to ask me out, but you never did."

"I know." He could feel the excitement and hope building inside. "I was too much in awe of you and I was painfully shy. I just loved and adored you from afar."

"Yes, I know. But what you obviously didn't know then was that I loved you, too. I'll always love you, Carl."

Carl's rapid heartbeat pounded in his ears. "I'll always love you, too," he told her. He couldn't believe how well this was going. To think that if he'd only had the nerve while they were in college, Elena would be his wife now. Mrs. Elena Overstreet.

"There's just something extra special about the love between old friends," said Elena between bites. "Our love has endured through the years and we'll always be there for each other." Elena smiled at the waiter as he set down her plate of shrimp crepes. "Oh my, but this is delicious," she marveled as she tasted it. "How is your salmon?"

Carl picked up a forkful of salmon and shoved it in his mouth, but he wasn't consciously aware of what he was eating. Friends? Carl mulled over the word. He took another sip of Scotch. What part of this conversation had he missed?

"Carl? Are you all right?"

"Huh?" Carl swallowed his bite of salmon.

"Is it good?"

"What?"

"Your salmon, silly." Elena giggled, reminding him of the many lunches they had shared at college. It hadn't taken much to delight Elena and send her giggling when she was younger.

"My salmon is excellent."

"I'm so relieved to hear that. After I picked this restaurant, I remembered that you never really cared for fancy, gourmet food and especially foreign food. But this place is usually quiet during the lunch hour. It primarily caters to career professionals. Students rarely come in here. I thought we could have a more pleasant conversation here."

"It's perfect, Elena. The food is delicious and the company is exquisite." And if I keeled over from a major coronary, he thought, there was bound to be at least one doctor in the house. While Carl was pondering ways to put the conversation back on track in the right direction, Elena did it for him.

"You know, Carl, sometimes I wonder what it would have been like—what our lives would have been like, if you and I had married. Have you ever had such fantasies yourself?" Elena chewed her last bite of crepes and wiped her mouth.

"Of course I have, Elena." Okay, Carl, he told himself, this is it. Don't blow it. This may be your last chance. He opened his mouth to pour out his heart, but Elena jumped in first.

"I always pictured us living in the suburbs," she said, leaning back in her chair, her eyes looking off in the distance. "You would drive a conservative gray Honda Prelude and I would car pool the children around in a pale green Odyssey mini-van."

"Children?" sputtered Carl.

"Of course, silly ... six of them ... four boys and two girls ... and a large dog ... maybe a sheep dog just like Hamlet." She sighed wistfully and looked at him.

Carl laughed awkwardly. "Well, now, that's some fantasy, Elena. Wow... six kids?" In his fantasy, they lived in a spacious London flat, took skiing trips to the French Alps and spent long holidays on the Riviera.

"Yes, I love children. My one regret with being married to Paul is not having any children." She reached out and grabbed Carl's hands with her own. "Oh, Carl, I'm so happy you've moved to Southern Pines. It's like old times—you, me and Paul. You're better than any girlfriend and cheaper than any therapist." She giggled, again. "Having you around as a confidante feels as comfortable as wearing an old pair of shoes."

"Is that what I am to you, Elena? A friend?" He squeezed her hands tightly and looked directly into her eyes.

"Not just a friend, but a very dear and cherished friend. A very beloved, very discreet best friend. A friend I can discuss anything with and know you're always there to help me in any way you can." She released his hands and sat back.

Carl rubbed his head where it was starting to ache and finished off his Scotch. "But you said you felt unfulfilled being married to Paul."

"Oh, that? That's nothing to fret over, silly—just some premenopausal blues talking." She glanced down at her plate and then met his puzzled gaze. "It's like this, Carl. Sometimes I do feel lost in Paul's shadow and I get tired of being Mrs. Van Horne or the president's wife. But you know I love Paul dearly and I cherish our life together," she confided. "We get to travel all over the world and our social life surely must rival the Queen of England's. I have a closet full of party dresses and gowns that make me the envy of all my female friends and I live in the biggest, most expensive, most beautiful house in Southern Pines. I have household help and my own personal secretary. When I married Paul, I married success and power. Aside from the absence of children in our lives and the lack of a satisfying career of my own, I have no regrets."

She pushed back from the table and stood up. "Now my dear old friend, I have an appointment with the president of the Southern Pines Historic Preservation Society and I must be running."

Carl rose dazedly to his feet. "Must you run, Elena?"

"I'm afraid so, Carl. Don't look so forlorn, silly. There will be many more lunches together. Thank you so much for lunch today and especially for letting me bend your ear." She threw her arms around him and planted a kiss on his cheek. "You are the most absolute very best friend a girl could have, Carl Overstreet. Try and be nicer to your staff. I don't want anyone calling my best friend an ogre." She touched his cheek and looked into his eyes. "Be good." She turned and walked away.

Frowning, Carl collapsed into his chair. That didn't go the way it was supposed to go, he thought. At least he now knew that she loved him—but only as a friend, you idiot. The question was, would he be able to live with that?

•　•　•　•　•

Marina was 10 minutes early for her afternoon appointment with her boss. "Come in, Marina," welcomed Walter Sigman, indicating for her to sit in the chair beside his desk. "This is working out to be quite a phenomenal day and it could very likely only get better."

"How is that?" she asked, somewhat puzzled.

"Otis Brookstone, class of 1948, dropped dead last night," he replied, grinning broadly. "Ah, but wait, it gets better: Henry Chitwood, class of 1952, is not expected to make it through the week. We're talking a total of more than a billion dollars for the university foundation coffers."

Marina tried to conceal her revulsion over Walter's "phenomenal" news. There was always talk in the development office about rich, aging alumni and the large sums of money being left to the university in wills and from life insurance. Sometimes the university received acres of land covered with lumber or maybe a swamp and other oddities, including a $2-million yacht, a $400,000 prize hog, a Tuscan *palazzo* full of costly18th and 19th century paintings and sculptures, and a case of 1953 Chateau Lafite Rothschild.

"I'm glad that the university will inherit such generous sums of money, Walter," Marina said softly. Walter smiled jubilantly and nodded his head. "But I'm terribly saddened to hear about the death of poor Mr. Brookstone." Walter's smile faded. "He was such a loyal alumnus throughout the years. He loved to go on all the alumni tours and he never missed the annual President's Holiday Open House. I will certainly miss him."

"Ahem ... uh ... yes, of course, you're right, Marina. He was an outstanding and generous alumnus. We, of course, plan to stay in touch with the family and we'll definitely want to do a feature story on him for the donor magazine. Now, what was it that you wanted to see me about?"

"Edward Ansley Liverpool," said Marina, pulling the audio-player/recorder from her purse.

Walter groaned loudly. "Marina! I thought we agreed this little misunderstanding between you and Mr. Liverpool was behind us. He called me last night and said you'd had a lovely lunch at the City Grill. He sounded excited about you flying down to Savannah to join him for dinner and personally accepting his generous check. You know the president is very excited about getting this $5 million for his new scholarship fund. It will help us attract more of those 'cream of the crop' scholars." And help us exceed that $500-million goal by year's end, he thought.

"Which helps the university recruit top-notch professors and researchers, which will make the university more pre-eminent and prosperous. Yes, Walter, I'm aware of all that."

Walter sighed and leaned back into his high back, overstuffed black leather chair. "Okay, Marina, what is the problem now?"

She placed the recorder-player on his desk. "I recorded our lunch conversation. Here is the proof that Mr. Liverpool has more on his mind than eating dinner and presenting me a $5-million check for university scholarships."

Walter leaned forward. His eyes narrowed as he picked up the recorder-player. He turned it over slowly in his hands and put it back down. He looked at his watch and suddenly jumped to his feet. "Yikes," he fussed. "I have to be in the president's office in five minutes." He held out his arm and led Marina to the door while putting on his suit jacket. "Marina, I'm so sorry. I promise to listen to the recording this afternoon and get back to you before the end of the day."

After Walter ushered Marina out of his office, he returned to his desk long enough to drop the recorder-player into his coat pocket.

• • • • •

Paul Van Horne turned off the recorder-player and pushed it across the desk to Walter Sigman. "Has anyone else heard this?" Walter shook his head. "Erase it then. Trash it. Get rid of it."

"Yes, sir." Walter dropped the recorder-player back in his pocket. "What are we going to do about this?"

"What are we going to do about it? We are going to do nothing. You are going to handle this situation," said Paul, his voice turning icy. Walter cringed and sank back into the high-back upholstered armchair. "Do you know how important this scholarship money is to me?"

"I believe ... yes, sir. Yes, I do."

"I want that scholarship money. The State Board of Regents gave me two years to bring in $500 million or they'll give me my walking papers. My time is up next year. If Liverpool is offended, not only will we not get his money, but he'll drop the university from his will, which will cause other donors to follow suit. So you do whatever you have to do to make Liverpool happy. Or I promise that **you** will be looking for a new job a long time before me."

• • • • •

Walter called Marina into his office right before 5 o'clock. "I listened to the recording, Marina." Walter paced beside his desk. He stopped beside her. "I don't know what to say. Frankly, I was shocked."

"See, I told you he's a perverted old man," Marina began, but stopped when she saw the expression on Walter's face. "What is it?"

"The audio sounds like you were leading him on."

"What are you talking about?"

"It sounded like you were looking forward to meeting him on his yacht. That you anticipated the time spent with him would be most pleasurable."

Marina jumped to her feet. "That's not how it was!" she shouted. "I only said those things so he would come out and divulge his true plans."

"In other words, you were deliberately setting him up?"

"No, of course not. Well ... not really."

"Edward Liverpool is an important, influential alumnus and a wealthy and generous donor for the university. He has nothing but the highest regards for you. Have you ever had a date get out of hand?"

"Yes, who hasn't?"

"Exactly! Just look at Mr. Liverpool as an aging adolescent with raging hormones."

"But, Walter, this is NOT a date. This is business. This is me accepting a very large check that comes with indecent strings attached. Can't you see that?"

"What I see, Marina, is that you are going to Savannah as part of your job. You will eat dinner on the yacht with Mr. Liverpool and bring back the $5 million. You act professional and I'm sure he'll behave himself. Marina, if you aren't up for the job, then put your resignation on my desk in the morning."

• • • • •

The news that morning from Steve Smith at the State Board of Regents office was good news for Paul. The board overwhelmingly approved GCU's request for the $50-million research center and the $15-million performing arts center. The research center would be number one on the list of new building projects requesting funding from the Georgia General Assembly. The performing arts center was number seven on the list.

"Of course, Paul," Steve said, "you must understand that getting on the governor's list doesn't necessarily mean the research center project will be funded. Depending on the year's budget, the state legislators could approve to fund none or only a couple. Or they could even reshuffle the priority of any project on the list."

"What are you saying, Steve?"

"That the legislators could move your research center to the bottom of the list and fund the top two. But the chancellor and the board will be lobbying to get the research center funded. It is in everyone's best interest, right?"

"Of course, it is," Paul agreed loudly. "Who would think otherwise?"

"Any influential senator you might have alienated along the way."

# Chapter Fourteen

Carl arrived at the office before security unlocked the building for the day. He fumbled with the large ring of keys, searching for the one Sandra told him fit the building's front door lock. His brain felt like that old television commercial—"This is your brain on drugs." Only his brain was suffering from cheap Scotch and lack of sleep. He couldn't get Elena off his mind. He'd spent the best years of his life loving her from afar, only to discover she loved him, too—but only as a best friend and confidante. "Dammit!" he yelled, kicking the door.

"Do you need some help?" came a male voice from behind him. Carl jumped and quickly turned around.

"Man, you look awful. Were you out drinking all night?" asked Paul, grabbing Carl's keys and opening the massive oak door.

"No, I was drinking all night at my place. Thanks." Carl put his keys back in his pocket.

"You haven't been here long enough to have job problems, so it must have been a woman." Carl felt a flush creep out from under his shirt collar and spread up his neck to his face. Paul laughed. "I see. Well, I won't press you for the embarrassing details this morning."

Paul reached out and slapped Carl on the back. "Look, I need you to do me a favor. You know that confidential for-your-eyes-only report I gave you on the senator?" Carl nodded glumly. "Please e-mail that to Steve Smith at the regents office."

Carl nodded, again. "I'll take care of it. How is the senator's grandson doing?"

"Not as good as I'd like. I heard he squeezed his mother's hand earlier this week and smiled, but he still can't feed himself or talk. I'm afraid the senator is still angry at me, which is complicating everything I want to do to move the university to greatness."

Paul stepped back from Carl and shook his head. "But don't you worry about it, buddy. You worry about the public relations office. And a word to the wise—whoever broke your heart, she isn't worth all the grief. Grab you one of these hot-blooded Southern women and move on."

Carl growled out a thanks to Paul. As he headed down the hall to his office, Paul's laughter echoed in his ears. Carl hung up his jacket and collapsed in his chair. While waiting for his computer to come to life, he downed a couple of extra-strength Tylenol with some Scotch and water.

• • • • •

Georgia had just settled down behind her desk with her first cup of morning coffee when she received a call from Vivian Kearny, vice president of external affairs at the University of Florida in Gainesville. Vivian, a doctoral student in the journalism school when Georgia was an undergraduate, taught Georgia's beginning news writing and reporting class. They became friends and kept up with each other through e-mail. Frequently, they were able to reconnect at regional and national conferences of the Council for Advancement and Support of Education (CASE).

"What a pleasant surprise to hear from you, Vivian. How is everything down there in Gator country?"

Vivian laughed spiritedly. "Apparently much better than things are up in Southern Pines. I received your note and a copy of your résumé. After reading about what happened in the Atlanta newspaper, I wasn't surprised to hear from you. Is the work situation becoming unbearable for you now?"

"Hold on one second, Viv." Georgia walked over and quietly shut her door. She never knew when someone like Latifa or Richard might be loitering in the hallway. "I'm sorry for the interruption, but I wanted to shut my door for privacy."

"Sounds like things really are heating up."

"Actually, things have improved some this week, but I'm remaining cautious."

"And wary?"

"Yes, that, too." Both women laughed. "So what's up?"

"Well, my director of media and corporate relations is retiring and I thought you would be perfect for the job. I doubt if I could pay you what you're making now at GCU, but it would be a challenging, satisfying job and would get you away from the back-stabbing politics. I've already interviewed several people, but nobody excited me. Then I get your résumé and the fireworks go off. What do you say?"

"Wow, Vivian! That's the best offer I've had this week. Actually, the only one. I tell you what ... could you please download and e-mail me the job description, size of staff, what kind of money you're talking about, and any other pertinent information? Then I'll get back to you in a day or two. Is that fair?"

"Georgia, that's fine. I'll wait to hear from you."

Georgia leaned back in her chair. So there it was. A job possibility hanging like the gold ring on the carousel. Ready for her to reach out and grab. But did she want it?

• • • • •

Carl wasn't sure why Paul was sending the report on Wittick to Steve, but it was politically motivated he was sure. Ever since the hazing incident involving the senator's grandson, Steve and Paul's working relationship had cooled. Maybe the report contained information that could possibly incriminate the senator. Maybe those rumors about the senator accepting cash payments in exchange for using his position to influence a development project were true. Maybe Paul had found evidence to use against the senator. Whatever it was, he didn't want to know.

Carl opened his mailbox and clicked on "new message." *I hate you, Elena,* he thought as he typed in "Steve" and hit return twice. *You're one big fool, Carl Overstreet!* Under "subject," he typed in "From

President." *Focus, Carl, you idiot!* He typed in "President Van Horne asked me to send you this confidential report." He clicked on "Attach File," attached the report to his message and clicked "Send." It was only in the last second before the e-mail disappeared off the screen that Carl noticed the e-mail was going to Steve Erwin, office intern, and not Steve Smith, State Board of Regents. "Carl Overstreet, you ignoramus!" he screamed out loud.

Carl's office door burst open and a frightened Sandra rushed into the room. "Mr. Overstreet, are you all right?"

"I'm a dead man, Sandra. I just e-mailed something sensitive to the wrong person. Can you save me?" he asked hopefully.

"No, but call Georgia. She knows all those folks in the computer center. I bet she'll know what to do."

As Sandra closed his door, Carl banged his forehead on the top of his desk.

• • • • •

Marina marched into Walter's office as soon as he arrived for work. She closed the door behind her and stood in front of his desk. Walter stood on the other side of his desk. They stared at each other like warriors before the fight.

"What is it, Marina? I haven't even had time to get my coffee. Can't this wait?" He pulled off his suit jacket and hung it on a coat rack in the corner.

"No, sir, I need to talk to you now." Because she knew if she didn't do it now, she would not be able to do it later.

"Oh, all right. Sit down and spit it out."

"I prefer to stand."

"Fine, but I'm sitting." And he did.

"Walter did you not promote me because my work was excellent and always exceeded expectations?"

Walter leaned back speculatively, slowly tapping his tented fingers. "Yes, Marina, I certainly did. Your work since my arrival has always been exemplary. I can always count on you to do what I ask, no matter how distasteful. You haven't let me down yet. Now where is this leading?"

Marina paused briefly, her mouth open, waiting for her brain to transmit her next words. "You wouldn't want me to do something that might bring me harm, would you?"

"No, of course not," he responded, somewhat irritated.

"I believe that if I go to Savannah to meet with Mr. Liverpool, I will be harmed."

"That is preposterous, Marina, and this discussion is over. Leave my door open on your way out." Walter glanced down at his phone, picked up the receiver and started dialing.

"Walter, I am not going to Savannah and let some rich old man fawn all over me or worse just so you and the president can get $5 million," she blurted out, her voice rising.

Walter slammed down the receiver and stood up, leaning over the desk menacingly. "Then go to your office and write me that letter of resignation."

"No, sir, I will not go to Savannah and I will not resign." Then Marina turned around, stomped out of Walter's office, slamming his door behind her. In her office, she pulled an audio player-recorder out of her jacket pocket and smiled. "Gotcha, Walter!"

● ● ● ● ●

Carl's voice on the other end of the phone sounded desperate. His message was curt. "Come to my office immediately." The line clicked.

Poopie on you, thought Georgia. How rude! No please, no good morning, no nothing. It might be worth a cut in pay not having to deal with Mr. Cranky Pants. Georgia literally stomped down the hall, past Sandra, who rolled her eyes and shrugged, and into Carl's office.

"Shut the door. Quick, I have a problem. Tell me how to fix it."

Knowing she would not be invited to sit, Georgia selected a chair and sat down. "What's wrong?" she asked, astonished at how bad he looked. He was definitely hungover. His eyes were blood-shot, his face pale and she could smell liquor.

Carl rubbed his hands over his face. "I did something really stupid, Georgia."

Wow, she thought, a confession. Could he be human, after all? "We all do stupid things from time to time."

"This one stupid thing could cause real trouble. I mistakenly sent a sensitive file to the wrong person. Paul asked me to send a copy of a confidential report to Steve Smith at the board of regents and I accidentally sent it to one of the student interns named Steve."

"That's no problem, we'll simply explain it to Steve when he comes in today. He can delete it from his e-mail box and forget he ever saw it."

"No!" shouted Carl. "That won't work! It can't be read by anyone. If the media gets wind of this, there will be serious repercussions."

His unexpected outburst shocked Georgia. She noticed that he was so rattled, he was starting to sweat. She decided she had two choices: one, do nothing and let him drown, or two, take advantage of the situation and save his ass—maybe earning brownie points for her efforts? She cleared her throat. "Well, there might be a way."

Carl leaned in her direction. "What? Tell me!"

"Hand me the phone. The campus e-mail postmaster might be able to help."

Carl handed her the phone. "How?"

She started dialing. "It's possible he might be able to delete the message from the student's e-mail box before he checks his mail."

"Can this person be trusted?"

"He's a personal friend of mine and you really don't want this student to read the email, right?" Carl nodded. "Well, okay, then. I'll put the call on speaker." Georgia pressed the button.

The phone rang three times before someone picked it up. "Gene Williams here."

"Hello, Gene. This is Georgia Davis in the public relations office?"

"Oh, yes! Good morning, Georgia. How are you?"

"Just fine, thank you. How did your daughter like the Babymetal concert?"

"She loved it. Don't think her mama did though. She was stone deaf for two days after the concert. Thank you, again, for helping me get those tickets. Anything I can ever do for you, just let me know."

"Actually, Gene, that's why I'm calling. Our office needs a big-time favor."

"You name it, Georgia, and I'll take care of it for you."

"Our new vice president accidentally sent a dynamite-sensitive piece of email to a student by mistake. The email should have gone to Steve Smith at the board of regents. Think you could sneak into this student's box right this minute and delete this miss-sent message?"

"Sure I can do it, but will I get into trouble with Mr. Van Horne if I do something like that?"

"It will be with his blessing, let me assure you. The student's name is Steve Erwin."

"Okay, hold on a bit."

Georgia glanced over at Carl who was fidgeting in his chair like a young boy sent to the principal's office. "It's going to be all right, Carl."

"Good," Carl replied nervously. "Ask him if he can tell if the student has read it?"

"Gene?"

"Wait ... okay, it's gone ... clean as a fresh-washed baby's butt."

"Good. Could you tell if Steve has read it?"

"No, ma'am, he has not. Before you ask, I deleted it without reading it myself. Just in case you wanted to know. Also, I deleted it off every file in his machine, too."

"Thank you, Gene. Everyone here in our office and the president's office thanks you. You did us a great service and saved us from an embarrassing situation."

"You're welcome, Georgia. Any time I can help, you got my number."

"On speed-dial, Gene!" Georgia hung up the phone. "There you go, boss. Problem solved. Now you can resend it to the correct Steve."

A bleary-eyed Carl walked around his desk and cleared his throat. "Uh ... thank you, Georgia. You're a lifesaver." He reached out and squeezed her hand. "I won't forget this."

Georgia squeezed his hand back and smiled. "You're welcome, Carl. That's why you pay me the big bucks, isn't it?"

Carl released her hand and looked puzzled. "Why do I pay you the big bucks?"

"To watch your back. To make you look good." She looked at him standing there like a lonely, forlorn little boy on the verge of tears. Something tugged inside her.

Carl rubbed the back of his neck and cleared his throat. "Thank you, again, Georgia."

Georgia couldn't believe it. He'd thanked her twice in less than five minutes. She didn't realize the words were in his vocabulary. Maybe he had a soft side under all the gruffness, after all. "You're most welcome. Anything else?"

Carl pinched the bridge of his nose. "No, Georgia, that will be all." He willed her to leave so he could take another drink of Scotch. He needed to feel better. He needed to think straight.

"Excuse me for noticing, but you don't look well? Are you all right?"

"Yes, I'm fine!" he replied grumpily. But seeing Georgia's eyes widen, he spoke softer. "I'm sorry, Georgia. I have this tremendous headache on top of everything else this morning. Please, go. I'll live."

Georgia was shocked. He had actually uttered more nice words— "I'm sorry" and "please"—more words she didn't think he knew. "Okay, I'm leaving." She walked over to the door, then hesitated. "Guess I'll see you at the reception tonight?"

Carl looked up at Georgia through parted fingers. "What reception?"

"The one at the ballroom in Lancester Hall? Paul is going to announce the winner of the General James Oglethorpe chair?" Georgia saw only a blank stare from Carl. "It's a prestigious award. An annual stipend of $25,000 will be awarded to an outstanding professor. It should be on your calendar." Georgia returned to Carl's desk and turned the page on his calendar. "See, here it is."

Carl glanced down to where Georgia was pointing. To where he had written with a red Sharpie: Oglethorpe Chair reception, 7 p.m.,

Lancester Hall, MANDATORY. "Uh-oh," he cried. "That thing!"

"Yes," agreed Georgia, "'that thing' at which **every** vice president must be present—no exceptions, by order of President Paul Van Horne. Don't be late."

· · · · ·

Georgia's mother greeted her at the front door when she arrived home. "Goodness sakes, daughter. I do declare you have a smile on your face," said Eula Mae. "That's the first smile I've seen on you in weeks. You must have had a very good day at work."

"Let's just say it was better than usual." Georgia dropped her briefcase and took off her suit jacket. "How was your day? Did you play bridge?"

"Yes, but before I tell you about it, you need to call your favorite reporter, Norman Brewster."

Georgia kicked off her heels, collapsed on the sofa and started thinking about what she would wear tonight. "Norman is NOT my favorite reporter at the moment. And I have to get ready for tonight. I'll call him tomorrow."

Eula Mae put her hands on her hips. "He said it was urgent."

Georgia glanced at her watch. It was already 6 o'clock. She had to shower, dress and walk out of the door in 45 minutes. Norman would have to wait. After all, if it was all that urgent, he could have called the office.

· · · · ·

In the shower, Carl felt the full force of the cold water hit his chest. He gasped at the chilly harshness and turned to torture his back. He hoped this drastic physical measure would revive him long enough to endure the reception and having to be in the same room with Elena. He promised himself he would smile and exude health and happiness to hide his shredded heart and lost dignity. Facing himself in the mirror to shave, he decided some eye drops couldn't hurt and laying off the Scotch would be beneficial, too. One more drunken scene in front of Paul and he could kiss his vice presidency good bye.

●　●　●　●　●

Still marveling at Carl's personality change earlier at the office, Georgia donned her new Moroccan-look outfit she bought for the reception. She drove all the way to Macon to the Shoppes at River Crossing in search of something special. The saleswoman at Dillard's told her this exotic style was the "hot" new look. The earthy desert colors went perfect with her dark hair and olive complexion. The coppery skirt was literally a tight girdle that encircled her waist and hips with a cascade of two-inch pleats reaching down around mid-calf. An off-the-shoulder top with an ornate embroidered pattern, open-toe brown leather heels with gold Moroccan charms around her ankles, and long gold earrings that matched the shoes, completed her ensemble. Not the usual conservative dress that one desiring to be vice president would wear to an academic function, but just the thing for showing the world that Georgia Davis was alive and well, and not licking her wounds in a dark cave.

By the time Georgia arrived at Lancester Hall, the reception was well underway. Paul and Elena Van Horne were at the head of the receiving line, followed by his cabinet of vice presidents and spouses. At the end of the line was a very uncomfortable-looking Carl Overstreet. Georgia was impressed that not only had he made it to the reception, but also that he resembled a living, breathing person and not the "zombie" she had seen at the office earlier.

Carl, who was concentrating on staying focused on each individual who shook his hand, was not aware of Georgia's presence until he took her extended hand and looked up to see who she was. He appeared startled and dumbfounded. "Georgia?" was all he could gulp out of his mouth.

Georgia couldn't help but smile at his astonishment and dismay. "Hello, boss. I see you made it." She released his hand, but he continued to grasp hers. She waited for him to let go and cleared her throat. She looked pointedly down at his hand.

He finally realized he still had her hand in his and immediately dropped it. "I'm sorry, it's just that ... I mean ... you look different tonight."

"You mean I look better than I do in the office?"

"Yes ... no ... yes, you look very nice this evening, Miss Davis." Carl, the man in control, took over. "Good to see you. Thanks for coming." He looked to the next person waiting in line. Georgia had been dismissed.

• • • • •

Finished with the receiving line and wishing he had a Scotch in his hand, Carl watched Georgia "work" the room. She was impressive. Faculty and staff hung around her, like humming birds and bees drawn to a flower's nectar, he thought. And they honestly and genuinely liked her, he realized. He rubbed his finger on the annoying achy spot on his forehead. Nobody was fawning over him. Not even his "best buds" Paul and Elena.

He leaned against the wall and wondered how much longer he would have to stay at this boring reception before he could escape to his place and a bottle of Scotch. His eyes continued to follow Georgia. Suddenly she looked in his direction and tilted her head. He pulled back from the wall and straightened up. She smiled and started in his direction, but was distracted by the admissions director. What was his name? Donovan? Yes, Al Donovan.

Carl had been warned by Paul to keep his eye on Georgia, and Paul had even suggested he might want to let her go, but like his secretary Sandra, she was turning out to be a valuable player. Unless he found out that she was plotting against him behind his back, he didn't see any reason why he should act any more despicable than he already was. After all, firing someone who had such a large fan club on campus could only bring him one huge headache.

• • • • •

132

The GCU Culinary Institute students catered the evening's affair. Students in white coats and puffy chef hats were everywhere, replenishing student-made gourmet creations spread on silver trays on white linen-covered tables. Guests walked around the food-ladened tables, helping themselves to tasty shrimp-stuffed mushrooms, paté crostini, mini-eclairs and raspberry-chocolate tarts. And tonight, Georgia promised herself that she wasn't going to worry about fat or calories. She had a job offer—although not a great one—and life was looking good.

As Georgia headed for a plateful of chocolate eclairs, she saw Dr. Oliver Betts chatting with a man she did not recognize. She decided it was an opportune time to speak to him about taking time to talk to the media regarding his research. "Dr. Betts," she said, reaching out to shake his hand. "Good to see you tonight." She turned to the stranger next to him and offered her hand. "Hello. I'm Georgia Davis, associate vice president of public relations here at GCU."

He took her hand and smiled, brushing a lock of his graying black hair out of his eyes. "It's a pleasure to meet you Ms. Davis. I'm Dr. Doyle Rothman."

Dr. Betts leaned forward. "Doyle holds the Gregor Mendel Chair in Genetics at the University of Georgia. He's visiting campus, so we can discuss a genetic research project we're working on together."

Georgia pulled her hand from his grasp. "How exciting for you. Dr. Rothman, I hope you will encourage Dr. Betts to share your research results with the media once you're finished." Georgia smiled and turned to leave, but pivoted back. "Dr. Rothman, recently, our museum exhibited a dozen watercolor portraits by a UGA art student—Missouri Rothman. Any relation to you?" She thought she observed a slight flush to his cheeks.

Dr. Rothman chuckled. "Yes, that's my ex-wife. She's quite talented."

"Yes, she certainly is. I enjoyed speaking to her about her opportunity to study art in Florence, Italy, and how that changed her life. One day I hope to go to Italy, too."

"You should do that," Dr. Rothman said. "I took our sons to Italy while my ex-wife was studying there."

"Did you enjoy your visit?" Georgia asked.

"Yes, but it didn't turn out like I'd hoped." Dr. Rothman nodded to her dismissively and abruptly turned toward the food.

How odd, Georgia thought. She remembered talking to Missouri about her art studies in Italy and a professor at the academy who had inspired and challenged her. Georgia's eyes followed Dr. Rothman's retreating back. Perhaps she received more than a little inspiration from the art professor.

• • • • •

Georgia was swallowing the last bite of her third chocolate eclair, when she spotted Carl moving in her direction with two glasses of punch. "Would you care for something to drink? I seem to have two." Georgia relieved him of one glass and motioned for him to sit beside her.

"Thank you," he said as he sat down. "I feel like I've been standing up for a week. If I have to smile one minute longer, my face will crack and fall off."

"You seem to be in a better frame of mind tonight, Mr. Overstreet."

"Yes," he said as he finished off his punch. "You look much better tonight, too."

"Okay, I'm taking that as a compliment," Georgia said, but she still wasn't sure if he meant it as one.

"That's good, because that's how I meant it."

Suddenly the room stilled as Paul stepped up to the podium. He welcomed everyone to the reception and thanked the culinary institute students for their hard work. Then he announced that the Oglethorpe chair would go to Dr. Oliver Betts for his outstanding genetics research, specifically his breast cancer-related research. As Paul posed for official photographs with a grinning Betts, Carl nudged Georgia with his elbow and whispered in her ear. "Let's slip out of here. I'm fighting a strong urge to stand up and scream." He smiled at her and winked.

Oh, why not, she thought. Maybe while he was in this positive frame of mind, she could learn more about what made him tick. She nodded, and amid applause for Betts, Georgia and Carl slipped through the crowd of mostly faculty, staff and spouses and out a side door.

A brand-new garnet red Rogue hybrid was parked behind the building under a blue-and-white sign identifying the slot as being reserved 24 hours a day for university vice presidents.

"That's a nice looking ride, Mr. Vice President. You traded your Camry for this?" Georgia walked around the car, admiring front, back and sides.

Carl looked sheepish. "Paul suggested I get a newer car. He didn't want folks thinking he wasn't paying his vice presidents enough money to live on." He opened the passenger door for Georgia.

"Where are we going?" she asked, settling into the passenger seat and enjoying that new-car smell.

"A comfortable place where we can talk in private," he said. "My place. Is that okay with you? I promise to be on my best behavior."

Georgia frowned in the darkness of his car. She did not make a practice of going to strange men's homes. Her mother had taught her better than that. But then he was her boss and not all the advice her mother had given her had turned out to be good. Her curiosity won over her cautious nature. If you can't trust a university vice president to behave himself, then what is the world coming to. It obviously was the old rich geezer alumni you had to worry about. "You don't live in some wild bachelor's pad, do you?"

"Hardly," he replied, cranking the motor.

And he didn't. He lived in Sunrise Forest, a gated community of upscale condos and townhouses. The complex included a club house, a heated pool, tennis courts, an 18-hole golf course, and paved trails for runners, bikers and golf carts. Carl lived in a two-story grey-brick townhouse with garage.

Inside, Georgia was surprised, again. The foyer, hallway and living room walls were covered with original art work—photographs, pencil-and-ink drawings, pastels, watercolor and oil paintings. The artwork included several beautiful nudes, as well as well-known landmarks and people around the world: the Eiffel Tower in Paris, the Duomo in Florence, Roman ruins in Rome, a flamenco dancer in Spain, a Geisha in front of Mount Fuji, two Eskimos chasing a polar bear, the Golden Gate Bridge in San Francisco and the French Quarter in New Orleans. "I didn't realize you had an interest in the visual arts."

Carl pulled off his jacket and tie. "I've always loved art."

Georgia walked up to an exquisite oil painting of a nude female lying on a blanket under a shade tree. "Oh my gosh!" she exclaimed looking at the initials in the corner: DH. "Is that a David Harris nude?"

Carl looked surprise. "Why, yes, it is. Are you familiar with his work?"

Georgia turned to face Carl. "I met him and his Italian wife in New York at an opening reception for an exhibit of his work," she said, glancing back at the painting. "Such sweet and innocent nudes. I love his work. Whatever happened to him?"

"I met him in a coffee bar in Florence, Italy, a few years back. He was happy to meet a fellow American. We sat and talked for hours. He said he'd lost his wife to cancer and along with her loss, he'd lost interest in painting. He said he was teaching art at one of the academies in Florence and trying to find his way back to painting. After I returned to the States, I found that painting online and bought it."

Georgia nodded. "That's sad. I hope he was able to find his muse, again."

Carl raised an eyebrow. "I think he might have. I read a story about him a few months back in the *Sunday New York Times Magazine*. Some gallery in Chelsea—maybe Hauser and Wirth?—was showing half a dozen new paintings by him. They were calling it his 'comeback' show. Seems like he had been inspired by one of his students at the academy in Florence."

Georgia blinked and sat up straight. She smiled, lost in her thoughts. Could it be that Missouri Rothman and David Harris had connected as student and teacher and inspired each other to create great works?

"Georgia?" Carl nudged her shoulder with his finger.

"Huh? What?"

"Where did you go? What were you thinking about?"

Georgia cocked her head and smiled innocently. "Well ... I look at all of these wonderful pieces of artwork and I can't help but wonder — Carl, are you a closet artist?"

Carl laughed. "Doodled all my life, but my high school art teacher told my parents I had no artistic talent. So I've contented myself with collecting original art from every place I visit."

"You must travel a lot," she commented, examining each piece of work.

"I don't have lavish spending habits. I don't like new, expensive cars."

"Your Nissan Rogue is not a cheap car," Georgia was quick to point out.

"No, but it isn't a Mercedes or a BMW or a Cadillac or a Tesla, either. I'm frugal with my money, because I want to see as much of the world as I can. How about you?"

Georgia edged over to a large burgundy-and-navy-blue striped, overstuffed armchair with plump burgundy pillows and sat down. "No, I haven't done much traveling."

"You've never been abroad?" Carl opened a cabinet and pulled out a bottle of Scotch.

"Not really, though I did take a 10-day cruise to the Caribbean and West Indies last summer. The year before that I went to Los Angeles and Hollywood. I've traveled with my mother to New York City and Washington, D.C. It's only been recently that I started making enough money and accruing enough vacation time to take a nice holiday. I spent several years saving money for a down payment on a home. After that I was 'house poor' for quite a while."

"Look, Georgia, I need a drink after that reception to de-stress me.

What can I get you? I have some white zinfandel in the fridge."

Georgia's mother had always told her never to drink anything alcoholic on a date because you needed to keep one's wits about you. She also told her to watch when her drink was poured to make sure no one put any drugs in it. She thought about this when Carl disappeared into the kitchen and returned with a glass of wine. Some of the worst advice her mother ever gave her was — "It's better to date any guy on Saturday night than sit home alone." The one time she followed that advice, she regretted it. Her date — a boring computer nerd with bad breath — took her to a matinee showing of "Barry Bear Meets Witchy Wolf." They were the only people in the theater, and she spent the entire movie fending off his roaming hands.

Carl handed her a glass and sat next to her on the sofa. He took a long swallow of Scotch and sank back into the pillows. "You just don't know how good and smooth that feels going down. It has been a real bitch of a day."

Georgia found the one glass of wine was mellowing her, too. Receptions and other obligatory social functions always left her exhausted. It took a lot of energy to keep smiling and carrying on a conversation and pleasantries with dozens of individuals. Remembering names, occupations and connections was mentally challenging and draining. Tonight, because most everyone present was a university colleague, was easier than other events where she was mixing with alumni and donors or foundation trustees and members of the board of regents.

Georgia startled when a cell phone started ringing. "It's not mine, I turned mine off," Carl said with a grin. He pointed to the end table where she had placed her purse.

She grabbed the phone from her purse, just in case her mother was having a stroke or something. "Hello."

"Georgia, where are you? I've been trying to reach you all evening."

"Norman, I don't have time to talk now. I'm in a – uh — meeting." She glanced at Carl who was taking yet another swallow of his drink.

"Your meeting will have to wait. This is important. It's about the information you e-mailed to the newspaper today."

Georgia vaguely remembered sending a news brief about the pharmacy college being recognized in *US News and World Report.* "What about it?" she asked impatiently.

I want to verify that you sent it. Harold Lepzig wants to use pieces of it in his opinion column tomorrow."

"Fine, fine, whatever. Thanks for calling."

"Georgia, are you sure you don't want to reconsider?" But Georgia had already hit the "end" button and turned off the phone. She could not believe that Norman had called her over something as trivial as that. Well, at least the pharmacy college dean would be pleased to see some positive media coverage on the editorial page. And in the managing editor's column, too.

· · · · ·

Managing Editor Harold Lepzig leaned back in his chair as far as it would go without tipping over. His interlaced fingers and hands rested on his slightly protruding belly. "Well? Did you reach her? What did she say?"

"I believe her exact words were 'Fine, fine, whatever. Thanks for calling.'"

Lepzig sat up straight. "Did she say why she picked today to be openly critical about her new boss?"

"She hung up on me before I could ask."

Lepzig reached for his phone. "Maybe I should call her. I don't think you two have good rapport."

"Won't do any good. She's not at home and when I called her back, I got her voicemail. She must have turned off her cell as soon as she hung up."

Lepzig sat back in his seat and smiled. "That's too bad, but it's no biggie. I have quite a file on Carl Overstreet. Lots of personal background based on facts. He's made himself very unpopular since his arrival. I personally checked on everything in Georgia's e-mail and it appears to be accurate. I only wish I could ask her a few questions before we go to press. I could run the piece without Georgia's information, but my column will be stronger with it. So, why do you think she did it?"

Norman twisted his mouth around thoughtfully. "Don't know. I just hope she has a job lined up somewhere else."

•　•　•　•　•

Georgia was on her third glass of wine. Normally, she didn't drink more than one or two. But Carl continued to put down the Scotch, so she was trying to hold up her end, against her better judgement. Her mother would not approve, of course, but then she wasn't here. Besides, the more Carl drank and mellowed, the more interesting the conversation became. She couldn't believe how many frustrating years he'd spent at Gabriel College. She couldn't imagine spending any length of time at a job she hated. Now she understood why he wanted to come down to Georgia.

"Yes, I was very upset when Paul named you vice president," confessed Georgia. "But I decided to be a team player while I looked for a job. I figured there had to be a good reason you were hired over me."

Carl reached out and squeezed her hand. "I'm glad you stayed and helped me settle into the job. You and Sandra certainly make things easier for the new guy. I can't thank you enough for everything you've done. For all those times you bailed me out of trouble—like the email crisis this morning." Carl rubbed his face just thinking about it. "You're damned good at your job! I don't deserve such a great associate vice president."

Georgia blushed in embarrassment. When she finished her wine, Carl poured more before she could protest. "Thank you for your kind words, Carl. I think you're doing a lot of good things for the office, too. That media update newsletter that goes out to the administrators and department heads is excellent. Everyone loves it. And I've had lots of compliments on the Thursday morning tip sheet for reporters and editors that goes out nationally."

"You're serious about searching for a position elsewhere?" Carl asked. "Can't say I blame you. But if you stay at GCU, I think we would make an award-winning team." Paul is absolutely wrong about you being a troublemaker, thought Carl. One day he will admit that he was wrong.

"I think you should know that I did get a job offer this morning from the University of Florida."

"You'd leave me, just like that?" He leaned towards her looking hurt. "I need you, Georgia, but I won't ask you to turn down a chance to accept a better job. Goodness knows I'm not an easy person to work with. Nobody in the office likes me." He covered his eyes with his hand. "You know no one on this campus likes me, except Paul. And he has to, since he hired me." He turned and looked at her sadly. "But if I don't get a top-notch public relations staff in place really soon, he won't like me either."

Well, thought Georgia, the proffered job wasn't exactly the perfect one she was searching for. But was she willing to remain at GCU while waiting for something better to come along? She glanced at Carl. His hair was disheveled and his bluish-green eyes pleaded with her to stay. She felt her resolve crumble. This vulnerable almost childlike side of Carl was unexpected. Apparently, his callous, uncaring persona was merely a role he was playing to weed out the losers on the staff. Not the way she would have done it as vice president, but clearly effective for him. They were as different as night and day, she thought. Like oil and water. Like peaches and pickles. "All right, Carl, I'll think about it."

"Thank you, Georgia." He leaned closer to her. He really loved her dark curly hair. Gently he kissed her lips and felt her respond. Paul could have Elena.

# Chapter Fifteen

It was almost 5:30 a.m. when Carl dropped Georgia off at her car on campus. They had driven from his townhouse in utter silence, both deep in thought. "Carl," began Georgia, as they stood beside her car. She felt like someone needed to say something.

"Hush, shhhh." Carl's finger touched her lips to silence her. "Don't say anything." He wrapped his arms around her. "Whatever happened last night is just between the two of us. It won't affect how we relate to each other in the office. I'm still your grumpy, irritating, despicable, ill-mannered boss and you're still the gracious, responsible, knowledgeable associate who attempts to keep her boss out of trouble."

"Would you say I'm sweet like a Georgia peach?"

Carl nodded. "Most definitely. The sweetest Georgia peach I know." He tugged on one of her dark curls. "What fruit does that make me?"

"A pickle."

"What?" He stepped back from her. "Pickles aren't fruit!"

"No, but cucumbers are, and they make pickles out of them."

"Are you saying I'm sour as a pickle?"

"Uh-huh. It's right up there with being grumpy, irritating, despicable and ill-mannered." Georgia saw him frown. "Those are your words, Carl, not mine."

Carl burst out laughing. "Let me guess. And I'm always getting myself into a pickle?"

"Again, your words. But yes. There was the email pickle and the meningitis pickle."

"Stop! That's enough, Miss Georgia Peach." He reached out and pulled her close to him.

Georgia tilted her face upwards and kissed Carl's lips. "Okay, Mr. Vice President Pickle. I'll see you in a little bit."

Carl helped her into her car and shut the door. He leaned over and kissed her, again, through the open window. "I like after-hour executive sessions. We accomplished more than I anticipated, Miss Davis."

Georgia started the engine, backed out of the parking space and headed toward home. As she turned out of the parking lot, she saw Carl in the rearview mirror, standing by his car, watching her leave. "Georgia," she talked to herself out loud, "your mother would not approve. You and Carl really are just like peaches and pickles. I hope this doesn't come back to bite you in the ass."

• • • • •

After a quick shower, Georgia dressed and was eating a bowl of Grape Nuts Flakes cereal, when her robe-wrapped mother banged her coffee mug on the table and sat down across from her. "You were awfully late getting home from your fancy reception, Georgia. I didn't know if you were lying dead in a ditch or what."

"Oh, Mom, I'm so sorry. I would have called, but I didn't want to wake you up."

"You know I can't sleep until you get home."

"Mom, we've had this discussion before. I'm not in high school any more. You don't have to stay up and worry about me." Georgia stood up and took her dishes to the sink.

"You're my daughter. I'm your mother. I will always worry about you."

Georgia leaned over and kissed her mother on the cheek. "I appreciate that you are concerned about my welfare, Mom. And from here on out, I will call and wake you up if I'm going to be late." She picked up her briefcase and opened the door. "See you tonight."

As soon as Georgia reached her office, she grabbed the phone immediately and called Vivian Kearny at the University of Florida.

143

"Good morning, Viv!"

"Am I glad you called. I planned to call you in a few minutes. You sound absolutely cheerful. I hope that means you've decided to come on down to Gator country."

"I appreciate your offer, Viv."

"But you're really looking to move up. I understand, hon. I gave you a call just in case your situation was desperate and I could save you and, at the same time, win myself a well-respected, seasoned professional at a bargain price. Does that offend you?"

"On the contrary, it gives me warm, fuzzy feelings and bolsters my morale. Believe me, Viv, if things were unbearable here, I'd jump at the chance to work with you."

"Thanks, Georgia, that's good to hear. I appreciate you letting me know this morning so I can offer the job to a man I interviewed yesterday after I talked with you. He's not up to your caliber yet, but I think he's malleable. Good luck. Hope to see you at CASE."

Georgia hung up the phone and walked over to the window where the bud on Evan's orchid was starting to look promising. She ran her fingers up and down one of the hard, waxy leaves. "Evan, if you were here right now," she spoke softly, "I know you would be fussing at me for turning down that job. My brain is screaming, 'Run, Georgia, run for your life,' but my heart is saying, 'Let's stop and think about this.'"

• • • • •

Before Carl could get out of the house to leave for campus, the phone rang. Hoping it might be Georgia, he grabbed it on the first ring. "Have you seen today's paper?" barked Paul.

"No, it's sitting on the coffee table. What's up?"

"Read it, Carl," Paul snapped. "Read Harold Lepzig's scathing editorial column and come straight to my office." The connection ended with a bang on the other end.

Rolling his eyes upward, Carl pulled the paper out of the plastic bag and unrolled it on the table. He pulled out the front section and turned to the editorial page. The headline on the lead column caught his eye: "New VP runs off staff members; turns off alumni." Suddenly weak-kneed and with ice-cold dread creeping through his chest, Carl sank down on the sofa and began to read.

The editorial column crucified him big time and reminded "the reader" that Carl Overstreet had not been recommended by the selection committee. Lepzig, who proposed that President Van Horne send Mr. Overstreet back to New York, had done his homework. He'd interviewed several of his former colleagues at Gabriel College and listed a few of his less-than-shining inebriated moments that he would have preferred to keep buried: a soccer game when he bloodied the nose of an obnoxious alumnus who had shoved him to the ground; and another incident, during a press conference, when he threw out a belligerent reporter. Lepzig also quoted some of Carl's infamous public outbursts since his arrival in Southern Pines, especially those in front of GCU alumni, donors, faculty and staff. A few of these quotes and information about four staff members who had left the public relations office since his arrival were attributed to Georgia Davis.

In anguish, Carl dropped the paper. How could Georgia do this to him behind his back? Not that it wasn't all true, but Georgia, of all people. Visions of dark curly hair splayed across his pillow, her fingers caressing his face, went through his mind. His chest heaved, his hands trembled, his head began to pound and instantly, he wanted a drink. He turned toward his bottle of Scotch, but quickly reconsidered. No, he couldn't go into Paul's office this early in the morning reeking of alcohol. He wasn't sure he could face Paul and discuss the situation without a drink, but he would have to try. He washed his face in ice cold water instead. Fighting feelings of nausea, he grabbed the paper and headed out the door. Funny, he thought, how one's life could change so drastically in just one second.

• • • • •

Marina didn't like the idea of being summoned to Walter's office so early in the morning. What could he possibly want now? Just for insurance, she popped the audio-player recorder in her jacket pocket and turned it on before opening his door.

This time he didn't greet her warmly or ask her to sit down. "Marina," he said sternly, "have you given any more thought about meeting with Ed Liverpool in Savannah?"

"No, Walter, I am not going to Savannah and spend the evening on a yacht alone with an old sexual pervert and that's final."

Walter's mouth twitched. "I'm sorry to hear that's how you feel. And do you have your resignation ready?"

Marina gasped. "I most certainly do not."

"Then it pains me to have to do this." Walter handed her an envelope.

"What's this?" she asked opening it up and pulling out a letter.

"That is your two-week notice. As part of a new reorganization plan for the office, we've decided to eliminate your position and use the money somewhere else."

"What?" exclaimed Marina in disbelief.

"You heard me, in two weeks you will be history in the development office. Good day." In shock, Marina walked toward the door. As she opened the door, Walter looked up. "However, if you should change your mind about doing your job and going to Savannah as originally planned, let me know and I'll happily reconsider."

• • • • •

A grim-looking Paul was sitting behind his desk when Carl arrived. Without speaking, he indicated for Carl to shut the door and sit down. "Ahhhh, my friend. You have definitely gotten us into a bit of a mess," Paul began quietly.

Carl threw up his hands and opened his mouth to speak, but Paul silenced him. "Let me talk. I'm the president, and this is my meeting."

Carl slunk back into the seat. "You told me you had everything in your office under control. I told you that Davis woman was a troublemaker. You said that wasn't the case. I told you to fire her. You said she was a big help. Well, how much is this helping you or this university?" By the end of his question, Paul's voice had crescendoed until it vibrated around the room. He shook the newspaper angrily at Carl.

Carl cringed. The last time he had seen Paul this angry was when he was running for Student Government president at Princeton and the opposition started a smear campaign against him. Paul was furious, especially when he realized the election might go against him. If he closed his eyes, he could still see Paul ranting and raving in the student newspaper office. In the end, the opposition resigned and the race went to Paul. Carl felt at the time that Paul had used blackmail or worse—physical intimidation—to get what he wanted. But Carl didn't pursue it, because he thought it better not to know.

"My first thought was to sue those imbeciles at the paper for slander and libel. However, you and I both know it can't be slander, because it's all true. I'm not sure about libel either. After all, it is on the editorial page, but I've made a call to the legal affairs office to make certain." He paused for breath.

"Do I get to speak yet?" asked Carl.

"No, I'm not finished. What we have to be concerned with now is 'damage control.' Although you would normally be the person to handle this, we'll have to get one of the other vice presidents to write a letter to the editor with a more positive look at you and the outstanding improvements you've made to the public relations office in the short time you've been on board. Maybe Walter would be a good choice for this." He cleared his throat, appearing somewhat calmer now that a "game plan" was in place. "Now, my old friend, here is what you are going to do."

"What's that?" asked Carl warily.

"Go back to your office and get rid of that trouble-making Davis woman like you should have done months ago. She's not loyal to you."

"But there has to be a mistake. I'm not sure she's responsible."

"Shut up, Carl! Go! Now! Get out of my sight before I really lose my temper! Things are rocky enough for me right now with the State Board of Regents and the situation with Senator Wittick and his grandson. I don't need you to torpedo my accomplishments and blow me off my throne of power."

•  •  •  •  •

Georgia was humming "I Feel Pretty," her favorite song from *West Side Story*, and spraying the orchid on the window sill when her door slammed shut with a bang. She turned in time to see Norman Brewster hurl a copy of the newspaper onto her desk and stand with his arms folded across his chest.

"Well, my lady, are you in need of rescuing yet?"

Georgia laughed. "From what or whom would I need to be rescued?"

Frowning, Norman dropped his arms. "We are in a good mood. I'd be nervous if I were in your shoes."

"Nervous? I don't understand. Why should I be nervous?"

Norman leaned over her desk and shoved the newspaper under her nose. "Harold Lepzig's column, of course."

"Why? Did he say something about me?" Georgia grabbed hold of the newspaper and started to read. "Oh my God!" She collapsed onto her chair. "Oh, no!" She looked up at Norman. "I never said any of this. Why didn't you tell me he was writing this?"

Norman stomped to the door and back. "I don't believe this. I tried the entire evening to reach you. I finally get you on your cell phone, and you barely say two words to me. Remember? Then you hung up on me."

"No, you were asking me about the news brief I e-mailed to the news editor."

"No, Georgia, I was calling to verify the e-mail you sent to the editorial page editor. Where were you? In bed with some man?"

Georgia looked at Norman in horror, a bright flush painting her face. His eyes widened in surprise. "I was at another person's home, all right? I wasn't able to talk freely," she said, hoping she didn't look as guilty as she felt. "Where I was or who I was with is not important," she declared, though deep inside she knew if she had not been with Carl, she would have been willing to talk to Norman and would not be part of this PR nightmare. "Who really sent the information on Carl is the important question."

"The e-mail arrived from your computer. If you didn't send it, then someone must have gone into your office and accessed your computer while you and Sandra were gone."

A knock sounded at the door and Sandra's head peered through the cracked door. Georgia didn't like the expression on her face. Bad news, she thought. "Yes, Sandra, what is it?"

"Excuse me, Georgia, but Mr. Overstreet insists that you come to his office immediately." Georgia's heart dropped and her stomach lurched. "And he's in a foul mood, too. Probably because of Mr. Lepzig's column."

"Thank you, Sandra. Please let him know that I'll be right there." Sandra closed the door.

Norman walked over to Georgia and put his hands on her shoulders. "What are you going to do?" he asked, full of concern. After all, he was still very much in love with Georgia and would marry her in a heartbeat. They had been the perfect couple for four years until he proposed, but he wanted what his parents had—the brick home, two or three kids, family vacations at Daytona Beach. Her dream was to be a college president.

She twisted and stepped away from him. "What do you think? I'm going to tell him the truth. That information didn't come from me. I'm sure he'll understand."

"Hah!" spat out Norman. "In a pig's eye! You'll be split open and roasted by the time you put one foot in the door. Let me go with you."

"You're crazy," she said, opening her door. "The man is not some miscreant. He's really a reasonable person. He'll listen to my explanation and then we'll plot how to handle the situation."

Norman reached over her shoulder and shut the door, trapping

Georgia between himself and the door. "Norman, what are you doing?"

"You slept with him last night, didn't you?" he asked bitterly, his face so close to hers that she could feel the warmth of his breath.

"It's none of your business with whom or even if I am sleeping with anyone. Now get out of my way."

"Georgia, the man took your job. No one likes him. He's a loser."

"You don't know anything, Norman Brewster. Move before I scream."

Norman stepped back from the door, allowing Georgia to open it and step out into the hall. "I have one more thing to say," he called out after her as she walked rapidly away. "I hope you have another job waiting for you in the wings."

• • • • •

Trying to calm her rapidly beating heart, Georgia willed herself to breathe slower as she entered Carl's office. Carl sat with his elbows on the desk, his hands supporting his head. He did not acknowledge her presence. A lump rose in Georgia's throat as she watched him sitting there. He looked very young and hurt. Her mouth was dry. She cleared her throat. "Carl?" she walked over to his desk. "Are you all right?"

No," he whispered, not moving.

"We have a problem here, but I think if we both put our heads together, we can come up with a solution."

Slowly he raised his head to look at her. "Yes, Georgia, there is a problem," he said softly and sadly. "You're my problem. I'm ruined, thanks to you. Why did you do this to me?"

"But I didn't do it!"

"Yes, you did," he shouted, rising to his feet. Frightened by his outburst, Georgia stepped back, almost losing her balance. "You were angry that I got the job instead of you." He waved the newspaper wildly in the air. "This is your revenge!"

"I've never denied that I was angry," she said. "I admitted that to you last night, but I'm telling you I did not say anything to Lepzig about you or anything going on in this office."

He looked away from her, so she couldn't see the pain in his eyes. "Ever since I arrived, you've been plotting how to get rid of me. You pretended to help me and be a team player, while all the time you were gathering information about me to pass on to your friends at the newspaper."

"That's not true."

"You certainly performed a good show last night. I actually believed you cared for me, and I had strong feelings for you. But now I see you for what you really are—a vindictive, revengeful, cold-hearted woman. Well, Miss Davis, this battle is over, but I'm going to win the war." He smiled coldly and walked around his desk. "You're fired. Go clean out your office. I want you out of the building before 5 o'clock today. Campus police will send someone by to make sure you make the deadline." He opened his door and ushered her out, slamming the door behind her.

Carl snatched a bottle of Scotch from his lower right-hand drawer. Not bothering to locate a glass, he unscrewed the cap and gulped down the burning liquid. How could he ever believe that Georgia Davis might be someone special—a woman heads above Elena, whom he'd fantasized over for years. How could he have been so wrong about Georgia? He took another swallow and another. Women! Were they all manipulative and conniving? One more drink and the pain he had felt all morning started to melt away.

•   •   •   •   •

Tears streaming down her face, Georgia ran past Sandra. A few staff members, including Latifa Benedict and Richard Henry, watched with curiosity and concern as she ran by. Norman, who had waited around to pick up the pieces, grabbed Georgia, pulled her into her office and slammed the door. He cradled her in his arms, while she sobbed quietly onto his shoulder. Even if she were sleeping with Overstreet, Norman thought she didn't deserve this. That bastard! He should be fired, tarred and feathered, and run out of town.

Georgia pushed back from Norman's embrace. "I can't blame Carl for this, Norman. It's not all his fault." She sat down behind her desk and pulled out a box of tissue from her bottom drawer. She wiped her eyes and blew her nose. "He fired me because he thinks I'm conspiring behind his back to get him fired." She blew her nose again. "He thinks I'm a mean vindictive person," she wailed.

When Norman reached out to comfort her, Georgia shoved him away. "Leave me alone. Please, Norman. I'm fine."

"Yeah, right, I can see."

"Go back to work. You have a deadline to meet or you'll be out of a job, too. And I have to start packing my personal effects."

Norman sighed in frustration. "You're right as usual. Okay, I'm leaving, but I'll be back to help as soon as I finish my story."

As Norman opened the door to leave, a distressed Sandra Gibson walked in. "Georgia, I'm so sorry." She sat down across from Georgia, her eyes watering. "I can't believe it. I read Harold's column, and everything you said was true."

"Sandra, I didn't say any of that."

"Then why did he say you did?" she asked, confused.

"Because the information arrived in an e-mail from my computer."

Sandra thought this over. "Someone went in your office while you were gone and sent the e-mail to the newspaper? When?"

Norman said they received it yesterday."

"I don't remember seeing anyone in your office, and I locked it up when I went to lunch."

"Is that the only time you were away from your desk?"

Sandra paused to think. "Except when I had to help Latifa un-jam the copier. She had it so screwed up, it took nearly half an hour to straighten it out."

Georgia sat up straight. "Did you see Richard?"

"Hmmmm, yeah ... in fact, if he hadn't stopped by when he did, I probably would have called auxiliary services to send someone over."

"Are you saying he fixed it?" Georgia asked, her eyes narrowing.

"Well, yeah," said Sandra. "He turned a few knobs, opened and slammed a few drawers, and pulled out an accordion-folded piece of paper that was stuck who knows where. Why are you looking at me that way?"

"It's nothing, forget it," she told Sandra, but she certainly wasn't going to forget. No way. "Could you please find me a few boxes?"

Sandra dabbed at her eyes with a pink handkerchief. "Yes, I'll take care of it. I just wish it hadn't come to this."

"Yes," replied Georgia, "me, too."

• • • • •

After Carl sent Georgia scurrying for her office, Latifa Benedict and Richard Henry left the building separately and met at Caffeine Supreme downtown. Unlike the three locally owned coffee houses, which were usually packed at mid-morning with GCU faculty, staff and students, and local townspeople, the three-month-old Caffeine Supreme had only half a dozen customers—thanks to most everyone protesting the arrival in town of this national chain coffee house. A group of business students at the university convinced local coffee drinkers to avoid Caffeine Supreme so small independently owned coffee houses in town would not suffer.

Latifa was already sipping on the gourmet coffee flavor of the week, "Costa Rican Dynamita," when Richard arrived. "Sugar, do you believe it?" blurted out Latifa, as Richard sat down across from her.

"I can't believe he fired her," Richard said, stirring his coffee worriedly.

Latifa leaned over conspiratorially and hissed, "Isn't that what you wanted, sugar?"

Richard glanced over his left shoulder to see who had come into the coffee house. "No," he whispered back. "Not necessarily. I would have preferred for the bad man himself to leave."

"Oh, phooey! Georgia's out the door. Her position is now up for grabs, just waiting for you to fill it." With a long fuchsia-painted nail, Latifa flicked up some whipped cream from the top of her coffee and licked it off with the tip of her small pink tongue. "All you have to do now is ingratiate yourself and make yourself indispensable."

"No, I think what we need to do now, is figure out how to get rid of Carl Overstreet."

Latifa reached out her finger and poked Richard in the center of his forehead. "Sugar, that man is already doing a good job of that all by himself. He is in self-destruct mode."

• • • • •

With help from Norman and Sandra, Georgia had everything boxed up and moved to her car and Norman's Ford pick-up truck before everyone returned from lunch. Although Georgia left the building as quietly as possible, she knew that with Latifa's gossip mongering communication system, word of her firing would be all over campus before the end of the day.

When Norman dropped the last box of her personal belongings on the living room floor, Georgia collapsed on the sofa. She envisioned the scattered boxes as symbols of the end of her long climb to the top. Norman disappeared into the kitchen and returned with a tray containing two glasses of iced tea and two pimento cheese sandwiches. "Here, you must be famished," he said, as he put down the tray on the coffee table and plopped down beside her.

Georgia sipped the tea slowly and stared off in the distance. "What time is it?"

Norman looked down at his Walmart Timex. "After two o'clock. Aren't you going to try the sandwich? I washed my hands before I made it, really."

She turned to look at him and almost smiled. "Thank you, Norman. You've been a really good friend today. And I appreciate you making me a sandwich, but I'm just not hungry," she mumbled and sighed.

"In order to assemble an action plan, my lady, you have to have strength. To get strength, one has to eat." He handed her half of a sandwich. "I won't take 'no' for an answer." Georgia took a small bite. "That's my girl."

"So what's the plan?" asked Norman, finishing off the last of his sandwich.

Georgia ate a small second bite. "I don't have a plan. My mind is numb. I wish I could talk to Evan. He would know what to do."

"Evan Bradshaw? Now that's a name I haven't heard in months. What happened to him? Is he still alive?"

"Of course he's still alive."

"Don't get indignant on me. If a retired person doesn't make an occasional appearance around town, it's only natural to wonder if they're still among the living."

"Norman!"

"Well, is he still alive? Have you seen him and talked to him recently?"

Georgia pushed her unfinished sandwich aside and absently rubbed her neck. "Well, not exactly. He sent me a postcard from Rome a few weeks ago."

"Rome? Maybe he's home by now."

"No, he said he would call me if and when he returned. He hasn't called."

"So you think he's still traveling around somewhere?"

"Yes, I think so." Georgia stood up. "Norman, I appreciate your help, but I don't want to keep you from anything important." She started walking toward the door.

Norman rose to his feet. "I hate to leave you here all alone. Can't I do something else for you?"

Georgia opened the front door. "Norman, you've been a dear. Mom will be home soon from her bridge group. I can manage not to slit my throat until then. Thanks, again, for everything." She leaned over and kissed him on the cheek. Bye."

Reluctantly, Norman departed. Georgia watched through the window as he drove off. She carried what was left of lunch into the kitchen. She picked up the phone and dialed Marina's office, but was told she had gone for the day. Georgia thought that was odd. She dialed Marina at home, but got her answering machine. "Marina, I'm home. Please call when you get in."

• • • • •

Carl Overstreet asked Sandra to cancel all of his afternoon appointments. He did not return to the office after lunch. He went home and sat in the kitchen with a bottle of Scotch. He refused to answer the phone. Mentally, he declared this day as the worst day of his life.

• • • • •

Paul Van Horne was furious when Sandra told him politely that Mr. Overstreet was gone for the day and that she did not know where he was. In an effort to pacify the president, she suggested the possibility that Carl did not look well when he left and therefore might be at home. Paul called Carl at home, but received no answer.

• • • • •

Around 4 o'clock, Georgia's home phone rang. She decided to let the answering machine pick up. She didn't feel like talking to sympathetic friends and acquaintances who might have heard the news. After the sound of the beep, a familiar voice cut in: "Georgia, I know you're there licking your wounds, so you better pick up this phone and talk to me, young lady."

The iced tea glass in her hand slipped through her fingers and bounced on the thick carpet. She snatched up the receiver. "Evan? Evan, is that you?"

"Yes, it's me. Sandra called and told me what happened. How are you doing?"

"I'm ... uh ..." she began blubbering. "Oh ... I'm so-o-o-o sorry."

"It's ok. Go blow your nose and we'll try again."

Georgia did as she was told. She felt like such a child, but she was happy to hear from her old mentor. "All right, Evan. I'm okay, now. I was sitting here wishing I could talk to you and now I am." She felt a catch in her throat and paused.

"Dammit, Georgia, I thought you were going to get out of there," he fussed at her in a fatherly way.

"I sent out letters and résumés, and I've been networking just like you told me to do. There's nothing opening up."

"What about that job at the University of Florida?"

"How did you know about that one?" asked Georgia suspiciously.

"I heard it through the grapevine." Georgia did not respond. "Oh, okay," confessed Evan. "I heard there was a vacancy coming up and called Vivian. She said she'd talked to you already. She called you, right?"

"Yes, yesterday, and she basically offered me the job, but it was less of a job with less pay."

"But yesterday you still had a job and weren't desperate enough to take it?"

"Yeah, something like that."

"Amazing how quickly one's circumstances can turn around, isn't it?"

Georgia sighed. "Yes," she said softly.

A few seconds of silence passed. "Sandra says you think somebody set you up?"

"If I had to place any bets right now, I'd guess Latifa and Richard."

"Ah hah! Why am I not surprised that those two would stoop that low. So what are your plans?"

"That's what everyone keeps asking me. Evan, I don't know what to do or where to turn. I was hoping you might have some thoughts. You know I've never been good at office politics."

"My suggestion is for you to get out of Dodge for a while and regroup."

"And just where do you think I should go to regroup? You want me to take my mother on a Caribbean cruise?"

"To be mothered to death? Who are you kidding? Come visit me."

"Visit you where?"

"Venice, my dear."

"Venice, Italy?" she asked in surprise.

"Do you find it hard to believe that a nice old retired gentleman like me could enjoy an indefinite stay in Venice?"

"I guess not, but I couldn't come visit you."

"Why not?" he asked.

"I need to be here to straighten out this misunderstanding."

"What misunderstanding is that, Georgia?"

"Once Carl calms down and rethinks the situation, I'm sure he'll realize he made a mistake firing me."

"Ahhh, Georgia, Georgia, Georgia. Just listen to yourself. You're in denial. Overstreet took the promotion you'd been working toward, and now he's fired you. You're unemployed. Get angry. Pack a bag. Come to Venice for a few days, and let me help you plot a strategy."

"Yeah, right, I can just hear my mother now: Let me get this straight, Georgia, you were fired today, so you thought you would fly off to Italy to recover."

Evan laughed. "If she says that, then you tell her that you need to spend some time with me because I know all the ins and outs of dirty politics and I can help you through this crisis."

"And if that doesn't satisfy her?" she asked laughing.

"Then tell her I'm an old decrepit retiree who won't be around to provide assistance for too much longer."

"Evan!" Georgia squealed in horror. "Don't talk like that. It's not funny."

Evan chuckled at her reaction. "Making light of one's immortality is better than sitting around depressed about getting old. Now say you'll come to Venice. You've worked so hard over the years that you never took time for a real vacation. This is an opportunity. How can it hurt?"

Georgia hesitated. "I don't know what to say." She really wanted to say "yes," but didn't want to admit it. She'd never been one to run from life's problems, still ...

"Listen to me, Miss Davis, I have a lovely, small, two-bedroom/two-bath apartment right off the Grand Canal and the kindest feisty old Mama Mia who keeps the place clean, serves me three meals a day, and prevents me from seducing any unmarried women who should drop by. How soon can you get here?"

Georgia laughed. Maybe Evan was right. Her nerves were raw

and the emotional stress was draining her. The thought of having to face everyone in town she knew was more than she wanted to handle at the moment. Just hearing Evan's voice was uplifting. A few days with Evan would be good, but first she had to take care of Richard and Latifa. Then she could say yes. "You know, Evan, I could definitely benefit from a short holiday. I'll get on the Internet tonight and see if I can find any bargain fares to Venice."

"*Fantastica, ma bella signora!*"

"But before I can leave town, I have to take care of a certain situation."

"I understand. Anything I can do from here?"

"Thank you, Evan, but I want to handle this myself."

•  •  •  •  •

Carl's Rogue was parked in the driveway when Paul pulled up in front of his townhouse. Paul rang the doorbell, but no one opened the door. He pounded on the front door, but heard nothing. Not a person to give up easily, Paul sprinted around the townhouse to the backdoor. Through the glass panes he saw Carl with his head resting on the kitchen table, his right hand gripping a nearly empty bottle of Scotch. Paul banged noisily on the glass and yelled, "Carl, open this door!"

Carl's whole body jolted so violently at the loud racket behind him that the chair toppled, sending him sideways onto the kitchen floor. He turned groggily and tried to focus his eyes on a disgusted Paul, whose face was pressed against the glass.

"Let me in!"

Carl rubbed his eyes and hanging on to the table leg, managed to pull himself up off the floor. Unsteadily, he walked 3 feet to the door and fumbled with the doorknob until the lock clicked and the door opened. Paul stepped in and grabbed Carl in time to prevent him from falling down, again. Slowly he maneuvered him down the hallway to his bedroom and hoisted him into bed. Carl rolled over moaning. "I feel awful."

"That's because you're drunk, Carl. What a pathetic excuse for a vice president you turned out to be."

"Wha'cha doing here?" Carl asked as coherently as he could.

Paul loomed over Carl and glared down at him. "I couldn't reach you at the office. What are you doing at home?"

"I'm drunk." Carl guffawed.

"Carl, did you fire that Davis woman?"

"Did I! Oh yesh I diddle-dee did. I did you proud." Carl cackled hoarsely.

"I don't understand you. I've fired many people over the years. Sure, sometimes I felt badly for what I had to do, but I never had to get drunk afterwards."

"Yesh, but ... how many ... did you sleep with first?" Carl asked groggily.

Paul leaned down closer to Carl. "What did you say? How many did I sleep with? Carl!" Paul reached down and shook his shoulder. "Carl, you were sleeping with that woman?"

"Elena wouldn't sh-leep wish me."

"What?" Paul slapped Carl across the face. "Carl, talk to me!"

Carl opened and shut his eyes. "Go now ... sh-leep."

Paul stepped back from Carl's bed. He wanted answers, but that was something that would not be forth coming from the unconscious drunk stretched out in front of him. A disturbed Paul left the townhouse and returned to his office.

• • • • •

Marina arrived on Georgia's doorstep around 6:30 that evening with take-out from the local sushi bar: one tempura roll, one California roll, one tuna roll, one rainbow roll, and one salmon *nigiri*. A solemn Eula Mae ushered her into the kitchen where Georgia and Marina hugged each other tightly and tearfully.

"Mrs. Davis, would you care for some sushi?"

Eula Mae wrinkled up her nose. "Thanks, but I only eat cooked seafood. You two enjoy your smelly, raw fish. I made myself a peanut butter and banana sandwich." She poured herself a glass of milk and headed out of the kitchen. "I'll let you two plot revenge without me. I'll be in the living room watching David Muir. He's such a hottie!"

Marina sat down and wiped the tears from Georgia's face with a sushi bar napkin. "I was absolutely blown away when I heard Carl fired you and sent you packing. I'm so sorry. You deserve better than that."

"Yes, Carl blind-sided me. When I went to work this morning I was happy and carefree."

"How ironic that we were both fired the same day."

"Everything was wonderful. I even turned down a job offer at the University of Florida. Can you believe I did that?" Georgia paused and jerked her head around to look directly at Marina, her eyes widening as her brain started to register what she'd heard. "You were fired, too?" she hissed.

"Yeah, Walter said if I didn't go meet Mr. Liverpool in Savannah, then he was going to eliminate my position as part of an office reorganization."

"How rude!" Georgia leaned back on the sofa and mulled this over, then she sat up straight. "Marina, you're taking this too well. What aren't you telling me?" she demanded.

"I have something here that should get me a seat at the big boys' table." Marina reached in her pocket and pulled out her audio player-recorder.

"Marina!" Georgia squealed, giving her a hug. "You have it all on audio?"

"Not only from this morning when Walter actually fired me, but also from an earlier conversation after he heard the recorded conversation between me and Mr. Liverpool and told me I had set the whole thing up. You know, like a sting operation? Then he told me to either make plans to eat dinner with Mr. Liverpool or turn in my resignation. When I went back the next morning to tell him I was not going to resign, and I was not going to Savannah—well, I have that conversation, too."

Marina played both recorded conversations for Georgia to hear.

"Where's the conversation you recorded between you and Mr. Liverpool in Atlanta?"

"You know, I'm not sure. When Walter returned the player-recorder to me, the recording was erased."

"Sounds like he wanted to get rid of the evidence," Georgia pointed out. "But you have the other two recordings now. What are you going to do with them?"

"To be safe, I copied them to my PC at home and emailed file copies to my brother in Los Angeles. Then I spent my entire afternoon shaking things up. First, I wrote down what was said on the recordings and printed out several copies. Then I went to see Bob Kelly."

"Who was kicked upstairs to serve as the president's personal assistant?"

"Yes... and then to Rodney Feldman at EOC."

"Nice guy."

"Followed by a visit to Alexa Stewart, director of Legal Services."

"Whoa!"

"And last, but not least, a visit to Clarice Crace, a lawyer who specializes in employee grievances."

"You have been busy. No wonder I couldn't reach you. So what did you say and how did they respond?"

"I told each one my story of what I perceive as sexual harassment and wrongful dismissal. Bob commiserated, but he's afraid for his job."

"Yeah, he's been treated very shabbily. But I bet Mr. Feldman told you he would be only too glad to file a grievance for you."

"Yes, he did, so I'm filing a grievance against Walter as soon as Mr. Feldman gets the paperwork drawn up."

"Great! What about Alexa Stewart? I don't really know her."

"She's a cold fish. Shows absolutely no emotion. Couldn't get a reading on her at all. I gave her my spiel and gave her copies of what I recorded. Then she asks, 'And what do you expect me to do?' So I told her, 'I expect you to do whatever it takes to prevent the university from getting involved in a sexual harassment and wrongful dismissal suit that they can't win.' Then I got up and walked out."

"Sorry I wasn't there to see that. How about your lawyer?"

"Ms. Crace was very professional. Fortunately, she doesn't charge for the first visit. Guess she figures she'll get her money later if I need her for my lawyer. She said I had an excellent case, but she thought it was best for now if I just filed the grievance on campus and see what happens. So what have you done to shake things up?"

Georgia sighed and pulled her legs up under her on the sofa. "I feel like raw steak that's just been ground into hamburger. I don't know what to think or do."

Marina reached out and squeezed her shoulder. "I'm sorry. When I read the editorial this morning, I thought you might be in trouble, but I didn't think Carl would fire you without hearing your side."

"It was almost like he didn't have a choice in the matter."

"You mean like the president told him to fire you?"

"I don't know. It hurts my head to think about it. That's why I've decided to go away for a few days to lick my wounds and decide what I want to do."

"Where are you going? Jekyll Island? Savannah? Hilton Head?" Marina named some of the resorts where Georgia liked to go for a mental health vacation.

"I haven't decided yet. What I really need to do is find another job. If only I'd waited an hour or two to turn down that job in Florida."

"No way! You turned down a job in Florida?" Georgia filled her in on the position at the University of Florida. "So you turned it down because it was less money and more of a lateral move?"

Georgia nodded, avoiding eye contact. "Yeah, something like that." She knew she had to be careful. She didn't want Marina to suspect that there might be something going on between her and Carl. Especially since there wasn't anything any more.

"I don't know what to tell you. I want to help you, but I'm not sure how."

Georgia reached over and hugged her friend. "I know you want to help, but goodness Marina, you have enough to worry about. I think I'll feel better and have a better grip on my life after I talk with Evan."

"Evan? Is he back in town?"

Georgia grabbed her friend's hands in her own and squeezed. "Marina, I'm going to tell you something—just between me and you—something very confidential."

Marina's gaze did not falter. "You're my best friend, Georgia. Haven't I always kept your confidences?" Georgia nodded. "Tell me. I'm dying here."

"I'm going to see Evan."

"Yes."

"In Venice."

"What?"

"Is that all you can say? What do you think?"

Marina shook her head. "I think leaving Southern Pines might be a good thing. I can't think of a better place to go than Italy to start the healing process. If anyone can help put your life back together and help you find another good job, Evan can do it."

Georgia felt relieved. "So you don't think I'm crazy or rash to leave town?"

"Definitely not. Unless you have something incriminating somewhere?"

"No, I do not. But before I leave town, I need a way to strike back at the two culprits who caused my downfall."

"Latifa and Richard?"

"Yes, those two troublemakers," Georgia said with a yawn.

"How about let's get a few heads together in the morning. I bet over a pot of coffee we could come up with a workable scheme." Marina pushed herself up from the sofa. "Why don't I head out. You look like you could use some sleep. I'll call Sandra and we'll see you here in the morning."

Georgia locked the door behind Marina and collapsed on the sofa. She wasn't sure that she had enough energy to make it to her bedroom.

# Chapter Sixteen

Dressed and ready to leave for the office, Paul Van Horne sat on the edge of his king-sized bed and rubbed his wife's back. "Elena, I don't want to upset you, but I'm really worried about Carl's drinking problem. It's starting to interfere with his job. You had lunch with him, how does he seem to you?"

Elena sat up and propped her arms on her knees. "Yes, he did have several drinks at lunch and I remember the night he came over here for dinner and drank too much. But getting a new job and moving to a new state are two big stressors, Paul. Add that to the stress piled on by a very demanding boss."

"Yeah, right." Paul stood up and walked over to the window, where he could see the groundskeeper trimming the English ivy away from the trees. "Yesterday afternoon when I stopped by Carl's house, he was so drunk he fell out of a chair onto the floor."

Elena frowned. "Kind of early for him to be drunk, wasn't it?"

"Yes, that's what I thought. But then I decided after trying to talk to him that the heavy drinking was probably brought on by his having an intimate relationship with that woman he fired."

Elena's head snapped around toward her husband. "What did you say?"

Paul turned around to face his wife. "Does that shock you?"

"Why, yes, of course."

"Because he loves you?"

Elena looked down at her hands briefly before facing her husband. "Yes, Paul. Carl has always loved me and you know that."

Paul turned back to the window. The groundskeeper was attacking the holly bush with clippers. "Yes, I know, but I never took it seriously. He never mentioned it."

"No, but it was always so obvious. He was absolutely devastated when we told him we were getting married."

"Yes, I remember, but his love for you has never affected our friendship."

"Because he loves you, too."

"And because we both love Carl," corrected Paul.

Elena joined Paul at the window. "Yes, I love Carl very much." She caressed Paul's chest with her hands. "But I married you, not Carl."

Paul reached up and tugged on a lock of her hair. "You gave up a lot to marry me."

"Yes, I could have married Carl and had a grand career and a couple of children with a house in the suburbs, but I married you, Paul Van Horne, because I was in love with you. Also, I knew one day you would be important, famous and powerful." She turned away from him. "And because you asked me before Carl did." She turned her head back around and grinned mischievously at him.

Paul laughed and grabbed her hips, pulling her to him. He kissed her lips softly. "Even if Carl had proposed to you, I think you would have been too much woman for him." His arms moved up to her shoulders. "Elena, I need to know what is eating away at Carl. Something has happened and I think it happened when you two had lunch together."

"Something like what?"

Paul turned and walked over to the bed. "You tell me what Elena. Did our beloved Carl finally get around to acting on his feelings?" Elena turned away from Paul. "What did you talk about, Elena?"

Elena stiffened and sighed resignedly. "All right, Paul, if you really want to know." She looked him straight in the eye. "Yes, he finally confessed that he loved me, okay? But I made it very clear to him that even though I cared for him, my love for him could only be that of a close friend and that was the only kind of relationship we could have."

Paul sighed with relief and sat down on the bed, gathering Elena in his arms and hugging her tightly. "I'm so glad to hear you say that," he murmured, burying his face in her hair. "Now I think I understand what devils Carl is fighting. I need to find a way to save Carl from himself and save the university from Carl before everything gets out of control."

"What you mean, Paul, is that you don't want him to jeopardize your job." Elena smiled sweetly as she left the bedroom.

• • • • •

Georgia smelled the coffee and bacon before she was fully awake. She stretched and frowned when she realized she was still on the sofa. "Hello, Sleeping Beauty. I thought my lady was going to sleep all day," a familiar voice sounded from above.

A groan rolled out of Georgia's mouth as Norman Brewster loomed over her. She swung her feet to the floor and sat up, rubbing a nagging kink that had worked its way into the left side of her neck. "How did you get in here?"

"Ahhh, my lady sounds a wee bit irritated this morning."

"Blame me," Eula Mae called out from the kitchen. Her voice grew louder as she made her way into the living room. "The poor dear was sitting on the porch when I went out for the newspaper. I took pity on him after he filled me in with the latest news." She sat down beside her daughter. Her own dark hair was trimmed to a short bob parted on the right side. "Why didn't you tell me we were having a meeting this morning to plot revenge?"

Georgia looked sharply at a smiling Norman and glared at him, turning back to her mother. "Mom, first of all, I was in shock last night and, secondly, you were asleep when Marina and I planned this. I didn't want you to worry and fret."

"But that's what mothers are for. It never bothered you when you were in college. How many times did you call me up in the middle of the night just to tell me you had menstrual cramps or a fight with your roommate? What's changed? Do you think I'm too old and fragile now to hear your problems?" Her mother brushed some stray hair away from Georgia's eyes with her fingers.

"No, I'm sorry. I'm glad you want to help."

"You just need a 'warm fuzzy,' dear. Come here," said her mother, giving her a big hug.

Georgia hugged her mother back tightly. Her mother's "warm fuzzies" had gotten her through lots of life's problems and tears. "Thanks, Mom."

"Now, while I check on the grits and buttermilk biscuits, you go take a shower. I won't put the eggs on until you're all ready to face the day," said her mother, pulling her daughter up from the sofa.

"Thanks, Mom. Everything smells good," said Georgia, who figured the biscuits came from the freezer section at the grocery store, the grits were instant, and the bacon pre-cooked. The eggs would be scrambled, but her mother always managed to cook them without making them unedible.

"I'll be glad to help my lady," offered Norman.

"Young man," said Eula Mae, "you'll do no such thing. You can help 'my lady's' mother in the kitchen by mixing up some of that frozen orange juice."

"Party pooper," groused Norman, but he gave Eula Mae a wink and headed dutifully into the kitchen.

●　●　●　●　●

A wicked, skull-splitting headache brought Carl instantly awake around 11 a.m. Holding his head in both hands, he walked slowly into the bathroom to relieve himself. After a long, soaking shower, some extra-strength Tylenol, and two strong cups of black coffee, he decided he might live. He opened the front door to reach for the Saturday paper and was nearly knocked unconscious by the bright sunlight. He stumbled back inside and shut the door.

He stood still by the door for a long time, willing the throbbing pain to settle down to a dull ache. Then he moved to the kitchen table with his coffee, turned to the editorial page and began reading Walter Sigman's "Letter to the Editor." In his letter, Walter wrote that he took exception to Harold Lepzig's column and expounded on Carl's wonderful qualities as a human being and as a public relations professional. Walter listed outstanding things Carl had accomplished since his arrival on campus to improve the public relations office. The letter made him sound so good, Carl became teary-eyed. Whatever they pay you, Walter, it's not near enough, he thought. The letter was signed, Walter Sigman, Vice President of Development, Georgia Central University.

Directly beneath Walter's letter, in italics, was a note from the editor alerting readers that yesterday, after the publishing of Lepzig's column, one of his named sources, Georgia Davis, had been fired. Carl let out a howl that vibrated the coffee in his mug and sent his headache back into the "red zone" of pain.

• • • • •

Just as the breakfast dishes were cleared from the table, Sandra Gibson and Marina Roberson arrived at Georgia's house. Eula Mae, exuding Southern hospitality and charm, passed out mugs of coffee and leftover buttermilk biscuits with butter and fig preserves— purchased from Publix.

"The campus is buzzing about your dismissal," said Sandra.

Norman handed the morning newspaper to Georgia. "Now that you're functioning, you should read Walter Sigman's 'Letter to the Editor' and the 'Editor's Note' that follows."

Marina read the letter over Georgia's shoulder. "That Walter," exclaimed Marina. "He's certainly defending Overstreet to the hilt. It's a shame he can't do that for his own staff."

"I bet Walter wrote this letter at the request—no, make that insistence—of the president," pointed out Georgia. "I bet the president is furious about the 'Editor's Note.'" Everyone agreed.

"The president probably told Overstreet to fire you, Georgia. Maybe he told Walter to fire me, too," said Marina thoughtfully.

"The president does what he has to do to protect the university," said Sandra.

"But especially himself," added Norman.

"When all of you are through griping about Van Horne and something we can't do anything about, let's put our heads together to help Georgia," suggested Marina, as she turned to face her long-time friend.

"I guess the question is, is there something that can be done about Latifa and Richard?" asked Georgia, as the five of them sat around the dining room table. "Richard is totally incompetent."

"He must not be too incompetent, if he could get you fired," Norman pointed out.

"Being devious has nothing to do with being competent," replied Marina.

"He's a slacker," continued Georgia. "He tries to avoid hard work and any work considered beneath him. Take the statewide high school visual arts competition held here in March. The entire writing staff was busting buns to get out hometown press releases on award winners throughout the state. He managed to disappear until too late to help. We ended up dividing his share of the press releases among the rest of the writers."

"Latifa is no angel," mumbled Sandra.

"She may be the office gossip," said Georgia. "But she's good at what she does."

"All the male interns would agree with that—especially Wiley," said Sandra.

Georgia, Sandra and Marina laughed boisterously. Norman and Eula Mae looked at each other and shrugged. "Is this an inside joke?" asked Norman, who knew Latifa only by sight.

"Yeah," said Eula Mae. "We need a chuckle over here, too."

"No one knows anything for sure," Georgia was quick to point out.

"But it's obvious something is going on, Georgia," said Sandra. "Wiley spends a lot of time in there with the door shut and locked, and I can hear Latifa's raunchy giggles from time to time."

"Even folks in development talk about her sexual exploits," added Marina.

"But it's all rumor and speculation," reiterated Georgia firmly.

"We don't have a shred of evidence to the contrary."

Everyone turned and looked at Georgia. "Georgia, why do you keep defending those two idiots after what they did to you?" asked Marina.

"Because I don't want to be part of a lynch mob," replied Georgia, her chin rising. "Because I know how it feels to be unjustly accused," she added softly, her eyes watering.

Sandra squeezed her shoulder. "Georgia, we appreciate where you're coming from, but we know that deep down inside you know those two are guilty on all counts, right?"

Everyone waited quietly until Georgia responded. "Yes, I think they're responsible, and I want to get back at them, but what can we do? We can't prove Richard sent the email from my computer."

"Maybe not in court," said Sandra regretfully.

"Hey, wait ... hold on a minute." Norman looked thoughtful. "If there really is some 'hanky panky' going on in that office, maybe we could use that to our advantage to bring down Latifa and Richard."

"We'd have to catch them in the act," pointed out Marina.

"How could we do that and be assured that Richard would be part of the group?" asked Sandra.

Georgia gasped and her eyes widened, as she brought her left hand to her mouth. "I just had a thought. How about this? It might work if we can get Gene Williams to help. If there is anything indecent or obscene going on in our office, then this just might flush them out into the open."

"Oh," squealed Marina, "I hope it is something deliciously wicked."

"You tell me." Then very quietly and in great detail, Georgia presented her idea before the group. "Okay, who's in with me on this?" Everyone raised their hand. "Great! Then let's do it. Latifa and Richard won't realize they've been conned until it's too late."

That evening, online, Georgia purchased a ticket to Venice, departing from Atlanta Hartsfield Airport on Wednesday.

# Chapter Seventeen

An irritated Walter Sigman received a copy of the grievance filed by Marina Roberson in the afternoon campus mail. He was getting ready to call her into his office to give her a hard time, when he received a call from Alexa Stewart, director of Legal Services. His presence was requested in her office immediately.

Alexa did not stand up or greet him warmly or offer her hand when he arrived. He'd heard she was a "real hard ass," who didn't take crap from anyone or mince words. Paul Van Horne's kind of person, he figured, as he sat down across from her desk. There were no niceties exchanged. She began to lash out at him before he was completely settled in the chair. "You are in deep trouble, Mr. Sigman. You have brought the university to the edge of a judicial precipice with your egotism and pomposity."

"Hey! You hold on a minute," he interrupted her. "What are you raging about here? I haven't done anything wrong."

"So we're going to play Mr. Outrageous and Indignant?" she asked, raising her right eyebrow. "Did you not receive a grievance today filed by one of your own staff members?"

"She doesn't have a leg to stand on."

Alexa leaned forward, her forearms resting on the desk. "Did you not fire her a few days ago?"

"I certainly did. She refused to do the work I assigned her, so I gave her the standard two-week's notice. Refusing to carry out work assignments is just cause to dismiss anybody in my book," he said smugly.

"Not if the work you asked her to do would put her life in jeopardy. There's no war on this campus and she's not enlisted in the military." Alexa rose to her feet, her hands flat on the desk top.

Walter jumped to his feet and glared at Alexa. "All I asked her to do was meet with an old alumnus and pick up a $5-million donation. I didn't ask her to jump out of an airplane or run through a mine field."

Alexa walked around her desk and confronted Walter, nose to nose, inches apart. "What you asked her to do, Mr. Sigman, was to spend the evening on a yacht with a wealthy womanizer known for his sexual exploitations of the opposite sex."

"Mr. Liverpool?"

"Yes, Mr. Sigman. Your Mr. Liverpool. I did what you should have done when Miss Roberson complained. I made some discreet inquiries with the proper authorities. There have been numerous complaints of sexual battery and assaults brought against Mr. Liverpool. All cases were settled out of court."

A pale and shaken Walter fell back into the chair. He quickly pulled himself together. "Well, I didn't know that. She still won't win the grievance."

Alexa's eyes narrowed. "She told you on more than one occasion that he was a perverted old man and that she didn't want to meet with him. In spite of her being an excellent employee, you told her she had to go or she would be fired."

"Yes, I did. And she refused to go, so I fired her. No, wait ... we're eliminating her job as part of office reorganization."

"Office reorganization? I see." Alexa sighed. "Mr. Sigman, do you know what sexual harassment is? Give me an example." She spoke with her soft voice of reason.

"Hmmmm. Say some CEO has an attractive secretary and he tells her he'll promote her if she sleeps with him."

"Very good. Now what about a vice president of development who tells his assistant vice president that unless she endures the sexual advances of a rich alumnus and brings back a $5-million check, she will be out of a job?"

"That's not the case here!" he yelled, standing back up and almost butting heads with her.

"It's not, is it?" she raised her voice. "Well, Mr. Sigman, I have a transcript of two audio recordings that say otherwise."

Walter sat back down, in shock. Alexa walked around to her seat and waited.

His hands on his knees, Walter sighed and slowly started talking. "When Miss Roberson first came to me and said Mr. Liverpool was making advances toward her, I figured it was a case of an old man admiring a younger, good-looking woman. You know how 'touchy-feely' these good old Southern boys can be." He paused, but Alexa didn't respond.

"I didn't take what she said seriously. Then she came back with an audio recording she had made during a lunch meeting. I took the recording to Paul Van Horne."

Alexa's eyes widened in surprise. "How did he react?"

"Basically, he told me to handle the situation myself. That he had to have that $5 million or else."

"Or else what?"

"I took it to mean that if he didn't get the check, then I would lose my job." Alexa nodded and made herself a note. "He also told me to dispose of the recording."

Alexa jerked to attention. "Did you?" she asked softly.

"Yes, I did. How did you get a copy?"

"The two recorded conversations I have are between YOU and Miss Roberson."

Walter frowned. "No, that's impossible."

"Not impossible, Mr. Sigman. Of course, I have only written transcripts, but trust me when I say both conversations are quite damaging for you and for the university. I recommend that you meet with Miss Roberson and come to a mutual understanding."

"Like what?"

"Do I have to spell it out for you? Apologize. Give her a raise or a promotion. Whatever it takes to get her to drop the grievance. With those recordings and Mr. Liverpool's past history, if Miss Roberson ever brought a sexual harassment and wrongful dismissal suit against the university, not only would we lose big time, but we'd be crucified in the media. Now get out of my office." With shoulders sagging, Walter walked over to the door. "Oh, and Mr. Sigman, if I were in your place, I would send a man to get that check from Mr. Liverpool."

•  •  •  •  •

While her mother puttered around the house straightening up and muttering about the mess and how they should call Two Maids and a Mop to clean the place—"It would be money well spent," she shouted—Georgia spent most of the day talking to sympathetic friends in Southern Pines and networking with others on college campuses throughout the Southeast.

Vivian Kearny, University of Florida Vice President of External Affairs, was disturbed to hear about Georgia's job loss. "Too bad you didn't get fired a day earlier. Oh wait, that didn't sound nice at all, did it?"

"It's okay, Viv, I've been thinking the same thing." Georgia gave her Evan's number in Venice, in case she heard of a job opening.

Her last call of the day went to her friend Gene Williams, the email postmaster for campus. After filling him in on Richard Henry's "dirty deed" with her computer, he agreed to be part of the conspiracy to bring Richard and Latifa Benedict down.

•  •  •  •  •

Wednesday morning, Eula Mae drove Georgia to the Atlanta airport for her flight to Venice. During their drive to Atlanta, Georgia's mother turned off the car radio with Rush Limbaugh in mid-sentence. The sudden silence in the car jolted Georgia from deep thoughts about her extreme feelings for Carl Overstreet and her stupidity in letting her guard down and allowing her emotions to take control.

"Mom," protested Georgia, "I thought you liked Rush."

"Can't stand the man. He's a complete moron. Makes my blood pressure go up, which keeps me awake at the wheel. Any time my mind starts agreeing with him, I always turn him off."

175

"Oh. What did he say you agreed with this time?"

"Nothing." She glanced briefly at her daughter. "I thought you might want to talk."

"What's there to talk about?" Georgia turned to watch a UPS 18-wheeler pass on their right.

"This trip to Italy, for one thing. Seems to me you should stay here and search for another job."

"That's really funny coming from you, Mom," exclaimed Georgia. "Is this the same mother who told me to take some time off and go on a nice vacation?" Georgia watched her mother's hands tighten on the steering wheel. "Didn't you tell me that getting away was rejuvenating? That it energized the batteries? That it made one a better worker?"

"Stop throwing my advice back at me. You had a good job, and you were overworked when I told you that." Eula Mae blew the horn at a red compact that pulled in front of her and immediately slowed down. "You nincompoop!" she shouted.

"See," pointed out Georgia. "Maybe you need a vacation, too."

• • • • •

About the time Georgia and Eula Mae were halfway to the Atlanta airport, an agitated Paul Van Horne sat behind his desk, scowling at a nervous Walter Sigman. "After you knew she recorded old Liverpool, it didn't cross your mind that she might do the same with you?" asked Paul.

Walter looked down at his shoes. "No, sir, I never considered that possibility."

"Dammit, man!" roared the president. "You let this sweet, little Southern belle take advantage of you."

"I tried to force her to go to Savannah, so you could get your stupid money!" he yelled back.

"I thought you could handle the situation better than that."

"All right, so it didn't turn out like we planned. Do you want me to follow Alexa Stewart's advice and apologize?" Walter asked with a "hang dog" expression. "I can always promote her to associate vice president."

Paul leaned forward in his seat, pointing his finger at Walter. "If you do, you'll be perceived as weak and in the wrong. That's not good for any vice president of mine. If two recorded conversations are all she has to discredit you, get rid of the recordings. Then it will be your word against hers."

"How do you expect me to do that?" a flustered Walter asked.

"Do I have to spell it out for you, Walter? Find the recordings. Destroy them. Do whatever it takes," he literally hissed at his vice president. "And while you're at it, Walter, find another 'hot babe' with a sexy Southern drawl and send her to Savannah to collect my $5 million."

# Chapter Eighteen

The Delta 767 jet lifted off on schedule for its nonstop flight from Atlanta Hartsfield to Venezia Marco Polo. Mentally and physically drained, Georgia settled into her window seat with her pillow and blanket for the nine-hour flight. As soon as the dinner hour was over, she planned to skip any movies and sleep as much as possible, since she would reach the Marco Polo Aeroporto around 9 a.m. Marina, as a parting gift, had given her noise-blocking ear phones and elastic-backed, soft velvet eye covers to keep out the light.

While a flight attendant droned on about seat belts, oxygen masks and life rafts, Georgia's mind returned to the conversation with her mother. As Georgia had expected, her mother was not pleased with her decision to fly off to Italy.

"I need to get away for my sanity," she explained to her mother. "My mental health has to come first. Besides, I gave everyone Evan's phone number, I'll only be gone a few days, and I'll be checking in on a regular basis."

"I know dear, I understand that. I just don't know about you staying with Mr. Bradshaw." Not giving her daughter a chance to interrupt, Eula Mae continued. "Yes, I've met the man. Yes, he's a real fine Southern gentleman. Yes, he's trustworthy."

"Then what's your problem, Mom?" she had asked, very frustrated. "This is the 21st century."

"You are in a very vulnerable state right now," her mother pointed out. "Your vulnerability and his kindness could equal trouble for both of you."

"Mom, you've been watching too many soaps," she had quickly replied.

"Georgia, the man loves you."

"I know. I love him, too."

"No, Georgia, you aren't listening. Evan Bradshaw really loves you."

Georgia remembered the shock that vibrated through her body as she finally realized what her mother was saying. "That is preposterous," she told her mother, while not convinced now that was the case. "Evan is old enough to be my father."

But somewhere in her subconscious, she knew there rang a little bit of truth in what her mother was saying. As the plane sped across the Atlantic, she promised herself not to let her guard down with Evan Bradshaw like she had with Carl Overstreet. Just in case her mom was right.

· · · · ·

Georgia spotted Evan and his thick head of white hair immediately outside the exit of Italian Customs. He looked tan, robust and healthy. Very relaxed and happy, she thought. "Evan! You look fabulous! The Italian lifestyle agrees with you."

Evan gathered Georgia into his arms and gave her a welcoming "bear" hug. "Georgia, it's not so much the Italian lifestyle that agrees with me, but retirement from the university. No more stress, no more politics and no more crap to deal with." He held her in front of himself for inspection. "Visually you don't look stressed out or unduly frazzled. Maybe a little tired, but that's probably from no sleep on the plane."

Georgia smiled lovingly at Evan as he picked up her bag. Then she crooked her arm through his. "To be honest, I just feel an enormous surge of relief at getting away from Southern Pines and the university. Now, which way to the car?"

Evan grinned mischievously. "No one owns a car in this town. We'll take a taxi," he said, leading her outside.

She blinked in the strong sunlight and looked around puzzled. "I don't see a taxi anywhere."

"Sure, you do," he said, directing her toward a dock where several small boats were tied up. "A water taxi."

"Can't we take a regular taxi, Evan? I have this thing about boats."

Evan laughed heartily. "My dear Georgia, there are no streets or cars in Venice. Only waterways and boats."

"What about fire trucks and ambulances?" she asked as Evan helped her into the water taxi.

"Boats."

"Delivery trucks and buses?"

"Boats."

Georgia marveled over these revelations, as the boatman helped her into the water taxi, secured her luggage and pushed the boat back from the pier. Across a large span of water that Evan called the *Laguna Véneta*, Georgia could see Venice through the morning haze. As the boat neared the island on which the city of Venice is located, Evan pointed out the lagoon islands of *Murano*, known throughout the world for its beautiful glass.

They passed the *Isola di Michele*, the cemetery island, on the left side of the boat and headed toward the *Canole di San Marco*. Their water taxi slowed its speed as water traffic congestion increased. Georgia was awed by the number of *gondolas* or small boats everywhere and the *vaporetti* or water buses carrying tourists and Venetians. As they passed the *Piazza San Marco*, Georgia dug out her cell phone and took photos of *Doge's Palace*, the *Campanile* and the *Zecca*. Then she turned in her seat and took a photo of Evan's profile in front of *San Giorgio Maggiore* across the canal.

"Evan, this is a wonderland," she said.

Evan grabbed her left hand and held it in both of his. "Yes, my dear, it is. Now you can relax and let Venice work its magic on you. Soon you won't want to leave either."

• • • • •

The public relations office was the last place Carl Overstreet wanted to be—especially sober. When Paul Van Horne called him at home that morning—at the ungodly hour of 7 o'clock—he tried to tell Paul he was too sick to come in for a media crisis. But an angry, agitated Van Horne implied that if Carl wanted to keep his job, he'd be in his office before 8 o'clock. "And sober, dammit!" Paul yelled at him before slamming down the receiver.

Carl dragged himself to his office by 7:45 a.m. Sandra Gibson handed him a bottle of Tylenol and a large mug of strong, black coffee as he passed her desk. He bolted down the painkiller and several gulps of the hot black liquid, flinching as it burned its way down his throat. He tried to focus on work, but all he could think about was Georgia lying in his arms and the bottle of Scotch that was calling his name from the bottom desk drawer.

Paul called promptly at 8 o'clock. "Are you drinking?" he asked as soon as Carl picked up the phone.

"Black, unadulterated coffee. Should I put my secretary on the line to verify that?"

A grunt on the other end was Paul's only response. "We have two media crises to deal with this morning, so you better be up to it," Paul began threateningly.

Oh, great, thought Carl. Like I don't have enough to deal with already. "What's happened?"

"First off, Dr. Oliver Betts."

Carl rubbed his aching forehead and tried to focus his thoughts. He knew he recognized that name. "Betts? Is that the genetics professor who recently received the Oglethorpe chair?"

"Yes, he's the one," responded Paul, seemingly relieved that Carl remembered something. "A former PhD student of his has publicly accused Betts of publishing a paper on some genetics research that the guy claimed he did for his dissertation. He alleges Betts, who was his major professor at the time, was the reason he washed out of the PhD program."

"Not good," began Carl.

"I'm not finished yet. As if that isn't enough to get your adrenaline going this morning, we have rumblings coming out of anthropology that the department head has misappropriated some grant money. In addition, Walter Sigman's assistant vice president has filed a grievance against him for sexual harassment and wrongful dismissal. Hopefully, we can keep this away from the media until it disappears by itself."

"All right, Paul. I'll get to work on these right away. We'll have something out to the media this morning."

"You do that, Carl. I want those press releases on my desk before noon." Paul hung up without even a good bye.

"Well, Mr. Van Horne, you have a nice day, too," mumbled Carl as he dropped the receiver into its cradle. He yanked open the bottom drawer and snatched out the half empty bottle of Scotch. Banging it down on his desk, he sat and looked at it for a few seconds. Then he grabbed his coffee mug, unscrewed the bottle's cap and shakily poured two inches of Scotch into it.

• • • • •

When Richard Henry checked his email, he found a "high priority" note from Latifa Benedict: "Richard, my Sweet, to celebrate our recent success, you are invited to a private soiree for three on Saturday night in the small meeting room. Our little *menage a trois* will begin promptly at 9 p.m. Come play with me and Wiley. We won't take no for an answer. Bring a really nice bottle of sparkling wine and glasses and I'll bring the other essentials—candles, blankets, pillows, whipped cream, massage oil, etc. Sugar, I guarantee you'll remember this night forever."

Richard smirked and felt himself becoming excited at the thought of an evening with Latifa and her intern. Geez, he thought, maybe all those rumors about her and those frat boys are true.

• • • • •

Down the hall, Latifa reread for the third time the "high priority" email she'd received from Richard: "My dearest Latifa, to celebrate our recent success, I propose a private soiree—a *menage a trois* with you and your sexy intern Wiley this Saturday night at 9 o'clock in the small meeting room. You've been titillating me for a long time with your provocative dress and sensual body. Now's the time to prove you're more than a tease. Won't you and Wiley come play with me? I won't take no for an answer. I'll bring a really nice bottle of sparkling wine and glasses, if you'll bring the other essentials that will make the evening more pleasant—candles, blankets, pillows, whipped cream, massage oil, etc. If you and Wiley are brave enough to show up, this should be a night that we will all remember forever."

Latifa leaned back in her chair, licking one of her long fuchsia-painted nails, deep in thought. Then she tipped back her head and cackled. "Richard, my sugar sweet'ums, are we going to have a hot time Saturday night!"

• • • • •

Marina Roberson was surprised to hear from Bob Kelly, the former associate vice president of development, who had been forced "upstairs" to serve as a personal assistant to the president. She was even more surprised when he invited her to be his guest for lunch at Georgianna Hall, a restored antebellum home in Macon that had been turned into a popular pricey restaurant. Her surprise turned to a feeling of unease, when she was ushered into a private dining room, where an uncomfortable looking Kelly sat waiting. He stood when he saw her and waited for the *maître d'* to assist her with her seat.

"Well, my dear," purred Bob, as he replaced his napkin in his lap. "I hear that we've caused quite a bit of trouble in the development office."

"Bob, you know what's been going on in that office. Last time we talked, you didn't want to get involved. Now you've suddenly invited me here to dine with you in the private dining room. What's going on?"

Bob squirmed in his seat. "I've been asked to discuss certain matters with you to see if we can come to some sort of an agreement."

"Really?" Marina sipped her water and opened the heavy, leather-bound menu. "And what matters would those be?"

He leaned forward across the table and whispered, "You know ... those delicate, sensitive matters?"

"You mean those matters where I was fired for refusing to be sexually exploited by a rich alumnus so the president could get $5 million?" questioned Marina loudly as the waiter entered the room.

"Puuuhhh-llleeese ... not so loud," Kelly hissed as the waiter approached.

Marina smiled at the waiter and ordered a glass of white zinfandel and a cup of *crème de champignons soupe* for an appetizer, to be followed by *salade de homard, poule de jeu rôtie, asperges cuites à la vapeur* and *pommes de terre au beurre.* Under normal conditions, she would have ordered something simple and reasonably priced, but since Kelly was footing the bill, she decided to really enjoy the moment with a glass of quality wine and end it with a nice dessert and coffee. She stifled her laughter when Kelly wiped his perspiring brow with a blue and white plaid handkerchief. "What were you saying, Bob?" asked Marina as the waiter left. "Something about sensitive matters?"

"Well, there is a new position opening up in the president's office." Bob paused and took a swallow of water.

"Really? What kind of position would that be?"

"An opportunity for someone with your special talents."

"I see ... and just what special talents do I have?"

Bob opened his mouth to speak, but the waiter returned with Marina's wine and soup, and poured more water into Bob's glass. Bob waited until the waiter started toward the door before he responded. "My goodness, Marina, you have so many talents. Do I need to list all of them?"

"Definitely not. Merely the ones that would be appropriate for this soon-to-be-created job." Marina smiled and tasted the soup. "Mmmmmm," she murmured. "Delicious!"

"Let me reflect on your question for a moment." Kelly looked at his hands and the ceiling and took another swallow of water. "Well, you are quite attractive."

"Are you saying that attractiveness is the number one asset for this position?"

"Of course, the president likes to have beautiful women in his office for the visitors, you know."

"Sort of office decoration should any old rich male alums drop by?"

Kelly strangled on his water. "No," he spluttered, "that's not what I meant."

"Oh, did I misunderstand? What did you mean?" Marina asked innocently.

After wiping his face dry, again, Kelly sat silently for a few minutes, watching Marina finish off her soup. The waiter removed her bowl and replaced it with the lobster salad. "Aren't you going to eat anything, Bob?" she asked.

"No, thank you, I'm not hungry." Marina raised her eyebrows in question. "I've been having a lot of gastric problems lately." He sighed. "See here, Marina, if you will drop the grievance you've filed against Walter and the development office, then you'd be eligible to be a personal assistant in the President's Office."

Marina kept eating and did not respond right away. "I like my job in the development office," she said at last. "Why would I want to be a personal assistant?"

"Because your job in development is ending. Besides, why would you want to continue to work for someone who doesn't want to work with you?"

"Why should I be forced to leave a job I like when I've done nothing wrong?"

"You'll love being a personal assistant," he said halfheartedly. "And the job is only temporary."

"What do you mean, only temporary?" she asked puzzled.

"The job will tide you over while you look for a development job at another college or university," he explained, finishing up the last of his water.

Marina dropped her fork in her plate. "Let me get this straight, Bob. You want me to drop my grievance for sexual harassment and wrongful dismissal against Walter, and in exchange, I get a temporary job as a personal assistant doing nothing except looking attractive to visitors."

Kelly scratched his head. "Yeah, well, sorta, I guess that's right."

"And then at some later date down the road, at the president's discretion, the position will be eliminated due to lack of funds in the budget?" Marina pushed back from the table and stood up. Her hands on the edge of the table, she leaned over and glared down at Kelly. "NO! Absolutely not!" she yelled at him. Throwing down her napkin, she turned and walked out of the room.

• • • • •

The InAcqua Restaurant was housed in an 18th-century palace on the Grand Canal that originally belonged to the illustrious Venetian family Tiepolos. Georgia and Evan dined on the waterside terrace and watched the gondolas and other boats passing in the evening, their lanterns and lights shining across the water. Georgia loved the gondoliers, attired in a traditional dress of striped vest, black trousers and beribboned straw hat. Each gondolier stood proudly at the helm of his boat, dipping the long oar continuously into the water. Often a gondolier could be heard crooning a romantic Italian love song to appreciative passengers.

Evan ordered a bottle of *Valpolicella* red wine and *frutti di mare* for the antipasto course. When the waiter placed the huge platter of cold seafood in the center of their table, Georgia gazed hungrily at the carefully arranged selection of prawns, small squids, mussels, a small lobster and a spider crab, dressed with olive oil and lemon juice. For the pasta course, Evan and Georgia had small servings of a deliciously flavored rice and asparagus dish that Evan called *risotto*. This was followed by the main course: *sardine in saor*, a traditional Venetian way of serving fish with a sweet and sour sauce. Georgia didn't see how she could eat another bite, but Evan insisted on a cup of *cappuccino* and *tiramisù* for dessert.

After dinner, they walked through the *Piazza San Marco*, where Georgia paused in awe in the middle of the great plaza. "Evan, it's beautiful—almost surrealistic with the lighting. And so many people everywhere."

"Mostly tourists, my dear." Gently he led her to the water's edge and a bench where they had a magnificent view of *S. Giorgio Maggiore* across the canal. Georgia sighed. Evan reached out for her hand and gave it a squeeze. "Happy?"

Georgia looked into her old friend's face. "Yes, Evan, very happy. I haven't felt this content in months."

"Since before you found out about Carl Overstreet?"

"Yes," she nodded and turned her gaze to a *vaporetta* making its way up the Grand Canal. "But being here makes it easy to forget any stress and frustrations."

"Yes, I know," he said, putting his arm around her shoulders and hugging her. "That's why I insisted you come over for a visit. You'll be a much stronger person when you return."

Georgia glanced back at Evan. "Do I have to go back?"

"Yes, you're going back—completely re-energized and ready to conquer all the Overstreets and Van Hornes of the world. We'll discuss that later, but tonight you are going to enjoy yourself and mellow out."

Georgia placed her head on Evan's shoulder. "That won't be hard to do."

• • • • •

Carl Overstreet was finishing the last of the Scotch when his office manager Sandra asked if he could talk to local reporter Norman Brewster. "What does he want to talk to me about?" asked Carl, who was considering leaving the office early and stopping at Pauly's Package Store on his way home.

"The misappropriation of funds in the anthropology department." Sandra entered Carl's office, shutting the door behind her.

"I don't want to talk to him," replied a belligerent Carl. "Can't Richard talk to him?"

Sandra picked up the empty Scotch bottle and dropped it in the trash. "It is against university policy to drink on the job," she said quietly. "You need to get a grip on yourself, Mr. Overstreet. And you ARE going to see Norman Brewster because you need to score points with the media." She glared down at him just like his mother used to do when she was very disappointed in him.

"All right, fine. I'll give him five minutes." Then, he thought, I'm leaving for the day.

Sandra opened the door and Norman sauntered in, all smiles. He plopped down in the nearest armchair and leaned back.

"How can I help you this afternoon, Mr. Brewster?"

"Isadora Duvall. Does that name mean anything to you?"

Carl repeated the name several times, but shook his head. "No, means nothing to me. Why?"

"Mrs. Duvall manages all the financial accounts in the GCU anthropology department. That includes all grants and special funding received by the various areas in the department. She keeps the books and writes the checks."

"So?"

"Did you know her last employer, Flat Rock College, charged her with check forgery and embezzlement? Charges were dropped after Mrs. Duvall agreed to leave and make full restitution of missing funds."

Carl breathed deeply and willed himself to stay focused on what the reporter was saying, but he kept thinking about the empty bottle of Scotch in his trash can.

"Is this something the university was not aware of?" asked Norman.

"Listen ... Herman, was it?" Carl struggled to remain focused and calm.

"Norman. Norman Brewster." Norman reached inside his jacket and brought out a pad and pen.

"Well, Norman, I'm sure the campus police are aware of this as they begin their joint investigation with the Southern Pines police and the GBI.

"Then why wasn't it mentioned in today's release?" he asked, pen poised.

"Because you are an investigative reporter and your editor expects you to do your job." Carl struggled to his feet. "Thank you for stopping by, Mr. Brewster."

"Can you say that the department head—Dr. Alton Weber—had nothing to do with the misappropriated funds."

Carl walked over and opened his door. "I'm sure he will be cleared of all accusations in due time."

Norman stood up, a look of disgust on his face. "And what about Georgia Davis? Will she be cleared of all accusations in due time?"

Carl froze. He could feel his calm veneer cracking. "What about Miss Davis?"

"She isn't the traitor you believe her to be. Someone else used her computer to send the letter to the editor. She was set up just like the anthropology department head. Only you're too stupid to figure that out."

Carl's face turned red. "That's enough out of you today, Mr. Brewster. Get out of my office." he said, fighting for control.

"That's fine with me. I just want to say one more thing—Georgia is too good for you, you pompous, ill-bred Yankee. And when they kick your butt off this campus, I'll be cheering from the sidewalk. Frankly, I don't think it will be long now."

• • • • •

In the President's Office, Steve Smith from the State Board of Regents and Paul Van Horne were engrossed in a discussion about the board's revision of the Major Capital Outlay Priority List. Paul was pleased that the proposed $50-million complex for the newly created College of Genetics and Molecular Sciences was number three on the priority list. He had lured the new dean away from MIT with promises of a multi-million dollar complex and the relocation of the Dwight Diamond International Research and Development Center in Seattle to this new complex, once completed. Diamond International would research, develop and manufacture small batches of experimental drugs for doctors to use in clinical trials, which could lead to future production of lifesaving drugs and make GCU's name known throughout the medical community.

"This list will be included in the regents' budget request for next year," explained Smith. Once the budget is submitted to the state's Office of Planning and Budget in September, then the governor will make recommendations for his budget, which will be considered by the state legislature when it convenes for the next legislative session."

"What are the chances funding will be approved for the new complex?" Paul asked.

"Last year the General Assembly approved the top six projects on the regents' list. The year before, they approved the top three. So unless the governor or the legislature decides to revise the list, your funding is literally a done deal."

The office door opened suddenly and Carl Overstreet came barreling into the room. Breathing hard, his face flushed, Carl ignored Smith and headed straight to the president. "I need to speak to you," he demanded loudly.

"Carl, I'm discussing something important with Steve," explained a vexed Paul. "Let me call you after Steve leaves and we'll discuss your problem then." Paul turned his attention back to Smith. "You were saying, Steve?"

"This won't wait, Paul," Carl interrupted, his voice increasing in agitation.

As Paul shot out of his chair to face Carl, Smith rose from his seat and headed to the door. "Paul, I'll be outside when you're finished. I need to check in with my office, anyway." Paul waved a hand at him in acknowledgment, but never took his eyes off Carl.

Paul shook his finger angrily in Carl's face. "What has gotten into you? Are you drunk, again? How dare you come barging into my office in the middle of an important meeting! You better be in here to report a major calamity on campus. What is it?" he asked, trying to keep his temper at bay.

"Dammit, Paul!" he cried out. "You made me fire Georgia and she didn't do anything to deserve it."

"What?" snorted Paul. "You crash in here and disturb me and my guest because of some woman you should have sent packing months ago?"

"She was doing a good job," said Carl, punching Paul's shoulder with his finger. "She was on my side."

Paul grabbed him by the shoulders. "Get a grip on yourself, man," he said, only two inches from his face. "You're disgusting, Carl! You smell like a distillery. Have you been drinking on the job, again?"

"How else could I do your dirty work and live with myself?" Carl shouted.

"You're caught up in some sexual fantasy. The woman's not worth it."

Carl pulled back his right fist and struck toward Paul's chin, but missed as Paul ducked, causing Carl to lose his balance and fall against the desk. "How do you live with yourself?" cried Carl, holding on to the desk. "You're ruthless. You get everything you want no matter whose life you screw up in the process."

"Carl, get out of here before I do something we'll both regret." Paul's neck and face were livid and he trembled visibly.

"Before you what?" snarled Carl. "Before you fire me? Well, let me save you the trouble. I quit." Carl rushed to the door and almost knocked over Smith in his haste to leave.

"Carl ... wait!" yelled Paul as he ran out the door after him, but he was already out of sight. Paul returned to his office slamming his office door.

"That guy has a problem," said Smith, sitting down in the chair. "You have enough other problems to deal with, Paul. You need to save your energy for the senator. That man means to bring you down."

"What?" asked a flustered Paul, his attention still on the departing Carl. His brain suddenly clicked and focused on Smith. "Who are you talking about?" he asked, sitting down.

"Senator Wittick," Smith explained.

"What does the senator have to do with anything?"

"Everything, my friend. You've been on his 'black list' since his grandson ended up in a coma."

"Yes, I know that, but I heard that his grandson was talking, feeding himself and in the process of learning to walk. I thought that by now, the senator had gotten over being angry at me and the university."

Smith shook his head. "The senator never forgets anything, and now he knows you've been accumulating questionable information on him."

Paul frowned and leaned toward Smith. "How does he know that?"

"The Wittick family has a long history in this state," Smith explained. "The entire family is rich, influential and powerful. Call them the Kennedys of Georgia. You know as well as I do that the senator himself has many alliances, both in and outside the political arena. He and his closest friends—a strong network of 'good old Southern boys'—have hatched many a plot over the years and unmade more careers than most folks down here can remember."

"He's just an old wind bag prima donna who's hung on way past his time," Paul said angrily.

"Don't be so sure about that, Paul. He's a force to be reckoned with. I'd tread lightly. Southern politics can sneak up behind you and lay you out flat on your face before you know what happened."

• • • • •

When the custodians finished cleaning the building, Walter Sigman let himself into the development office. Marina Roberson's office was located two doors down from his. First, he wandered throughout development spaces to make sure no staff member was working late. Taking out the master key ring he'd borrowed from his secretary's desk earlier, Walter cautiously opened Marina's door and went inside.

Marina's desk was clean and orderly. No stacks of paper or mail. The only items on top of her desk were a Mickey Mouse business card holder, a Minnie Mouse tape dispenser, a Goofy stapler, a Donald Duck pencil cup, a Pluto gem clip box, a Walt Disney candy canister, a standard issue campus telephone and four stacked, clear-plastic organizers with multi-colored files.

"Okay, Marina," Walter mumbled out loud, "where have you hidden your recorder?" He sat down in her chair and pulled out the top right drawer, which was full of GCU letterhead, second sheets and envelopes. He moved down to the second drawer and found one Tinker Bell coffee mug, one Tigger coffee mug, envelopes of hot chocolate mix, a partially used bag of miniature marshmallows, a box of assorted herbal tea bags, a plastic container of honey, instant ramen soup in a Styrofoam cup, several packages of peanut butter and crackers and an unopened one-pound bag of peanut M&Ms.

Walter slammed the drawer shut and moved down to the bottom drawer. The front of the drawer contained files on a variety of subjects, including health insurance, leave requests, mileage and expenses, and development publications. Behind the files, he found a box of Tampax and a large bottle of Aleve. "I can't believe I've stooped this low," he fussed, shutting the drawer. "They don't pay me enough to do this."

Turning his attention to the left side of the desk, Walter opened the top drawer and discovered a hodgepodge of office supplies. There among the Post-it Notes, index cards, thumbtacks, memo pads, labels, paper fasteners, rulers, stamps, rubber bands, boxes of new pens and pencils, colored markers and a rubber-banded stack of business cards, Walter found an audio player-recorder.

Walter turned it on and reviewed each of the six recorded files listed. Each recording was exactly what it was titled: recordings of development training and CASE conference sessions. "Utterly worthless," exclaimed Walter, tossing the player-recorder back into the drawer.

The middle drawer on the left contained printer paper, CDs, a USB flash drive, a small Webster's dictionary and a digital camera. The bottom drawer was locked. Walter muttered an obscenity under his breath. He reached into his pants pocket, pulled out a small pocket knife and jimmied open the lock. The drawer was full of files from front to back. Walter quickly thumbed through them. The last file in the back was unlabeled, but held a sealed envelope containing a small audio player-recorder. He clicked "play" on the first of two untitled recordings and heard his own voice and that of Marina's. "Yes!" he cried out with glee. "Marina, you are toast!"

• • • • •

Paul Van Horne was sitting in bed, going over some papers that Steve Smith had left with him, when his cell phone rang. Paul reached over to the bedside table and grabbed it, checking the caller ID before answering. "Hello?"

"Mr. Van Horne, this is Lt. Cassidy with the Campus Police."

Paul set his papers aside and swung his legs off the bed. "Yes, lieutenant, what can I do for you?"

"Sir, there was a one-vehicle accident on campus tonight."

"Anyone hurt?"

"The driver of the car is pretty banged up, but nothing serious. Fortunately, no one else was involved. I'm here with him at Crisp County Regional and the doctor says he's gonna be okay."

"I don't understand, lieutenant, why are you bothering me with this?"

Lt. Cassidy sighed. "Well, sir, the driver is that new vice president you hired—Carl Overstreet?" Paul's hand tightened on the phone. "Sir, he's very drunk. He totaled his car and pretty much destroyed a bike rack and four bicycles. The alcohol content in his blood is through the roof. I'm afraid the Southern Pines police are going to charge him with DUI. If he gets released tonight, he'll end up in jail, and I was thinking about how this might not look too good in the media tomorrow—what with all the other negative press we've been getting lately."

"Thank you, Lt. Cassidy, you were right to give me a call. I'll get dressed and be right down." As Paul hung up the phone, Elena came out of the bathroom dressed in a powder blue sleeveless nightie. "Elena, that was the Campus Police. Carl has been in an accident on campus."

Elena drew her hand to her mouth. "Is he okay?"

"Yes, the fool is going to live, but he's drunk and I need to get to the hospital to see what I can do before he gets carted off to jail." Paul reached for his trousers and shirt. "Maybe this will knock some sense into him."

"But, Paul," Elena put her hand on his forearm, "spending the night in jail might be good for him," she said.

"Maybe for Carl, but not for me and the university."

Lt. Cassidy met Paul at the entrance to the emergency room and directed him to the young doctor on duty who was looking after Carl. "Dr. Van Horne, this is Dr. Sidney Crockett. Doc, this is the president of the university," Lt. Cassidy introduced them to each other.

Paul didn't think Dr. Crockett looked old enough to have graduated from high school, much less medical school. He reached out his hand to the doctor. "Pleasure to meet you, Dr. Crockett."

"Same here, sir."

"What can you tell me about my vice president?" Paul asked.

"It was very fortunate he was wearing his seatbelt," Dr. Crockett pointed out. "He has a mild concussion, a few scratches and lots of bruising, but he'll live to talk about it."

"Will you be keeping him overnight?"

"Not necessary, and you know how those insurance folks are."

Paul eyed two policemen sitting in the ER waiting area. "Just between you and me, Dr. Crockett, Mr. Overstreet has been drinking heavily this week because of a major crisis with this woman he's romantically involved with," he whispered conspiratorially.

Dr. Crockett nodded knowingly. "Oh, man, that's rough. It's terrible how a woman can drive a man to drink and ruin his life."

"Yes, it certainly is. I just want what is best for Mr. Overstreet. The poor man needs to go to a special facility where his—uh—condition can be treated. Can you help us out with this?"

"Oh ... I don't know ... I think those police officers are waiting to take Mr. Overstreet to jail to sober up."

Paul paused in thought for a minute. "Dr. Crockett, do you like football? Are you a GCU Pelican fan?"

Dr. Crockett grinned broadly. "Oh, yes, sir! I love them Pelicans! I watch them on TV every chance I can."

Paul stepped closer to Dr. Crockett and whispered in his ear, "How would you like two season tickets to see the Pelicans play this fall? I bet we could get you seats on the 40-yard line, if you can just help us out with Mr. Overstreet. Do you think that might be possible?"

"Season tickets for two?"

"That's right."

"Could you include tickets to the away game at UGA? Those tickets are impossible to get."

"I think that could be arranged."

Dr. Crockett cocked his head and smiled at Paul. "Well, let me see then ... I reckon I could call the King's Crossing Substance Abuse Center and see if they have room for a patient."

"That would be good," said Paul with a nod. "Think we could get Mr. Overstreet on a stretcher and past those two officers without them knowing it?"

Dr. Crockett laughed. "For two season football tickets on the 40-yard line, I expect it won't be a problem."

# Chapter Nineteen

Carl's head was pounding furiously when he finally woke up and realized he did not know where he was. He was dressed in one of those disgustingly indecent hospital gowns that fails to properly cover the rear end, and he was attached to an IV. His achy forehead was covered with a bandage on the right side, and he had scrapes and bruises on his face and forearms.

"That's from the air bag," said a chirpy feminine voice beside him.

Carl turned his head and stiff, painful neck slowly to face the voice, which belonged to a twenty-something brunette in a nurse's uniform. "Air bag?" he questioned.

"Yes, don't you remember the accident?" she asked as she inserted a hypodermic needle into his IV.

"Accident?" he mumbled. He strained to remember. Bits and pieces of hazy memory floated teasingly just out of his conscious reach.

"I heard you took out a whole bike rack on campus and destroyed half a dozen scooters. Bet there will be some upset students today, huh?" She removed the empty hypodermic and discarded it in the 'hazardous material' box. "There, that should have you feeling spiffy in no time at all. How about some black coffee and a piece of toast?"

Before Carl could respond, Miss Chirpy was gone, but returned seconds later with a tray. She put the food tray down and cranked Carl's bed to a sitting position. Carl groaned. The vertical position made him dizzy.

"Oh, I'm sorry. Bet after last night you're feeling a little bit woozy, huh?"

Carl groaned, again. He wasn't too sure how much more of Miss Chirpy he could take. She was even more cheerful than his former secretary at Gabriel. "Where am I?" he asked, trying to decide if he wanted to drink the coffee or not.

"Wow," she exclaimed. "You really must have tied a big one on last night, huh?"

Yes, thought Carl, he did remember that he was pretty much snockered. But what else? Something was there ... something he needed to remember ...

"You're at King's Crossing," she responded cheerfully.

"What is King's Crossing?" Carl asked, somewhat irritated, his head starting to ache.

"A substance abuse center."

Carl frowned. Substance abuse center? Suddenly he remembered his arrival last night with Paul by his side, helping him sign some papers. Had he checked himself into a substance abuse center? "Oh no, hold everything. I'm getting out of here." He pushed back the sheet and made a feeble attempt to get out of bed, but was overcome by dizziness, a wave of nausea and squeals from Miss Chirpy.

"Mr. Overstreet, you can't get out of bed yet. Please wait. I'll get an orderly," she yelped, running out of the room.

The orderly, who Carl thought would have made a good body double for Jesse Ventura, arrived as he was making a second attempt to get up. "Whoa there, Buddy," said the Ventura look-alike, holding Carl in bed with one finger against his chest. Carl fell limply and exhausted back against the bed.

"That's right, just relax, that's a good fellow," he continued soothingly as though talking to an agitated Labrador Retriever. "Where did you think you're going?"

"Home," replied Carl, with what felt like one of his last breaths.

"Buddy, you ain't going no place until the Doc says so." The orderly leaned over Carl and smiled at him patronizingly.

"What if I have to urinate?" he croaked.

"Then I'll bring you a urinal, Buddy. Do we understand each other?"

"Yeah, yeah, I understand," said Carl, throwing his arm over his eyes. *I get it. I'm stuck in this hell hole with Genghis Khan as my guardian.*

"Is there a problem here?" sounded a familiar voice from the door.

Carl uncovered his eyes to see Paul standing in the doorway. He sat up. "Paul, get me out of here," he yelled.

The orderly backed away from the bed as Paul came forward. "Now, Carl, you've been in an accident. You need to rest and get well." Paul nodded to the orderly, who left the room, closing the door behind him.

"There's been some mistake here, Paul. The nurse told me this was some sort of substance abuse center and I'm no drug addict. Can't you tell them that, Paul?"

"Carl, your substance abuse comes in a bottle of Scotch. If you had not checked yourself into this facility last night, you'd be drying out in the city jail this morning, charged with driving under the influence. This is the only way to go."

"For me or for you and the university?"

"This is the best solution for everyone. You'll get the help you need."

"And there'll be no bad publicity for the university."

"My dear Carl, you sound rather testy this morning."

"If you were sitting here instead of me, you'd be testy, too." Paul didn't respond. He looked at Carl and shook his head. "It's all about power and control, isn't it, Paul? You put me in here so I will be out of sight and out of mind, didn't you?"

"Carl, you signed the papers to admit yourself last night. Don't you remember?"

"What little I remember of last night was you holding a pen in my hand so I could write my name. I don't remember much else."

"Like embarrassing me in front of Steve Smith? Or resigning your position as vice president in a fit of rage? Or telling Elena that you loved her? Or all of the above?"

"You jerk!" shouted Carl. "Get out of here!"

"Gladly, my friend. I won't be back until you're permanently sober and ready to apologize." Without a glance back, Paul turned and walked out the door.

"Never, Paul. You hear me? I'll never apologize to you."

• • • • •

After receiving the phone call Friday morning from Bob Kelly, the president's personal assistant, Sandra Gibson typed up a special memo and emailed it to every staff member in the public relations office. The email explained that Vice President Carl Overstreet was hospitalized following a one-vehicle accident on campus last night and would be out of commission for several weeks. In the meantime, Richard Henry would be in charge of day-to-day activities in the office until further notice and emergencies would be referred to Bob Kelly in the President's Office.

Latifa Benedict immediately e-mailed the contents of the memo to her friends and stooges all over campus. One of her acquaintances, Rachel Malone, a senior secretary in the dean's office at the dental college who was married to a King's Crossing orderly, replied to Latifa's e-mail with news of her own. By quitting time, the actual whereabouts of the unpopular new vice president was quickly making the rounds through e-mail, Twitter, Facebook and text messaging.

As soon as Richard Henry heard about his new office status, he strutted down the hall to Latifa's office. "Sugar, you just come on in and sit yourself down," she said, patting the seat of the chair next to her desk. "You must be proud enough to pop all the buttons off your shirt."

Richard plopped down in the proffered chair, grinning from ear to ear. " I think the first thing I shall do in my official capacity as vice president is to declare the rest of today a holiday and send the entire staff home."

Latifa leaned over laughing and fell backwards into her chair. "Sugar, you are just a rip-roaring hoot."

"I can't believe how well everything is coming together," remarked Richard. "I'll do such a good job, the president will surely want me in Georgia's old position."

"We'll have to double celebrate tomorrow night! Maybe we'll need more sparkling wine than you thought?"

"Maybe I'll cut out early today."

"To beat the rush hour congestion?"

"No," he replied with a smirk. "To allow extra time to purchase some really special sparkling wine."

Latifa held up her finger and licked her long fuchsia nail seductively. "Oh, Sugar, the good times will roll Saturday."

• • • • •

Georgia and Evan had just returned from a day of sightseeing around Venice when the call came in from Marina Roberson in Southern Pines. The last stop of the day had been a mask and costume shop in *San Polo*, where Georgia discovered a large assortment of Venetian masks and costumes made especially for the annual Carnival, a vibrant 10-day festival preceding the abstinence of Lent. The festival is used as an excuse to don a mask and costume and parade around the city.

Inspecting the delicate, ornately decorated mask that she had purchased in the shop, Georgia accepted the phone from Evan and settled into an overstuffed chair. "Marina, I'm so glad you called. I can't believe you're already missing me."

"I'm afraid it's not just me. Dozens of folks are missing you. Maria Eddings wants you to go to Murano and buy her a small piece of glass and Al Donovan says to bring him back a Carnival poster."

Georgia laughed. "Okay, I'll make myself a note. What time is it there? Are you at work?"

"No, I thought it was best that I call you from home on my lunch hour. I have so much news, I don't know where to start."

"Then start anywhere. Don't keep me in suspense."

"Someone broke into my drawer and erased all of my recordings."

Georgia gasped. "I don't believe it! Do you think it was Walter?"

"That's where I'd put my money."

"What are you going to do about it?"

"I called Lt. Cassidy. He looked at it and said someone had definitely forced open the lock. He dusted for fingerprints, but said he doubted if he found any good prints. I have an appointment with my lawyer this afternoon."

"Let me know what she says. What else?"

"Are you sitting down?"

"Oh, yes, is this juicy?"

"Carl Overstreet had a little car accident last night."

"Is he okay?"

"What do you care? But, yes, he's okay. Norman called me. He said his friends at the station are seething because he was quite drunk. They wanted to arrest him for DUI, but somehow he was sent from Crisp County Regional to King's Crossing before they realized he'd been released."

"This is all so weird," said Georgia, betting that the president played a role in it to avoid bad publicity for the university, as well as for Carl.

"Oh, you haven't heard the really weird part yet. Apparently, since no one knows how long Carl will be in King's Crossing, guess who the president put in charge of day-to-day office activities?"

"I can't imagine. There aren't that many staff members left."

"Would you believe Richard Henry?"

"No, be serious. Who is it?"

"Richard Henry!"

"That totally incompetent man has been placed in charge of day-to-day office activities??

"Yes, isn't that a scream?"

"Richard will self-destruct and destroy the public relations office in just a matter of days. Any other news I should know about?"

"As a matter of fact, the devious plot we hatched against Latifa and Richard is starting to come together."

"Oh, my gosh! Saturday night?"

"Yes!" she exclaimed ecstatically. "I wish I could be a fly on the wall in that conference room Saturday night when things heat up. Are you wishing you hadn't left town now?" asked Marina coyly.

Georgia turned around and glanced at Evan who was standing nearby waiting to hear what was happening. "No," she said, smiling at Evan. "I'm deliriously happy to be on this side of the Atlantic and what goes on in that office is of no concern to me." But they both knew that was a lie. That office had been part of her life all of her working years. She still felt connected. And then there were her secret feelings for Carl. By all rights, she should hate the man for stealing the vice presidency right out from under her and then firing her unjustly—but she didn't. Neither did she understand what about him appealed to her. And that frightened her.

● ● ● ● ●

Lt. Charles Cassidy stepped out of the shadows of the administration building Saturday night as reporter Norman Brewster and a young camera-toting male sauntered up the sidewalk. Outdoor lighting provided ample light for positive identification. "Lieutenant," greeted Norman. "Our best nightshift photographer, Frank Toddy. Charles Cassidy with the GCU Campus Police." The two men shook hands.

"Man, but this campus gets quiet and eerie in the middle of the night. Has everyone arrived?" Norman asked Cassidy.

Cassidy tilted his head down. "Last one arrived about 45 minutes ago. The curtains on the conference room windows have been drawn and the lights are off. I saw some flickering candles through cracks in the curtains."

"Did they lock the conference room door?"

"Affirmative, but I have the master key." Cassidy dangled a bronze key on a labeled chain.

"Are we ready to rumble?" asked the photographer, licking his lips in anticipation.

"Yeah" replied Cassidy. "Let's go."

Brewster and the photographer followed Lt. Cassidy up the front steps of the building and waited in silence for him to unlock the heavy, oak doors. Walking softly and as silently as possible, guided by

Lt. Cassidy's flashlight, they headed down the darkened hallway towards the public relations office. Arriving at the double-glass-doors entry, Lt. Cassidy quietly unlocked and pushed open the door. The three men stood in the small lobby area for a few seconds and listened. Faint sounds of music could be heard coming from the direction of the conference room.

"Sounds like somebody is having a good time," whispered the photographer as he shifted the camera bag strap on his right shoulder.

"Yeah," agreed Lt. Cassidy softly, his smile in the flashlight's illumination appearing more as a leer.

• • • • •

Richard Henry stood at the end of the long, dark oak conference table, finishing his third glass of wine and watching Latifa Benedict and Wiley Moore—in various shades of undress—wiggle around on a thick burgundy sleeping bag spread on the table top. As Wiley ran a bright dark purple feather tickler around Latifa's neck and ears, she squirmed, sighed and giggled obscenely to the strains of Stravinsky's *Fire Bird*.

Richard, his shirt untucked and unbuttoned, was starting to sweat. He had always suspected that Latifa was a wild woman, even before he heard any scandalous gossip circulating around campus about her sexual escapades. After all, where there is smoke, something must be smoldering and burning. But at the moment, it wasn't Latifa who was peaking **his** interest—it was the young intern Wiley.

Latifa lifted her head off a pink ruffled pillow and stared at Richard with "bedroom" eyes. "Sugar dumpling, what are you waiting for? Come on up and join the party. Don't be bashful. Oh, my," she cried as Wiley began teasing her arms with the feather. "Don't stop now. More, more, more." She rolled over onto her stomach and Wiley began running the feather across her back.

Richard dropped his shirt to the floor and unzipped his trousers. Wiley massaged and squeezed Latifa's shoulders, looking at Richard in his Minion-themed boxer briefs. Purring sounds began oozing from Latifa. As Richard heard the music crescendo, he climbed up on the table for his share of the fun.

• • • • •

Lt. Cassidy slowly inserted his key in the conference room door and turned the lock. With Norman and the photographer behind him, he stealthily turned the knob and pushed open the door enough to see three writhing, half-naked bodies in the candlelight. The three men furtively and silently entered the room and approached the conference room table.

Flashes of light from the camera temporarily froze the *ménage a trois*. When Lt. Cassidy turned on the overhead lights, two men and one female—all shrieking—scrambled off the table and onto the floor. Clutching clothes and sleeping bags to strategic parts, Richard, Latifa and Wiley crouched down and backed away from the intruders.

"I'm Lt. Charles Cassidy with the GCU Campus Police. May I see some identification, please?"

Warily eyeing the photographer and trying to keep their faces covered, Richard, Latifa and Wiley scrambled for wallets and produced Georgia Central University ID cards. Lt. Cassidy accepted the ID cards and checked their faces against the photos.

"See here, officer," began Richard huffily. "What's the meaning of barging in on a private meeting? All three of us work here in this office."

"Yes, sir, Mr. Henry, but I'm afraid I have to write you up and take you in to the Campus Police Station." Lt. Cassidy pressed the radio attached to the left shoulder of his uniform. "This is Lt. Cassidy requesting backup in the public relations office conference room."

"Backup?" spluttered Latifa. "But officer ... sugar ... we certainly aren't trespassing or anything."

"No," joined in Richard. "We're trying a new method of massage recommended by the health center as a way to destress after a long work day."

"I'm not going to lose my scholarship or get kicked out of school, am I?" asked a shaken Wiley, who was trying to put on his pants.

"Mr. Henry, Ms. Benedict and Mr. Moore, if you will please get dressed and come with me. We're taking the three of you in for inappropriate use of university facilities."

Latifa turned to Richard and glared, slapping him across the face. "You fool! I can't believe you got me into this. 'Come celebrate,' he says, 'We'll have a good time,' he says." She spit on him.

"ME?" he yelled. "You shameless harlot. You invited me here tonight for a *ménage a trois*. You told me to bring the wine."

"Liar!" she screamed. "I have the e-mail to prove it."

"No, I have the e-mail from you." Richard paused and looked strangely at Norman and the photographer. "You're from the newspaper?"

"Oh, no," squealed Wiley, slipping into his shoes. "Dad's gonna kill me."

Latifa's eyes widened. She looked at Richard. "Sugar, this is a sting operation. Holy crap! We've been screwed."

# Chapter Twenty

Sunday morning, Georgia Davis stood beside Evan Bradshaw on the Lido and gaped at the hundreds of colorful cabanas that lined the beach—row after row after row. Before they left that morning, Evan's housekeeper had packed them a lunch large enough for half a dozen construction workers: *panini* with slices of vine-ripe tomatoes, "buffalo" *mozzarella* and *pecorino* cheeses, thick slabs of *salami*, a bottle of *valpolicella* wine and *biscotti*. They took the fastest *vaporetta* (*Montonave No. 6*) for the 10-minute ride to the Lido, a slender sandbank that forms a natural barrier between Venice and the open sea.

Evan led Georgia through a maze of yellow and blue-striped cabanas to the one he had rented for the summer. While Evan set up deck chairs outside and pulled out the awning to protect them from the sun, Georgia went inside their cabana and slipped into her swimsuit, a dark green tankini she'd found in the L.L. Bean summer catalog. As she emerged from the cabana, Evan handed her an icy peach-flavored *Crodino* and they settled into their chairs, facing the sea.

Now that it was early September with schools back in session, Evan said the tourists were thinning out, but the beaches still seemed crowded to Georgia. The Lido beach area was very wide, she thought, so unlike the beaches along the Georgia coast at Tybee Island, St. Simons and Jekyll. The sand was dark, too. Not pristine white like the Florida beaches she had seen. But the ocean smell and the sea breeze were the same. She sighed and took a sip of her drink.

"Happy?" asked Evan, as he adjusted his blue-tinted sunglasses.

"Oh, yes," she replied, reaching out to squeeze his hand

affectionately. "And mellow and relaxed. If this is what being retired is all about, then I think I will retire early."

"But not now," he said with a serious tone.

Her smile left her face. "No, Evan. Not for another ten or fifteen years, at least." She paused and thought about it. "Argh! That sounds like an eternity away."

Evan smiled. "Trust me, my dear, it will pass faster than you know."

$$\bullet \quad \bullet \quad \bullet \quad \bullet \quad \bullet$$

Elena Van Horne hugged Carl Overstreet and kissed his cheek, rubbing a little bit of lipstick off afterwards. When he found out he was being released from King's Crossing after several weeks of treatment, Carl planned to take a taxi home, but Elena insisted on picking him up. "Friends are always there for each other," she said. And Elena had been there for him during his entire length of stay at the substance abuse center. At first, she just sent him funny little cards, then she started dropping by for short visits. She kept him informed about what was happening at the university—when he finally expressed interest. She avoided any mention of Paul until Carl asked about him.

During the first week at the center, Carl hated Paul for locking him away. But as Carl worked his way through counseling sessions with Dr. Bernard Franklin and in group therapy, he slowly recovered physically and emotionally. Gradually, he was able to look at his life differently. With Dr. Franklin's help Carl began to understand what had driven him to hide in a bottle of Scotch.

Toward the end of the second week of his treatment, Carl was able to talk about Elena. "Ahhh," muttered Dr. Franklin thoughtfully when Carl had finished talking. "The old unrequited love story." The psychiatrist took a black plastic comb from his shirt pocket and slowly groomed his gray beard. "Your Elena was a fantasy, my boy. You built her up as the perfect woman in your mind. You set her on a pedestal and worshipped her from afar. But reality blew your dream girl to smithereens, didn't it?"

"If only," Carl spoke, his teeth clinched.

"If only you had had the courage to speak up? If only you had looked more handsome? Been more athletic? Had more personality? Driven a red convertible? Had lots of money to spend on presents? Had a 4.0 average?"

"Yeah ... all of the above would have helped."

"You felt inadequate and undeserving of the perfect Elena. You perceived her as unattainable, therefore, you made no attempts 'to get the girl.'"

Carl squirmed in his seat. "Yeah, something like that."

"I think those feelings of inadequacy spilled over and affected your professional career. Your drinking made you feel better—more confident about yourself."

Carl grimaced and sat up straight in his seat. "Yes, that's right. Scotch makes me feel good," he explained in a louder voice.

"For a little while."

"Okay," he admitted begrudgingly, "for a little while."

"And this Miss Davis, before you fired her, did she make you feel good?"

"Yes," he hissed. "She made me feel like I could have it all. And now I have nothing."

Dr. Franklin smiled faintly and tugged on the ends of his bushy mustache. "Ahhh, my friend, you are wrong and you know it. Enough of this pity party. You have your health back, and you can conquer your drinking problem if you want to. You have good supportive friends."

Carl snorted.

"Who check on you regularly. Miss Gibson calls daily and comes by every few days, does she not?"

"Well, yeah," he admitted sheepishly.

"And your special friend Elena?"

Carl looked down at his hands and nodded. "Yeah, she's been here every day this week." He looked at the doctor. "She brings me a little piece of sunshine."

"And your feelings for her?" he pushed.

"Friendly feelings, Doc. We're simply the best of friends."

"Excellent! And your friend Dr. Van Horne, who checks on you every day by phone."

Carl's face darkened. "He's not my friend."

"If he weren't your friend, Carl, he would have let the police arrest you on DUI charges and cart you off to jail. By now, if you weren't still in jail, you'd probably be lying drunk in some public place. By bringing you here, that man has given you the opportunity to turn your life around. Where you go from here is up to you."

So where was his life going from here, Carl wondered, as he looked at a nervous, but smiling Elena who stood by the door waiting on him. He knew for certain that the first place he was going today was to Paul's office to discuss his job. He painfully remembered how he had resigned, but somehow Carl knew it was up to him now on how the rest of his life went, and he couldn't put the blame on anyone else.

•   •   •   •   •

Georgia reclined on a forest green chaise on Evan's balcony overlooking the canal. She sipped a small glass of sweet *vin santo* and watched the gondolas come and go down below. Evan had given the housekeeper the evening off. While he fussed about in the kitchen preparing dinner, Georgia washed off the salt water, sweat and sunscreen in the shower. The two of them ate a simple, delicious meal on the balcony—thick slices of Italian bread, a variety of cheeses and olives served with cold steamed prawns, lobster, small squid, mussels and spider crab—washed down with cold *bianco di Custoza*.

The day full of sun, fun, relaxation and lots of wine had taken its toll on Georgia. As she sighed and finished her last sip of *vin santo*, Evan returned from cleaning up the kitchen and sat down beside her on the chaise. The balcony was softly illuminated from an inside lamp. Evan took the empty wine glass from Georgia's hand and set it on the table. Suddenly she was very much aware of his presence and that he had recently showered. Strands of white damp hair clung to his forehead and he smelled faintly of bath soap and aftershave.

"Has it been a good day?" he asked softly, stroking her left hand with his fingers.

"Oh, yes, Evan, it has been a truly magnificent day," she replied, wiggling her toes and stretching her legs. "In fact, my whole visit here in Venice has been wonderful. You've been the perfect host. I feel relaxed and happy. It is difficult to think about leaving here and doing something about the rest of my life." But she knew she had to leave soon. She could not believe that her long weekend visit had stretched out to two weeks. The longer she stayed in Venice, the harder it would be for her to walk away. But staying in Venice was easier and more palatable than getting back to reality.

Evan leaned his face down towards hers. "Then don't leave," he whispered. "Stay here with me."

Somewhere, buried under too many glasses of wine, muffled alarm bells began to ring, but Georgia was only vaguely aware of them. She was thinking of how easy it would be for her to remain in Venice with Evan. She reached up and gently brushed his hair away from his forehead. "I appreciate your hospitality, Evan, but I need to get a job and get on with my life. You said so yourself just a few days ago. And my mom has been left alone too long. She has probably redecorated the house and is cleaning out closets by now."

"But I've grown rather fond of your company. Stay with me, Georgia, and you won't need a job. You know you don't want to return to the middle of all the academic politics and ugliness."

Georgia raised a brow in surprise. "What are you saying, Evan? I can stay here and sponge off you indefinitely."

Evan sighed. "That's not what I'm saying, Georgia. You know I love you. I've loved you from the first day you walked into my office."

Georgia looked at her mentor, her eyes softened. "I love you, too, Evan. You've been like a father to me."

"Ouch! You really know how to hurt a guy."

"Seriously, you've taught me everything about media relations, public relations and university relations. I'll never be able to pay you back." She reached up, placed her arms around his neck and hugged him.

Evan stroked her cheek with the back of his hand. "I don't want you to pay me back, my dear. I want you to marry me." Georgia gasped. She opened her mouth to speak, but Evan placed a finger on her lips to silence her. "Let me finish. I know I'm old enough to be your father, Georgia, but I'm quite well off. Marrying me wouldn't be that bad. We can travel all over the world and enjoy life together. I promise if you marry me, I will set you up on a pedestal and treat you like a queen. This may be an old man's fantasy, Georgia, but I think it could work. I still have a lot of good years left. I can name you at least a dozen famous men who have wives 20 or 30 years younger— Michael Douglas, Harrison Ford, William Shatner, Bruce Willis and Alec Baldwin, to name a few."

Evan stopped reciting names when Georgia started laughing. "What is so funny?"

Georgia stopped laughing and wiped her eyes. "I'm sorry, Evan. It's just that all of those men are really hot, sexy actors. They're rich, powerful and internationally famous. I understand how they can attract much younger women."

Evan frowned. "Are you saying some old boring, unimaginative, worthless retired senior like myself has no chance of attracting and marrying a younger woman like you?"

Georgia sighed. "Evan Bradshaw, there is no way anyone would ever use those words to describe you. You are one of the smartest, kindest, most caring and distinguished individuals that I know."

"But?"

"What do you mean, 'But?'"

"After you said those nice things about me, I felt there was a 'but' coming. Like, sorry Evan, but I can't marry you."

Georgia's lower lip began to tremble. She swallowed hard. "Evan, I do love you." His face relaxed. "But I see you as a father figure, not as a husband." Her voice faltered.

He smiled sadly. "But not as the knight in shining armor you've been waiting on to gallop up to your front door?"

Georgia pushed back from her former boss. "Evan, I'm sorry, I don't want to hurt you. I care for you very much."

"I know ... I know that," he whispered and hugged her tightly. They stood silently embracing for several minutes. "Georgia, it's okay."

"No," she said and sighed. "It's my fault. My mother said I shouldn't come over here and stay with you."

"Why not?"

"She thought you had 'feelings' for me."

"Eula Mae said that?" Georgia nodded, and Evan laughed. "Your mother has always been perceptive about people." Evan placed his hands on Georgia's shoulders. "My dear, you would have made me one very ecstatic old man, if you'd accepted my proposal, but I really had no expectations that you would be willing to marry a decrepit senior citizen like myself."

"Evan, don't sell yourself short. I know a lot of mature, unmarried women at GCU who would jump at the chance to marry you."

"Like who?"

"Priscilla Kuschner, for one."

"Dr. Kuschner in the College of Marine Biology and Oceanography? That daffy old professor? Bah! Humbug! I don't need an old lady for a wife. Especially someone I might have to nurse and wait on during my golden years. I need a strong, young woman with a sharp mind and a good sense of humor and the ability to get me into and out of a wheelchair without working up a sweat."

"Evan!" Georgia looked at her mentor in horror.

Evan smirked and winked. "Gotcha!" he exclaimed and laughed.

"You are so mean!" she said, playfully pushing him away in mock disgust.

"I know," he said. "Seriously, Georgia, you don't have to marry me, but please don't start trying to set me up with every single dowager you know." He tucked a piece of hair behind her ear and cupped her face in both his hands. "Never forget that I love you," he told her. "I'll always love you."

Georgia leaned up and kissed his cheek. "And I'll always love you, too, Evan."

Evan dropped his hands from her face, turned away. His shoulders slumped, his head down. In a few seconds he turned back around to face her. His eyes were red, his face strained. "Well," he said clearing his throat. "If you aren't going to be Mrs. Evan Bradshaw, then you're going to need a job." He gently pushed her into the living room. "But we'll talk about that tomorrow."

• • • • •

Carl and Elena rode in silence from the substance abuse center all the way to campus. A Macon FM radio station spewed out tunes from *Oklahoma*, *My Fair Lady* and *Phantom of the Opera*. Elena drove into a visitor's slot in the GCU administration parking lot and turned off the motor. "Carl," she said, pulling him from his thoughts.

"Yes," he answered hoarsely, turning his face to look directly at her.

"Are you all right?" she reached out and touched his cheek gently.

Carl took her hand, brushed his lips across her fingers and released them. "Yes, I'm fine, Elena." He smiled. "It's just difficult for me to return to campus after everything that happened. Paul has every reason to be angry with me." He paused. "You have every reason to be angry with me, too."

"How could I be angry with you? You've been through a rough patch these last few weeks. Paul and I love you, and we've been worried about you."

Carl looked out the passenger window, hiding any emotions that being back on campus had brought back to the surface. Feelings of inadequacy, longing and loss. He tried to focus on the campus as it came to life. The sidewalks were filling up with students carrying book bags and professors with briefcases. Class change, he thought, taking a deep breath. He turned back to face Elena. "I know," he began softly. "At King's Crossing I had plenty of time to think about my life and about you and Paul. I'm grateful that I have friends who love me and who're willing to stick by my side even when I'm acting the total jerk."

A tear rolled down Elena's cheek. She wiped it away quickly. "Sorry," she apologized. "I didn't want to get all blubbery on you."

Carl leaned over and gave her a quick hug. "It's okay, Elena, I'm trying not to get all 'blubbery' on you." They both laughed. The air was cleared. Carl put his hand on the door handle. "Well, guess I better get in there and hear what Paul has to say. I feel like the kid who's been asked to see the teacher after school."

"You'll be fine." Elena looked down at her hands. "But Paul is under a lot of stress." She looked back up at him. "Things aren't going well for him. Politics. You know what I mean?"

Carl sighed. "Yes, I know, and I'm sure the behavior of his vice president hasn't helped any," he replied grimly. "But how is the woman 'behind the man' holding up?"

"Okay, I guess. To be honest, I just don't read the local paper anymore." She forced a smile. "You better get going before Paul comes looking for you."

Carl opened the door and slid out of the car. As he shut the door, Elena let down the passenger window. Carl leaned down to look at her. "Elena, thanks for your visits and phone calls, while I was getting my life back together. Your support meant a lot to me. And thanks for the ride."

"You're welcome." She turned the key and the engine started.

"I love you, Elena," he said softly, as he waved bye.

"I know," she replied. She blew him a kiss and backed out of the parking spot. Carl watched until she turned out of the lot. Then he sighed and headed for Paul's office. The broken man heading for his impending doom, he thought, but this time he could handle whatever happened without a glass of Scotch.

• • • • •

Paul Van Horne ushered Carl Overstreet into his office and greeted him warmly with a hug and slap on the back. Carl sat down on the gold-and-brown striped sofa at the far end of the room. Paul sat opposite him in a matching armchair. A dark oak coffee table with ornately carved legs separated the two men. Issues of *The Chronicle of Higher Education* were scattered on top.

After briefly discussing Carl's recovery and well-being, Paul leaned forward toward him. "Carl, you know you are one of my best friends. Our friendship goes back many, many years."

Carl shifted uncomfortably in his seat. He didn't like the serious tone in Paul's voice. "Yes, Paul, our friendship has endured over the years, in spite of bumps along the way. It was this friendship that brought me down to Georgia. It was this friendship that saved me from jail and helped me straighten out my life."

Paul nodded his head and half-smiled. "Yes, and it is because of this enduring friendship that I know I can speak frankly with you about the situation here at the university." Paul rose to his feet and walked over behind his chair. "My job is in jeopardy."

Carl was startled. "No, Paul, I didn't realize that." He ran fingers through his hair and frowned. "I knew there were some terrible problems, but not that it was serious enough to affect your job. What's happened to exacerbate things? It's my fault, isn't it?"

"It's true, Carl, you have become somewhat of a liability to me."

"I'm sorry."

"But that is only a small piece in the plot against me." Paul walked over to the other end of the sofa and sat down. "Since my arrival, I have not exactly endeared myself to the faculty and administration. Early on I forced out a large number of older, ineffective college deans and top administrators—those I considered 'good old boys'—and brought in a few good men I knew I could trust."

"I hope they didn't disappoint you like I did," Carl said frankly.

Van Horne smiled sadly and shook his head. "On top of that, I made a huge mistake earlier this year with the senator's grandson. I'm afraid I underestimated the power of the Wittick family. When I did not cave into the senator's demands, I made a powerful, revengeful enemy."

"Won't the State Board of Regents stand up to him?" Carl asked.

"I'm not even sure about my standing with the regents any more. This year's fund-raising isn't going well. Partially due to the senator's influence and that of his rich, powerful friends in the business world and state politics. In addition, the development office is having internal problems and is being sued by a former employee. Then there's your office." Paul sighed and rubbed his chin and the back of his neck. "The staff member I placed in charge of day-to-day operations of the office ... what's his name?"

"Richard Henry."

"Yes, he and a female staff member."

"Latifa Benedict."

"And some male student intern in the office were caught in the conference room doing who-knows-what." Paul waved his hand in the air and rolled his eyes.

"Yes, I heard. We did get to read the local paper at Kings Crossing. What came of that scandal?"

"Fortunately for the university, we didn't press charges and both of them quietly resigned and crawled under a rock or something." He leaned his head back and rubbed his eyes.

"I'm sorry I let you down, Paul."

"Look, Carl, as far as bad publicity goes, after this, anything you might have done is now forgotten."

Funny thought Carl, but that didn't make him feel any better. "Is there anything I can do to help?" Carl doubted if he could, but at least he could make the offer.

"Thanks, Carl, but right now everything seems under control. Sandra Gibson—definitely one of the most capable women I've ever known—was able to help me bring back Delores Rinehart and Dudley O'Brien."

"Two of the news writers I scared off?"

Paul nodded. "In addition, graduate students in the journalism college have been a tremendous help. In the meantime, I've started a national search to fill your position. Although it may be too late, this time I thought I would pay attention to any suggestions made by the selection committee." Paul reached over and grabbed Carl's shoulder.

"As for you, my friend, I think we've found you another excellent administrative position."

Carl, who had been studying the floral pattern on the carpet under his feet, bolted up right. "A job?" He couldn't believe it. As big an ass as he'd acted, and with as many problems as Paul was dealing with, Paul had still taken the time and effort to help him find another position. But then getting him out of Southern Pines would be politically beneficial to Paul.

"Yes, and not just any old job." Paul leaned against the back of the sofa and smiled at Carl. "Have you heard about the prestigious women's college in Savannah that's located on Wilmington Island?"

Carl's eyes widened in surprise. "Rose Dhu College?" He remembered reading in *US News and World Report* that it was one of the top 10 women's colleges in America. "Yes, I believe the college is rated right up there at the top along with Mt. Holyoke, Bryn Mawr and Smith."

"What position do they have open?" Carl asked, hoping it was in the college's public relations office, but knowing he would be happy with any administrative position, considering his recent problems. He tried not to look too eager.

"Do you remember our old classmate Gaerter Jones?"

"Jabber-wocky Jones? Long straight orange hair, dressed like a gawky Bohemian?" he asked, incredulously. Paul nodded. "She had the hairiest legs and armpits I ever saw on a female. Last I heard of her, she quit school five hours short of graduating to go to Nepal to find herself."

Paul chuckled. "That's good, Carl. Well, she found herself all right, returned to school and eventually received a PhD from Brown University. She's been president of Rose Dhu for the last seven years."

Carl let out a whistle. "I never thought I'd see the day she would finish school, much less end up as president of an elite women's college. Sounds like she found herself quite well."

Both men laughed. "Well, she has created a new position to alleviate some of her work load and free her to work closer with the trustees and strategic planning. She's looking for an executive personal assistant to the president."

Carl tried to hide his disappointment. "What would I be doing?"

"You would basically become an extension of the president and an extra pair of eyes and ears. You would represent her at committee meetings and accompany her to important college functions, as well as be in charge of her office personnel. You would also send out special news releases from the president's office, arrange her personal press conferences and work closely with the offices of communications, marketing and development."

"Sounds like a gopher position," he mumbled, intently looking at the wooden chair arm he was rubbing.

"Carl, you'll have to look at this as an opportunity. If you work hard, do a good job, and eventually get a graduate degree along the way, you could use this position as a stepping stone to one day becoming a college president yourself. What do you think?"

Carl was silent for a moment. Savannah would be a great place to live, he thought. Going back to school for a graduate degree—maybe a master's degree in public administration—sounded like hard work, but then the idea of one day being a college president had appeal. Paul was giving him a chance to prove himself. He wondered if Jonesy was as entertaining and wacky as she'd been as a student. This could be fun. "Yes," he said softly. "You're right, it sounds like an opportunity for me." He looked intently at Paul. "Thanks, Paul, I appreciate your efforts. You didn't have to do this. You could have just handed me my pink slip and booted me off campus as an undesirable."

Paul and Carl stood up. "Nonsense, Carl. I have some remorse for dragging you down here to take over the public relations office. I feel like I threw you in a boiling lava pit." Paul extended his hand to Carl, who reached out and shook it. "I'll call Dr. Jones. She wants to interview you Friday. Could you be in her office by nine o'clock?"

"No problem."

"Remember, friend. All I did was get you the interview with Dr. Jones. It's up to you to sell yourself. Call and let me know how it goes." Paul clapped Carl on the back and gave him a farewell hug.

# Chapter Twenty-One

Marina Roberson sat calmly in her lawyer's conference room. Her lawyer, Clarice Crace, sat next to her. A legal pad, brief case and an assortment of papers were spread in front of them on the heavy wooden conference table. Across the table from them sat Alexa Stewart, vice president of Legal Services at the university, Walter Sigman, and Harry Stilton, another GCU lawyer. A court stenographer sat at the end of the long table, recording the questions and responses during discovery, an opportunity for counsel for both sides in a civil suit to ask questions of the claimant and defendant outside the courtroom. Such discoveries often resulted in the dropping or settlement of a case before trial.

Half an hour into her discovery period, Marina divulged information about her former job and its duties, as well as meetings with Walter about the potential donor, Edward Liverpool. "Ms. Roberson," said Stilton in a nasal twang, "you say Mr. Liverpool acted inappropriately towards you?"

"Yes, that's correct." Marina looked over to Clarice, who nodded encouragingly.

"Did you tell Mr. Liverpool he was acting inappropriately?"

"Not at first."

"Why not?"

"I didn't want to offend him."

"Why not?"

"Because he is a wealthy alumnus, and he indicated he planned to make major donations to the university."

"You complained about his behavior to Mr. Sigman?"

"Yes, I did."

"What was Mr. Sigman's response?"

"He indicated Mr. Liverpool's behavior was not a problem."

"What did you tell Mr. Sigman when he asked you to go to Savannah to receive the scholarship money from Mr. Liverpool?"

"I told him I didn't want to go, but Mr. Liverpool insisted that I be the one to collect the check."

"You gave Mr. Sigman a recording that you made of a conversation between you and Mr. Liverpool?"

"Yes, I wanted to prove that Mr. Liverpool had illicit thoughts about my going to Savannah."

"What was Mr. Sigman's response after hearing the tape?"

"He said it sounded like I was leading Mr. Liverpool on. He told me to go to Savannah or turn in my resignation."

"Did you go to Savannah?"

"No, I returned the next morning and told Walter that I had decided not to go to Savannah to be sexually assaulted by a perverted old man, and I was not resigning."

"What did Mr. Sigman say?"

"Nothing much then, but the next morning he called me into his office and asked if I had changed my mind about going to Savannah. When I told him 'no,' he said he was reorganizing the office and that my position was being eliminated."

"What did you do?"

"I recorded the last two conversations with Walter and took a transcript of the recordings to Alexa Stewart and explained my situation."

"Did you tell Mr. Sigman about the recordings"

"Yes, I did."

"Where are these recordings now?"

"I placed my player-recorder in my locked bottom drawer at work. One evening the drawer was forced open and the recordings were erased."

"Did you report this to anyone?"

"Yes, I did, and the campus police investigated."

"So these alleged recordings are no longer on your player-recorder?"

"Correct."

"In other words, Miss Roberson, you have no physical evidence that the alleged conversations between you and Mr. Sigman, regarding your position in the development office, ever took place. It is your word against Mr. Sigman's?"

"Not really."

"What do you mean?"

"I have copies of the two recordings on my computer."

The color of Walter's face turned from a healthy golfer's tan to a look of walking death. Stewart and Stilton held an intense muffled discussion behind Walter's back. Stewart rose to her feet and stuffed papers in her brief case. "I think we've heard enough here today. Clarice, I'll be in touch with you later this week." She turned and walked quickly out of the conference room, followed closely by Sigman and Stilton.

Walter paused and turned to look at Marina. Their eyes locked briefly before Stilton grabbed Sigman's arm and pulled him out the door.

"Whoa," exclaimed Marina. "Was it something I said?"

Clarice laughed. "That would be my guess." They hugged each other and laughed.

"What will happen now?" asked Marina, twirling a blond curl around her finger.

"That depends on them. The ball is in their court now. Based on how abruptly they left, I'd say they will probably make an attempt to settle this out of court."

"That would be good."

"Or," the lawyer said, "they could just proceed toward a court date and continue playing hard ball."

# Chapter Twenty-Two

"I have some bad news for you," Steve Smith began his phone conversation with Paul Van Horne.

Paul sucked in his breath and gripped the edge of his desk with his left hand. "What's that, Steve?"

"The governor has dropped the new building from number three on our priority list down to number thirteen."

Paul let out his breath in an audible hiss. "What does that mean?"

"That no matter what budget decisions the Georgia General Assembly makes in January, there's no way you're going to get funding for the new building in the near future."

"Then I'm in deep trouble," replied Paul matter of factly.

"You mean you're screwed?"

"Yes, that's exactly what I mean."

• • • • •

Carl Overstreet barely recognized Gaerter Jones when he was shown into her office at Rose Dhu College. Her long straight orange hair was now a shiny golden blonde and cut into a stylish Lady-Di hairdo. Her shapely body was dressed in a simple long-sleeved, snug-fitting, forest-green dress with a plunging V-neck that accented her figure and ample bosom.

She stepped toward him and held out her hand. "Hello, Carl. Good to see you, again," she greeted him in a low second-alto voice. "You look exactly like I remember you."

Carl shook her hand firmly. "Well, you don't, Dr. Jones."

Jones released his hand and chortled. "Yes, and thank goodness for that." They both laughed. Jones indicated a chair and they sat down. For the first hour of the interview, Carl told her about his academic background and work experience, and she told him what she expected a personal assistant to do.

"Paul has highly recommended you for this position. He told me about your drinking problem and your stay in rehab. He says your problems are under control. Is that true?"

Carl looked directly at Jones. "Yes, I'm putting my life back together."

"Very well, then." She stood up. "Here's the deal, Carl." Carl rose to his feet. "I'll give you six months to show me your stuff and impress me. If you slip up or if I don't like what I see, you're out of here immediately, and I'll start advertising to fill the position. If you're as good as Paul says you are or if you exceed my expectations, then I'll sign you on for a one-year contract." She stretched out her hand toward him. "Deal?"

Carl grinned and grabbed her hand. "It's a deal. I won't disappoint you."

"I certainly hope not. We don't have too many males working on this campus, and you're easy on the eyes." She winked and smiled.

• • • • •

Georgia Davis and Evan Bradshaw strolled hand in hand through the *Piazza San Marco*, scattering pigeons into the fall sunshine and blue skies. Along the edge of the huge *piazza*, Georgia saw Venetians and tourists sitting at outside tables, drinking an afternoon cup of *espresso* or *cappuccino* or eating a late lunch of *zuppa di cozze* or *risi e bisi*. As she walked along, she tried to memorize every detail. Since she would be returning to Georgia the next day, she wanted to take home as many wonderful memories as she could.

Evan squeezed her hand and put his arm around her shoulders. "Sorry you've decided to go home?"

"Yes, I'll miss Venice." Georgia paused. "I'll miss you, Evan."

Evan halted at the end of the *Palazzo Ducale* and the *Bacino de San*

*Marco.* "I can understand you wanting to put as much distance between me and you as possible, but how could you fly off and leave this behind?" He waved his hand in the direction of *San Giorgio Maggiore* across the canal.

Georgia leaned against Evan and took in the view of Palladio's church, appearing like a stage set across the water from San Marco. She remembered an earlier trip to the church to see two Tintoretto paintings on the chancel walls: *The Last Supper* and *Gathering of the Manna.* She and Evan had taken the lift to the top of the *campanile* for an unforgettable panoramic view of Venice and the lagoon.

Evan turned her around to face the *Doge's Palace,* the towering *Campanile* and the *Basilica San Marco,* graced with replicas of the Four Horses of St. Mark. "And this?" he asked, sweeping his hand before her.

"I know, Evan," she answered softly. She looked up into his face. "But I have to leave. I love Venice, and I love you. But I have to find a job."

"I know ... I know," he whispered, giving her a hug. "I don't want to let you go, but I understand." He pushed her gently away. "Speaking of a job," he said.

"Yes?" She pulled a wisp of her wind-blown curls out of her face.

"I talked to Sandra last night."

"And?" Georgia held her breath.

"Carl was released from King's Crossing and fired the same day."

Georgia stepped back from Evan and felt a coldness creep up her back, and it wasn't caused by any breeze from the Canal. She rubbed her arms as goose bumps broke out. "I guess I'm not surprised. Does this mean another search committee?"

"Yes, Van Horne has formed another search committee and the position is being posted nationally. Are you interested in applying?"

Georgia took a deep breath. Did she really want to put herself through that, again? Watching a couple warily settling into a gondola, Georgia asked the important question. "Van Horne will still get to choose the person he wants for the job, right?"

"Of course."

225

"Evan, I'm not sure I could go through that, again." Georgia walked over to a bench facing the gondolas. "You can't stand there and tell me that he doesn't already have someone else in mind for the job? Someone who would be loyal to him? Someone he didn't have fired?" She felt that burning feeling of anxiety in the pit of her stomach just thinking about it.

Evan sat down next to her and put his arm around her shoulders. "Then let's end the discussion on that thought. I also talked to our mutual friend, Luke Peridone. Since I seem to be enjoying retirement so much, he's decided to retire early. He says a search committee is starting to gather names, letters of recommendation and resumes of folks interested in his position."

"What?" Georgia pressed her hands into her face. "Get out of here! Are you serious? Luke Peridone, the vice president of communications at Rose Dhu College in Savannah, is retiring?" When Evan nodded, Georgia leaped to her feet and almost tap-danced into the Grand Canal.

"Does this mean you might be interested?"

"Don't tease me, Evan! Yes!" Rose Dhu College was like an ivy-league school for women in the South. The position could be a stepping stone to becoming a college president one day. She started tapping her feet, again.

Evan put his hand on her shoulder. "Hey, slow down. We're only talking about a job opening. You have to apply for the position and send them three letters of recommendation, along with your resume. Luke says he'll put in a good word for you, but there is an in-house applicant—an alumna of the college, who has already formally applied."

Georgia studied Evan's face for a few seconds. "Are you saying this is another one of those done deals? That I don't have a chance of getting the job?"

"That's not what I'm saying. Luke thinks the committee will be open-minded. But the woman has been at the college ten years, and she does have friends on the committee. You can relate to that, can't you?"

Georgia shivered. "I don't know about this, Evan. If I get the job, the woman will hate me."

"Georgia! This is nothing personal." Evan grabbed her shoulder and gently shook it. "It's a case of the best person getting the job. If you want the position, you'll have to work very hard to impress everyone. You'll have to convince everyone on the committee that you're their best choice. You'd love the job, wouldn't you?"

"Of course, I would." She let out a deep breath. "Okay, I can do this." She grabbed his hand and pulled him along. "Hurry, let's get back to the apartment and you can fill me in on the office politics at Rose Dhu."

"I thought you didn't want to involve yourself in politics?" he asked, scurrying along beside her.

"You know I've never understood politics, Evan. You know how much I hate it, but if getting a grasp on politics at Rose Dhu will make me a better candidate for the job, then so be it. Shoot, I'm all ears."

● ● ● ● ●

Ivan Nicoletti, the new dean of the College of Genetics and Molecular Sciences, greeted Paul Van Horne warmly. Paul ushered the dean to his sitting area, where a thermos of coffee, packages of cream and sugar, and GCU coffee mugs were spread on the oak coffee table. "How is your first week on the job going?" asked Paul as he poured the steaming coffee into the mugs.

"Quite well, thank you." Nicoletti stirred in one spoonful of sugar and took a sip. "I'm most impressed with the efficiency of the office staff so far. This afternoon I have my first full faculty meeting."

Paul sat down in his armchair across from the dean. "And do you have enough room in your office for your books and papers?"

Nicoletti tugged at the edges of a black, bushy mustache, peppered with gray and smiled. "Yes, the space is adequate for now. You did say my office in the new building would be much larger, right?"

"Yes, that is correct."

"Good. I'll just make the best of the situation until the new one is completed in—what did you say? Two years?"

"That was the original schedule, yes."

"Original schedule? What do you mean?" Nicoletti's eyes narrowed. He thumped his mug down on the table, sloshing coffee in the process.

Paul put down his coffee and smoothed out his trousers, avoiding Nicoletti's gaze. "There's been a setback," he started.

"What kind of a 'setback'?" Nicoletti asked, leaning forward.

"The governor moved the project down on the State Board of Regents' priority list." His eyes met Nicoletti's. "The complex will not be funded for next year."

"What?" Nicoletti jumped to his feet. "You mean I have to wait three years for the new building?"

"At the very minimum."

"You mean it might be longer?" Paul nodded gloomily. "You wooed me away from MIT with false promises? I should sue you for breach of contract!" Nicoletti yelled, his hands forming into tight fists. "What about Dwight Diamond? They're already making plans and commitments to relocate their research and development people to Southern Pines. They'll probably sue both of us and the university."

"Plus the Governor's Office, the State Legislature and the State Board of Regents."

"What happened?" he asked angrily.

Paul stood up and faced the dean across the coffee table. "Politics, Ivan. We've been screwed."

"Maybe you've been screwed, but not necessarily me. The president of MIT is still begging me to come back. One phone call and I can be back in my old office before the selection committee has its first meeting."

Paul looked startled. "Ivan, don't get hasty. Sit down and let's discuss this minor setback."

Nicoletti snorted. "There is nothing to discuss, Paul. I accepted this position because of the opportunity to work with Dwight Diamond. That group is known worldwide for their ability to research, develop and manufacture small batches of experimental drugs for doctors to use in clinical trials that could lead to future production of lifesaving drugs. Do you know what that could mean?"

"Yes, I do. International recognition and preeminence that would bring top scientists, researchers and faculty to your college and this university."

"Well, it's lost now." Nicoletti headed toward the door.

"No," shouted Paul, stopping Nicoletti in his tracks. "Only delayed. Stay and wait this out." Nicoletti took another step toward the door. "I'll make it worth your wait."

Nicoletti paused and looked back at Paul. "How?"

Paul licked his lips. "How about $50,000 more a year? I could create a chair just for you."

"$75,000."

Paul took a deep breath. All right, a $75,000 chair, in addition to your salary."

"And a $60,000 a year job for my wife."

"Doing what?" Paul asked, starting to sweat.

"I don't know. How about a position in the development office or a job as your own personal assistant?"

"That might not be so easy."

"Then we have no deal." Nicoletti reached for the doorknob.

"Wait!" Nicoletti dropped his hand from the doorknob and faced Paul. "I'll do it. Consider it done."

"Very well, then I'll stay."

"Thank you," said Paul with relief. "Now if you could please arrange a meeting between you and me and the 'top brass' at Dwight Diamond?"

"I'll see what I can do. Do you have any magic left to work on them?"

"I'm not sure," replied Paul as he wiped his forehead with a handkerchief, "but I'll look through my political 'bag of tricks' and see what I have."

"Better make it flashy and good."

• • • • •

Willing her knees not to shake and her teeth not to chatter, Marina Roberson entered Paul Van Horne's office to meet with him alone. Her own lawyer, Clarice Crace, was not aware of the meeting. But after President Van Horne had called her at home and asked to meet with her one on one, she decided to tell Clarice after the fact. Clarice had called her two days earlier to let her know that Walter Sigman had unexpectedly resigned from his position as vice president of development and that there might be an offer coming from the university very soon.

Marina passed up a seat on the sofa to sit in one of the large armchairs opposite the huge coffee table. Paul sat in the other armchair, facing her. Marina steeled herself against his gaze and waited for the president to say what he had on his mind.

Paul sighed loudly. "Marina, I appreciate your willingness to meet with me, just the two of us. Alexa Stewart would have my head if she knew we were doing this and your lawyer, Ms. Crace, would not be happy either."

"Then why did you want to meet without their knowledge?" she asked, her eyes searching his face for some sign of emotion.

"I thought that if the two of us sat down together and discussed the situation quietly without lawyers interrupting every second, then we might be able to come up with a plan that would be acceptable to your lawyer and to Alexa."

Marina relaxed. "So, you want me to run by my lawyer any offer you make."

"Of course, Marina. I'm not here to 'do you in' behind your lawyer's back. Is that what you're thinking?"

"The thought crossed my mind, Dr. Van Horne."

"Paul, please."

"Paul, then. During the years that I've worked here at the university, I have seen a lot of wheeling and dealing, dirty politics, back stabbing, underhanded actions of all kinds and frankly, I don't trust anyone—especially you," she said.

"I see." Paul studied her thoughtfully. "Marina, considering what you've been through this past year, I wasn't sure if you would agree to meet with me. I don't blame you for feeling the way you do. Now that said, shall we continue?"

Marina sat up straight and looked directly at Paul. "Yes, please proceed."

Paul slowly laid out his deal. "Marina, if you will drop your grievance and law suit against the university and certain staff members, then I will offer you the vacant vice president of development position and a one-year contract. Your starting salary would be increased 25 percent and your contract could be renewed, if it is determined you did a good job during your first year on the job."

"Who determines if I'm doing a good job and if the contract should be renewed?" she asked pointedly.

"Good question, Marina. Smart thing to ask." Paul smiled at her. "I think myself and two of the other vice presidents should evaluate your work and make that decision."

"As long as I get to choose those two vice presidents."

"Agreed. Anything else?"

"I think the 25 percent salary increase is not enough. Seventy-five percent."

"What? That's ridiculous and outrageous. Thirty percent."

"Paul, as an assistant vice president, I am woefully underpaid compared with other assistant vice presidents at GCU. I know what Walter was getting paid. Seventy-five percent or this conversation is over." She stood up.

Paul jumped to his feet. "Wait. Let's not be hasty." He paused and sighed. "All right. Seventy-five percent it is. Anything else?"

Marina smiled. "Not that I can think of, but that's not to say Clarice won't."

"Good, I'll write up a draft of my proposal and get it to your lawyer and Alexa this afternoon." Marina started toward the door. "Before you leave," Paul brought her departure to a halt, "there's one more item we need to discuss."

Marina frowned and a warning twitch rippled through her

abdomen. "Yes? What's that?"

"Are you aware of the new dean we hired to head up the College of Genetics and Molecular Sciences?" he asked casually.

"Of course," she replied with surprise. "We did some major fund-raising for a new building complex to entice him to come. He has an Italian-sounding name. Came here from MIT, right?"

"Very good memory, Marina. Ivan Nicoletti."

"What about him?"

"His wife needs a job."

"Can't she go to personnel, check out the job postings and fill out an application?"

"Not exactly. She's looking for—uh—a special position in the development office."

Marina's brow wrinkled as she looked uncomprehendingly at Paul. Suddenly her eyes widened. "You mean create a position for her in the development office?" she asked incredulously.

"Yes, that's exactly what I mean." He shook his head. "She could be an asset. She could attract donors with deep pockets."

"B-b-but—"

"No but, Marina. If you're going to be one of my vice presidents, then I expect you to do what I tell you. To be a vice president, you have to be a team player. Dr. Nicoletti gave up his position at MIT to move down here. To make him happy so he will stay, we have to find his wife a job."

"In other words, this is a 'political hire'?"

Paul nodded solemnly. "Yes, you could call it that."

"You want me to use money in my budget to hire this individual who may or may not have any experience in development work?"

"I'll ask Dr. Nicoletti to fax over her résumé."

"What kind of job do I create for her?"

"One of those gray-area positions with a vague job description. Once she's on board, I'm sure you can find some type of work suited to her skills and abilities."

"How much will I be expected to pay this woman to do whatever it is she might be capable of doing?"

"$60,000 a year."

Marina willed herself to keep her mouth shut while trying to keep her anger in check. She took in a deep breath and let it out slowly. "I see. Well, that certainly gives me something to think about." She took a step towards the door, then paused and turned. "You'll be hearing from me later." And you better believe I will have a plan in place when you do, she thought to herself as she left the president's office.

# Chapter Twenty-Three

"So it's a 'done deal'?" asked Norman Brewster, as he looked at Marina Roberson over a steaming mug of Jittery Joe's coffee. "You are officially the vice president of development now?"

"On paper and legally, yes. I dropped my suit against the university and they made me vice president. But I think I made a deal with the Devil."

Norman raised his eyebrows and set down his coffee with a thud. "What are you talking about? Are we celebrating a victory here or not?"

Marina sighed in exasperation. "I wish I knew, Norm." Briefly she filled him in on her conversation with the president, including creating a new position for the professor's wife, and her lawyer's counteroffer.

"What was the counteroffer?" Norman asked. "Did Van Horne accept it?"

Marina sipped her coffee and smirked. "What choice did he have? He knows we have the upperhand. He didn't blink at giving me a two-year contract in writing, but he was annoyed when Clarice told him I would give the professor's wife a job in development only if he paid for her salary. He sputtered and choked so badly, I thought we'd have to dial 9-1-1."

"How are you feeling about all this?"

"Numb and exhausted. I'm glad I have the vice president's job, and I'm relieved that the whole suit and grievance thing has gone away. All of this has created havoc with my health. I haven't been able to sleep or eat or think straight. My stomach hurts so bad most days I can barely sit up straight."

Norman reached out for Marina's hand and gave it a squeeze. "I'm sorry, I didn't know. I hope this means Van Horne is finished messing with your life." Suddenly Norman realized he felt badly when things weren't going well for Marina.

"I hope so, too. I was afraid when Clarice made the counteroffer that Van Horne would say forget it and I'd have to go to court. You know how many years court cases can drag on?"

Norman nodded. "You can deal with me now."

"How would I do that, Mr. Brewster?"

"By letting me take you out to dinner to celebrate your promotion."

Marina eyed him casually. "But I thought reporters were notoriously underpaid."

"Nothing fancy—just Pizza Hut." He finished off his coffee.

"Make it the Olive Garden and we'll go Dutch treat," she suggested, pushing back from the table.

Brewster stood up and helped her into her jacket. "I'm paying for it, because this is a date."

Marina froze. "A date? Who's going to explain this to Georgia?"

"Hey, this is her fault. She flew off to Italy and left us here all alone. Can we help it if we fell into each other's arms while providing support and sympathy?"

Marina put her arm through Norman's as they exited the coffee house together. "To be honest, Norman, I don't think she'll care."

# Chapter Twenty-Four

Carl Overstreet had just settled behind his desk at Rose Dhu College, when Gaerter Jones called him into her office. The president of the all-woman's college was standing at the window when he knocked and entered. Her hair shone like a shower of gold coins in the morning sunlight. She turned to face him when he closed her office door. She motioned him to his favorite chair next to her desk.

"Good morning, Carl," she said with a broad smile that showed nearly every tooth in her mouth.

"Good morning, Dr. Jones—uh—Gaerter."

She chuckled our loud. "Ahhh, Carl," she sighed happily as she sat down. "I cannot tell you how delighted I have been with your work. You have taken over and handled perfectly all the 'drudge' duties I hated. Thanks to you, I had time to visit the Craycraft Corporation in Atlanta and persuade their board to form a partnership with our business school. They were very impressed with your detailed report on the program and the success of our graduates in the business arena. Starting next semester, we will have students working internships not only at their Atlanta headquarters, but at their offices in Miami, Dallas, San Francisco and New York City. What a competitive edge this will give our business majors!"

Carl leaned back in his seat and smiled at her. "I'm pleased that our hard work has paid off, Gaert. Thanks, again, for giving me the opportunity to prove myself."

"Thank you for persuading me that you were worthy of the chance. Now, before I let you get back to work, I have a question for you."

"What's that?" he asked, his curiosity peaked.

She picked up a sheet of paper off her desktop and handed it to him. "Take a look at these names. They are the finalists for the vice president's slot and will be coming in for interviews this week."

Carl ran his finger down the list. His heart jumped as he stopped on one name: Georgia Davis, former associate vice president of Georgia Central University Office of Public Relations.

"Is that someone you know?"

"Yes," he said in a hushed tone. "Georgia Davis. She was my associate vice president at GCU." He looked up sadly at Jones. "I fired her," he said matter-of-factly.

"Should we alert the committee?" Jones asked startled.

"No," responded Carl. "Georgia Davis was outstanding in every way and exceeded my expectations from the first day I arrived on campus, in spite of losing her bid for the vice presidency to me."

"Then I don't understand why you fired her."

Carl closed his eyes briefly and swallowed hard. Then slowly he explained to Jones what had happened at GCU, but not mentioning the evening he spent with Georgia after the reception. When he finished, Jones sat in thoughtful silence for a few moments, her chin resting in her right hand, her elbow propped up on the desk. "You found this woman to be an exceptionally talented staff member?" Carl nodded morosely. "Yet you fired her without giving her a chance to defend herself. Why?"

"I thought that someone I trusted had betrayed me and was working against me and the president," he replied defensively.

"In other words, Carl, you were pressured by someone higher up to eliminate the source of probable embarrassment. Paul told you to fire her, didn't he?" Carl hung his head and nodded. "Did having feelings for her make it more difficult?"

Carl jerked his head up and stared at Jones. "What makes you think that?"

Jones stood up and walked over to Carl. "It's chiseled on your face. And it would be my guess that you still care for her."

Carl looked up at her thoughtfully. "Yes," he answered, pausing to consider her words. "I do care about her and I can't stop thinking about how unfairly I treated her after everything she did for me. I want to make amends."

·  ·  ·  ·  ·

Eula Mae gave her daughter a welcoming hug and kiss when she picked her up at the Atlanta airport to drive her home to Southern Pines. "Honey, you are a sight for sore eyes," she told Georgia as they loaded her luggage into the car trunk. "I've missed you so much."

"I missed you, too, Mom. Even though I had a lot of fun in Venice, it's still good to be back in Georgia."

Eula Mae forked over $3 to the short-term parking attendant and followed the signs to I-75 South towards Macon and Southern Pines. "You definitely look better now than you did when you left here," she told her daughter.

"I feel better, too. My stress is all gone and I'm relaxed, stronger and ready to face the world."

"Having a job interview this week helps, too," said Eula Mae.

"Mom, what are you talking about?"

"Ever hear of Rose Dhu College?"

"What?" gasped Georgia. "I didn't think they would call this soon. I just faxed them an application before I left Venice."

"Good thing your mother was here to take your calls while you were gone. I sounded so good I think they thought I was your personal assistant."

Georgia rolled her eyes. "Thanks, Mom, for sounding professional. When is my interview?"

"Friday at 2 o'clock. You can drive to Savannah that morning."

"Oh, no, I'll drive over Thursday afternoon and spend the night. I don't want to take a chance on having car trouble or getting held up by highway construction. Also, I want to appear cool and calm and not like some woman who rushed down I-16 at the crack of dawn. I'd be a nervous wreck."

"Okay, okay. Now tell me all about the important stuff. How was your visit with Evan? How did it go between you?"

238

"Mother!" Georgia hesitated.

"Georgia!"

She sighed. "All right, Mom, it was just like you said. Evan wanted more than friendship."

Eula Mae pounded the steering wheel. "Uh-huh. I knew it! Was I right or what?" She put the car on cruise control and glanced at her daughter.

"Yes, you were right—this time."

"This time?"

"Okay, the truth be known, Mom? Now that I'm an older mature woman of 55, I've looked back over my life."

"Yes?"

"You know all that advice you gave me throughout high school and college and beyond?"

"Yes?"

"Well, I wish I'd paid more attention to what you told me because you were right most of the time."

"Darn!" Eula Mae exclaimed.

"What's wrong?" asked a concerned Georgia.

"Where's a recorder when you need one?"

• • • • •

Chancellor Reginald Howell of the State Board of Regents shook Paul Van Horne's hand solemnly when he arrived at his office in Atlanta. Paul was nervous at being summoned to meet with Howell. He knew things were going badly, but he was prepared to defend himself, if necessary. He thought the expression on Howell's face did not bode well.

Chancellor Howell did not begin the meeting with the usual pleasantries or niceties. He went straight to the point. "Paul, you know I'm a man who doesn't 'beat around the bush.'"

Paul grimaced and nodded. "I know that, Reg. Please, come straight to the point."

"I'm being squeezed between the 'proverbial rock and a hard

place.' You received your marching orders when you were hired. You knew what we expected you to do, specifically in the fund-raising arena. You have not lived up to expectations of the board. The press has been all over you about the actions and behavior of two vice presidents that you yourself hired, as well as a number of campus scandals. The influential Council of Senior Faculty has given you a vote of no confidence. In addition, you have made a formidable enemy in Senator Wittick, who is using his influence with the Georgia State Legislature to sabotage next year's budget. I regret to say that your continuing on as president of Georgia Central is detrimental. Your contract will not be renewed. I'm sorry, Paul, it's out of my hands."

• • • • •

Marina Roberson invited Georgia and Eula Mae to her home for a Welcome Back dinner. Georgia was surprised to find Norman Brewster waiting when she arrived, but greeted him and Marina enthusiastically. Marina poured everyone a glass of Asti, a sweet sparkling Italian wine, to toast Georgia's return and Marina's triumphant promotion in the development office to vice president.

Over a dinner of grilled rib-eye steak, twice-baked potatoes and spinach and mushroom salad, Georgia shared the highlights of her stay in Venice. Marina filled in details of her suit against the university and the hasty departure of her former boss Walter Sigman.

"You know, up until the Liverpool incident, I thought Walter was an ideal boss," said Marina thoughtfully. "After my conversation with Dr. Van Horne, I can only wonder if Walter was forced into doing what he did."

"Why, what did the president say that made you think that?" asked Georgia, as she helped Marina clear the table and take the plates into the kitchen.

Marina explained how Van Horne expected her to be a team player and create a job specifically for the new dean's wife. "Thank goodness my lawyer was able to work things out. I still have to create

240

a job, but Paul will be paying her salary."

Georgia placed the last of the glasses in the dishwasher and turned thoughtfully to Marina. "If Dr. Van Horne put you on the spot, then odds are he did the same with Walter. And with Carl."

"And with who knows how many other university administrators," pointed out Norman, carrying in the last of the dishes. "Just how far would you be willing to go to protect your job? Or how low would you be willing to stoop?"

"Evan once told me that whenever folks in high places make decisions, it's never personal," remembered Georgia. "It's strictly business and it's all politics."

"Because the rules are made by men, too," insisted Marina. "And the men who make the rules don't understand why anyone who is fired or forced to quit their job would take it personally."

"Dirty, greedy, obnoxious, horrible old men," agreed Georgia. "If only there were more men like Evan in the work place."

"Allowing women to make the rules would make the work place a much better place, too," said Marina.

Eula Mae entered the kitchen quietly. "Not necessarily. The worst boss I ever had was a woman ... a back-stabbing, high finagling, self-promoting slut, who couldn't manage a pre-programmed robot, much less the six women who worked under her."

"Mom!" Georgia yelled.

"Thank you, Mrs. Davis. I thought I was going to have to slip out the backdoor before I got tarred and feathered," said Norman with a laugh. "What happened to your former boss?"

"She ran up against a woman with backbone and gumption, and I got her fired."

Everyone cheered. "Not only does Georgia get her good looks from you, Mrs. Davis, but I think I know who gave her that fiery spirit and feisty determination," said Norman. The cell phone ring of the theme song from *Les Miserables* interrupted the room full of laughter. Norman yanked his phone out of his pants pocket and headed into the living room.

Georgia was in the middle of describing the job at Rose Dhu

College, when Norman returned to the kitchen with a smug look of satisfaction on his face. "That was my managing editor, Harold Lepzig. They just received word from AP that Dr. Van Horne is being dethroned by the State Board of Regents. His contract will not be renewed at the end of the fiscal year."

"Whoa!" exclaimed Marina. "There will be some happy folks on campus when that news breaks!"

Norman reached over and picked up his wine glass. He raised it in the air. "A toast to the State Board of Regents for seeing the light."

"And a toast to Georgia for returning home," added Marina.

"Cheers, everyone," said Eula Mae, finishing off her wine. "Good luck to Marina and her new fellow."

"What?" gasped Georgia. Then after looking from Marina's blushing face to Norman's big, smug smile, she knew who the "new fellow" was. "Well, for goodness sakes," she cried out, giving Marina a hug.

"You don't mind?" asked a relieved Marina.

Georgia hugged Norman, too. "You have my blessing."

# Chapter Twenty-Five

Zechariah Smith, head of night-time security at Rose Dhu College, popped his head into Carl Overstreet's office around 8:30 p.m. "Mr. Overstreet, you burnin' the midnight oil this evenin'?" His four gold front teeth sparkled as he grinned at Carl.

Carl smiled back at Zechariah. "Good evening, Zechariah," he responded. "Anything going down on campus tonight?"

"No, Suh, everythin' is real quiet. Wha'cha doin' here so late?"

"Just not enough hours in the day to get everything done."

"Mmmmm, I know wha'cha mean. Doc Jones, she musta run out of time, too, cause she's still workin' hard." Zechariah tipped his navy blue security hat and turned away down the hallway. "'Night, now," he muttered as he disappeared around the corner.

Carl leaned back in his chair and stretched his arms up and yawned. He threw some paperwork into his brown leather briefcase and stood, reaching for his jacket. After he turned out his light and shut the door to his office, he hesitated briefly before heading for Gaerter Jones' office and knocking lightly on her door.

"Yes? Who is it?" asked a voice behind the door.

"It's Carl. May I come in?" Carl heard movement and footsteps, then the door was unlocked and opened by Jones.

"I didn't realize you were still here," she said, motioning him into her office.

"Same here. Zechariah told me you were here or I would have gone on home without checking. Is there something I can help you with?"

Jones returned to her desk and sat down, while Carl settled into his regular spot. "Oh, bother, Carl." She sighed discouragingly. "The selection committee sent me a short list of two finalists for the vice president's slot. Now I have to make a choice."

"Who are the two finalists?" he asked, not sure if that was something he should ask, but he had to know if one of them was Georgia.

"This is strictly confidential, Carl, but you are an extension of me, right?"

"So you keep telling me," he answered.

Her low, raspy chuckle filled the room. "The two names are no surprise: our faithful staff member and your former staff member."

He tried to mask his joy and appear neutral. "I see," he said as casually as possible. "And you are leaning toward which one?"

"Our staff member, of course."

"Because?"

"She's a graduate of our school, has been a staff member since graduation and knows everybody and everything. I personally know that she's loyal, trustworthy and hardworking."

Carl took a deep breath and crossed his arms across his chest. "She definitely sounds like a good choice. However—"

Jones frowned. "However? However what?"

"However, before you make a final decision, you need to think about what you want this person to accomplish for the college. If you just want to keep everything status quo, then I say, yes, go with the alumna. But if you want to grow and become the preeminent all-women's college in America, then you might want to reconsider that choice."

Jones crossed her forearms on her desk and leaned forward, her eyes narrowing. "How is that? Explain, please."

Carl stood up and stroked his chin thoughtfully, arranging his thoughts carefully. He knew he'd have to hook Jones with his next few sentences or Georgia would lose out. This was his chance to start making amends for what he'd done to her. He turned and looked directly at Jones.

"Your alumna sounds like a terrific staff member, but in order for this college to reach any level of preeminence, you need to bring in new blood, new thoughts, creative ideas, a deeper range of experience. If you want Rose Dhu to be a major player, you need someone who has already been out there in that arena playing with the 'big dogs.' You need someone who knows the writers and editors who cover the academic scene at the national level—because to move up, you have to get Rose Dhu College mentioned in national publications like the *Chronicle of Higher Education, USA Today, Washington Post, New York Times, Business Week,* and *US News and World Report.* You want your faculty members and researchers to get on the national talk shows. And you need someone like Georgia Davis and her proven record to help you accomplish this."

Jones stared at Carl in silence. Then she blinked and stood up. "Thank you, Carl, for your enthusiastic input. It's definitely something to think about before I make a final decision." She reached out her right hand to him and he shook it. "Good night, Carl. Have a great weekend and I'll see you Monday morning."

Before Carl realized what was happening, Jones had shut and locked her office door behind him and was walking down the hallway, out of the building and into the parking lot. Well, he thought, he did his best to convince her. Now the decision rested with Jones.

• • • • •

The tension had been building between him and Elena for months, Paul Van Horne recalled. He couldn't quite put a date on when things had started to change for them. Sometime after Carl had arrived in town or was it before that? But the deep freeze between them was noticeably chilling the air for sure after he'd taken Carl to King's Crossing for treatment. And after his catastrophic meeting with Chancellor Howell, life with Elena was like living on a glacier. Just when he could have used a little sympathy and a kind word, she froze him out of her life. But after an afternoon phone call from Massachusetts, he felt encouraged that a thaw might be coming.

When Paul arrived home with his news, Elena was on the chaise in the sun room writing in her journal, something he noticed she did a lot of lately. "Hello," he called out as he walked into the sun room, but received no acknowledgment from her. When he bent over and tried to kiss her, she pushed him away. He sat down on the chaise and she looked out the window to the backyard.

"I have some good news." She ignored him. "I've been offered the presidency of a small college outside of Boston," he continued.

Elena turned and looked at him stonily. "What college? Where?"

Paul's pulse quickened. "Parsons-Sifre College. It's a small liberal arts college with about 7,000 students in Lynn, Massachusetts."

"Never heard of it. How far is it from Boston?"

"It's about a 15-minute ride from the commuter rail station to downtown Boston."

"Aren't there publishing houses in the Boston area?" she asked pointedly.

Paul eyed his wife speculatively. "Why?"

"Because I'm not going with you unless I can start a belated career," she announced firmly.

Paul stood up and looked down at Elena. He rubbed the back of his neck. "We can talk about this once we move and settle down in the community. But why would you want to go to work? You can stay home and write a book or something."

"No, Paul," she shouted adamantly, jumping to her feet and facing him like an angry pit bull terrier. "I'm tired of being Paul Van Horne's wife. I have brains and a college degree from Princeton. I edited the student literary magazine. I loved doing that. I want to feel that I've accomplished something. I want to be happy. You do want me to be happy, don't you?"

A reddish-purple flush spread from under Paul's collar to his face. He could feel the anger welling up inside. Who was she to make demands of Paul Van Horne? "No, dammit, Elena!" he exploded. "I don't want you working. It will look like I don't make enough money to support a wife. It will make me feel like a total loser." His whole body trembling, his chest aching, Paul paused to catch his breath. Only then did he notice the look of horror on his wife's face.

"Thank you for your honesty, Paul. I just wish you had let me know your true feelings years ago. You can go to Lynn, Paul, but I won't be there with you. I plan to find a job. I want to have something to look forward to when I wake up in the mornings. I want to feel fulfilled."

# Chapter Twenty-Six

As soon as Georgia Davis moved into her new office on the Rose Dhu campus, she placed Evan Bradshaw's blooming orchid in a prominent spot on her desk. She felt an urgent need to pinch herself to make sure she wasn't dreaming. Imagine her, Georgia Davis, the vice president of communications at the prestigious Rose Dhu College. President Gaerter Jones had called her in for a second interview and offered her the job on the spot.

Very quickly after she accepted the position, the rest of Georgia's life fell into place, too. She was able to sell her house in Southern Pines the very first day it was on the market, and yesterday she had closed on a townhouse in the beautiful, historic city of Savannah. Eula Mae was so excited about the move, she bought several ebooks about Savannah and the Georgia coast. Who would have thought that her mother would be elated about relocating? How blessed could one person be!

Only a surprise call on her cell phone from Maria Eddings, who was once again heading up the search committee for a new vice president of public relations, caused her 30 seconds of reflection. "As you must know by now, President Van Horne will be leaving GCU the end of June. The State Board of Regents has already named an interim president to fill the position until a permanent president can be hired in about a year. While a search is underway for a public relations vice president, we are looking for a qualified, experienced individual who can immediately jump in and take over as interim vice president of public relations—until such time that a permanent vice president can be hired." Dr. Eddings paused. "Georgia, your name was the number one choice on our list. Would you be interested?"

Georgia felt her heart begin to race. She pictured herself finally at last sitting in Evans' chair and running the public relations office. Her dream come true. But if she agreed to serve as interim, what guarantee would she have that a new president would offer her the permanent position? And even if she were appointed, was it something she really wanted to do now that she had an opportunity to make prestigious Rose Dhu College preeminent? She sighed. "Maria, thank you for considering me, but I have already accepted the position of vice president of communications at Rose Dhu College in Savannah."

"Yes, Georgia, I heard that, but we were hoping you would jump at the chance to serve as interim vice president here, especially since the committee knows you would do a great job and that you have always wanted the job." Now Dr. Eddings sighed. "But I understand, and I wish you well in your new position. I hope Rose Dhu College realizes what a gem they have hired."

Georgia was unpacking books and framed photos in her new office, when someone knocked on her open office door. She turned and froze. Carl Overstreet stood framed in the doorway. "Hello, Georgia. I—uh—just wanted to welcome you to campus."

"You!" she uttered with astonishment. "What are you doing here?"

Carl's eyes widened in surprise. "You didn't know? I work in Dr. Jones's office."

Georgia fell backwards into her chair. "No! Oh no!" She groaned. "I knew things were going too well." She motioned him out of her office with her hand. "Please leave. I can't talk to you."

"But we need to talk, especially if we're going to be working together."

Georgia stared at him in horror as realization set in. "Oh my God, no!" She covered her face with her hands. "This can't be happening to me." She jumped to her feet and pointed her finger at him. "Carl, get out of here now!" When he hesitated, her voice sounded louder, "Get out ... get out ... get out!"

Carl backed out of her office and hurried out of the building. Curious staff members watched as he rushed by.

• • • • •

The Rose Dhu president looked down at the two letters of resignation on her desk. One had been given to her by Carl early this morning after he'd returned from the communications office where he'd gone to welcome Georgia Davis to campus. "I can't stay here," he'd explained, his eyes red-rimmed. "I thought she might be able to forgive me, but she hates me too much. One of us has to go. You can always find another personal assistant, but women like Georgia are hard to come by."

When Jones returned from lunch, she found Georgia's resignation on her desk. In her letter, Georgia wrote that due to personal reasons she could not go into, she regretted that she had to resign from her new position. She apologized profusely for any inconvenience. Jones re-read both letters, again. Her phone rang and she picked up the receiver. "Yes, Angie."

"Georgia Davis is here."

"Thank you, Angie, please send her right in and tell Carl to come, too."

Georgia was seated, grim-faced, in Carl's "usual" seat when he walked into the president's office. Jones pointed to the other chair by her desk and he sat down rigidly. Jones stood up behind her chair. "Thank you both for stopping by my office," she said. "I read over your letters of resignation."

"What?" exclaimed Georgia.

"You quit, too?" choked Carl at the same time. "How stupid of you!"

"Don't you call me stupid," Georgia yelled.

"People ... zip it for one minute," interrupted Jones. "I called you both here to tell you I refuse to accept your resignations." She quickly stuffed both letters into her small paper shredder. The grinding noise of the shredder echoed through the office, while Georgia and Carl watched in shocked silence. "You both signed a contract to work for me and I'm not going to let you out of it. So live with it." She walked around her desk and stopped between them, glaring at them both like a frustrated parent.

"Now I'm going to the faculty dining room for an over-due coffee break with my admissions director. During my absence, you two will discuss any problems and differences you might have. I need both of you here at Rose Dhu to help me accomplish my goal of getting national recognition for the college.

"Carl, as my executive personal assistant, you have become an irreplaceable fixture in this office. Georgia, I alienated a lot of faculty and alumni when I chose you over a favored staff member and alumna, but I wanted the very best person possible as my communications vice president. Carl made me see that you were that person." A startled Georgia looked at Carl and back to Jones. "Ten years from now, when a college-bound woman thinks about attending an all-women's college, I want Rose Dhu College to be her first choice. I expect you two to help make this happen."

Jones walked briskly over to the door and opened it. Looking back over her shoulder, she said, "If you haven't resolved your issues by the time I return, then you will remain in this room until you do." She left the room, shutting the door firmly behind her.

The silence descended throughout the office like morning fog creeping into a mountain valley. Only faint sounds penetrated the solid oak office door and the heavily draped, double-pane windows. So quiet was the room that the quartz movement of Jones's Seiko desk clock could be heard as distinctly as anvil blows by a village blacksmith.

Georgia wished she had followed her mother's suggestion last year to take yoga classes. She felt an urgent need to meditate and slow down her breathing before she hyperventilated. Focusing on the floor to ceiling windows, Georgia attempted to count the panes—six panes across, nine panes down, times three windows total. Carl cleared his throat. She held her breath and waited, but he didn't say anything.

She released her breath slowly and as soundlessly as possible. Bother, she thought. This was so stupid. She felt like she was in grade school, again. A trip to the principal's office.

"I'm sorry." Carl said quietly, rubbing his forehead with his fingers.

"Sorry? Sorry you fired me?" she asked softly, not looking up.

"Yes, I'm very sorry I fired you. I thought you betrayed me."

"You didn't even give me a chance to defend myself."

"I know, Georgia. I wanted to, but Paul told me to fire you. I regret that I listened to him."

Georgia looked at Carl with contempt. "So the evening we shared meant nothing to you? Nothing at all?"

Carl rose from his seat and knelt beside her. "Georgia, listen to me. I was really messed up when I arrived at GCU. I was an alcoholic with a crappy attitude, okay? A total loser. The position at GCU was my last chance to jump-start a stagnated academic career." He reached for her hand, but she yanked it out of his reach. "When you and I connected, I thought my life was finally turning around."

Georgia pushed him aside as she stood up and walked over to the windows. "While mine was going down the drain."

"If it makes you feel any better, after I ended up at King's Crossing, I figured my life was over. You hated me. My career was gone. I had nothing to live for. All I could think of was how I had lost you."

Georgia turned as Carl rose to his feet and walked over to her. She backed away and quickly put the desk between them. "Don't think your sob story is going to win any points with me. What about my life? My dream job? You stole it all away from me. And you broke my heart!" A sob escaped her throat.

"Georgia!" Carl took a step toward her.

"No, don't you dare come any closer." She stretched out her arm to fend him off. "I've put you and my feelings for you behind me. That's why I can't stay here and look at you and work with you in any sort of professional relationship."

Carl halted. "Georgia, please give me another chance. How many times do I have to apologize for my behavior. I'm sorry you didn't get the vice president's position at GCU. You certainly wouldn't have screwed things up like I did. I'm sorry I was a spineless jerk and fired you unjustly. I'm sorry I hurt you so badly that being in the same room with me makes you physically ill." Carl stared morosely at Georgia. "I'm sorry for everything, but I'm not sorry about loving you."

Georgia shuddered and turned her back so he couldn't see the tears rolling down her cheeks. Strong women don't cry, she fussed at herself. Suddenly he was behind her, grabbing her shoulders and turning her around to face him. He saw her stricken face. "You do still care for me, don't you?"

She looked away from him. "No, you were right before. I hate you passionately."

"Well, that's a start. As long as you have some sort of feelings for me, then I think there's hope." He released his grip, but now the hint of a smile curved his lips. "Listen and consider this proposal." She looked back at him, her eyebrows raised in question. "Dr. Jones is a unique individual, unpredictable and quite stubborn," he said, walking back to his seat.

"Yes, I've noticed that," replied Georgia.

"She is serious about keeping us locked up until we work things out. So I propose we let her think she's won."

Georgia sat down opposite Carl. "Go on."

"We'll agree to be civil to one another, no matter how distasteful it may be. I'll address you as Dr. Davis and you can call me Mr. Overstreet. Do you think you can manage that?"

Georgia lifted her chin. "I can, if you can."

"Good. Whenever we must communicate with one another, we will keep it on an absolute—but polite—business level. No unnecessary niceties or pleasantries."

"Okay. What else?"

"If I see you walking on campus, I will take a different route or do whatever is necessary to avoid you."

Georgia's mouth twitched slightly. "If I see you first, I will do the same."

"Perfect. We should also consider the dining hall. I usually eat after 1 o'clock."

"I prefer the noon hour, myself."

"Excellent. But if either finds it necessary to change the lunch hour, then we should warn the other person."

"Yes, by all means. What about meetings?" asked Georgia. "I'm sure we will have to attend some of the same meetings."

"Yes and that includes Dr. Jones's monthly cabinet meeting. I suggest whoever arrives last to a meeting be considerate enough to sit on the opposite side of the room. Does that cover it all? Are we in agreement on our rules of behavior?"

Georgia stood up. "Yes, I think we can say we have resolved our differences. Shall we let Dr. Jones know?"

Carl rose from his seat and stepped over to Georgia. "Yes, Dr. Davis, I think she will be delighted that we worked it out and are both unscathed."

Georgia moved toward the door. "Dr. Davis?"

She paused and faced him. "Yes, Mr. Overstreet?"

He moved up beside her. "Welcome to Rose Dhu College."

She swallowed hard. "Thank you, Mr. Overstreet. I'm looking forward to working hard and being a team player."

"As a team player, you must know that there is a reception tonight at Dr. Jones's house to meet the newest member of her staff. Will I see you there?" Carl bowed politely.

"Not if I see you first."

Carl smiled mischievously as he opened the door. "Then I shall endeavor to remain out of your line of sight."

Georgia muffled her laughter as she passed him in the doorway. Jones was waiting for them in the hallway. She looked from one face to the other. "Well, did you work everything out peacefully?"

"Yes," they both replied.

"Excellent," Jones responded. "I knew that two sane, intelligent people like yourselves could come to an agreement under duress." She eyed them speculatively as they walked down the hallway separately, but with smiles on their faces.

View other Black Rose Writing titles at www.blackrosewriting.com/books and use promo code **PRINT** to receive a **20% discount** when purchasing.

# BLACK ROSE
## writing™

CPSIA information can be obtained
at www.ICGtesting.com
Printed in the USA
LVOW12s0017310118
564694LV00001B/107/P